STOP CALLING ME PSYCHO

Alexandria May Ausman

This book is a work of fiction. Any references to historical events, real people, or real places, are used fictitiously. Other names, characters, places, and events are products of the author's imagination, and any resemblance to actual events or persons, living or dead, is entirely coincidental.

Copyright © 2022 by Alexandria May Ausman

All rights reserved, including the right to reproduce this book or portions thereof in any form whatsoever.

Book design and editing by Jon M. Ausman
Cover photo by Christian Axel

Library of Congress Control Number: 2022912065

ISBN: 979-8-9862745-1-5 (ebook)
ISBN: 979-8-9862745-4-6 (paperback)

Characters: Book Two

Bob: married to Mary, Psycho's grandmother
Boyd: a deputy sheriff
Brian Sloan: Julie's father, a trucker
Cathy: a deputy sheriff dispatcher
Cindy Sloan: Julie's mother
Crystal: a classmate of Psycho and Stephanie
Danielle: Simon's spouse
Debra: a deputy sheriff
Dennis: the county sheriff
Freak: the main character (this name will change over the years)
Green, Mr.: school principal
Higgs, Dr.: a contract psychiatrist to the sheriff's office
Huff, Dr.: a psychiatrist
Joni: a classmate and friend of Stephanie
Julie: a classmate of Crystal and Stephanie, an antagonist
Kelly: a schoolyard bully
Mary: female foster parent and Psycho's grandmother
Patty: principal office secretary
Psycho: another name for Freak
Scott, Dr.: new psychologist at mental health center
Simon Brag: a shard of Psycho/Freak
Stephanie: a schoolmate teased by Kelly
Vicki: a schoolmate friend of Joni and Stephanie
Wells, Mrs.: a teacher

Dedication:

This book is dedicated to my friends and family who inspired the writing of this book: Simon Bragg, Mad Maxx, Christian Axel, Amanda, Charlotte, Ravyn, Mike, and my loving husband Jon

Chapter 21: Head of the Class

Are we revved and ready to take the monster schizophrenia head on? Well, let me re-phrase that, keep your head on, instead of becoming a monster from schizophrenia. So, screw your neck bolts tight, grab the aluminum foil hat you made to keep out the static, and all the other 'stuff' as we are going on a road trip. No worries, I am here with you in the passenger's seat giving you the correct equations. Trust me, we won't get lost, I already know the way. Start your engines, ready, steady, go!

"Reality is merely an illusion."
- Albert Einstein

Everyone was trying to talk to me. That was not part of the plan. It just did not make sense to me. Even if the story had been true, and it was not, the cops are the good guys, right? I must have missed the meeting that explained why beating the good guys up made one "popular." Each class got worse with this strange adoration the students were showing for me. The more I ignored them the more "bad ass" they thought I was. It seemed to be a never-ending barrage of kids clamoring to get me to notice them. It was driving me, well, crazy.

I felt somehow that I should be interested. However, I was not able to be. Deep in there somewhere I wondered where all this had been when

I was alive to enjoy it? Now, as a delusion it seemed very cruel. All I had ever wanted once was to belong, be loved, to just be like everyone else. Now, I knew that could never be. I had long ago given up such fantasies. I no longer desired these things at all. I just wanted to be left alone. I had to laugh at the irony of it all. When I wanted to be one of them, they treated me like a pariah, and I was ignored. Now that I want to be ignored, they celebrate me. This thought kept creeping into my mind like my mother's poison that once had coursed throughout my veins. It was starting to make me angry.

"Why cannot I ever have what I want? Why is it always about everyone else?" was echoing in my shattered mind over and over in a loop. Between the noise, light, and kids, plus this infernal looping thought, I was sure I would explode into a thousand pieces.

I suddenly remembered my madness box. Shaking with sheer sensory overload I managed to get the ear buds into my ears as I blasted my beloved Sisters of Mercy.

There, better, calmer. I could no longer hear the students pestering me wanting to hear details of this unrealistic battle. I chuckled as I realized that the doctors say I am crazy, but really, they all are. Seemed to me I was the only idiot here that had any grounding at all. None of this is real, and I know it.

They all believe it is. I could think of nothing crazier than that thought.

Lunch time was coming. Kelly was gone forever, so I had no worries this time. Finally, I could just get a break from all of them. They all loved to eat so much. The thought that maybe that is why they are all crazy occurred to me. The food they are eating is laced with LSD, so it all makes so much sense. Now that I have stopped eating, I was feeling so much clearer, and everything was making sense again. No way I was going to be drugged now that my system was clear of that shit.

As a delusion, I would not require food anyway. So, let them get high. I would stay clear and keep an eye on all of them. After all I need to complete the mission. Drugs had only caused me not only to get into trouble but also confused me from my purpose. When the bell rung for lunch, I stood up laughing as I watched all the delusions go rushing for their daily dose of drugs and poison. Nope, not this girl. I went to the picnic tables with my paper and pencil to write out my equations on the mission. I had work to do.

"E is for electricity, which is what the static is made of. X is the correct result to acquire freedom of the imaginary. We will call the causal B and B2 with an unknown factor. A point of interest in this equation is the appropriation of items that may be useful in the solving of X to the 2nd degree," I write on my paper feverishly as I try to solve for X. There

had to be a way to get out of this delusional world and back to dead where I belonged.

It was just so damned simple. I was unsure how I had not already solved it, but for some reason I could not recall what it was for in the first place. I continued to write the formulas trying to work out the details. I did not even see Stephanie and another girl walking up as I babble and write, sometimes right off the paper onto the picnic tabletop.

"Hey psycho!" Stephanie said while sitting down. She looked to her companion motioning her to sit as well. "I see you are writing that crazy shit again. Hey, look at me!" she snaps her fingers in my face, "focus!"

I look up at the snapping sound. "What the hell was that?" Stephanie is here and she has brought the girl with the dimples, who gave me the useless blow pop and stupid note. "What was her name again?"

"Crystal, that is her name," I hear from behind me. Quickly I turn to see who just read my mind, both startled and angry. How rude to read my private thoughts.

No one is there. "Wow, that guy was a quick one. No worries, I will find him and kick his ass later," I think. I stand up and look to both sides of the yard to be sure I cannot at least get a sight of him.

"What is she doing?" I hear behind me. "Why is she writing this nonsense?"

I turn around, I had forgotten these two were there. I see this Crystal touching my equations trying to steal my work. In one sudden movement, I growl and snatch them from her. Yelling to keep her dirty fingers off my equations. Everyone here is so damned rude!

Crystal looks scared as she pulls her hands to her body and eyes wide at my behavior. Stephanie looks at me flashing anger, then rapidly calming. She turns to Crystal and tells her not to touch my things.

"You see Crystal, Psycho here is a real nutball. She has the schizzies for like real and stuff. I saw the records. So, mess with her or me and she will fuck you up real bad and stuff," Stephanie says while twirling her hair and smiling smugly.

"What the fuck," I yell at Stephanie. "Why? Why are you lying about me?" I wanted to kill her right there. She just casually spews those lies all around for me to mop the shit up! What a diarrhea mouth!

"Oh, stop it, Psycho! Oh, that is her nickname by the way, Crystal, because you know she is like all Norman Bates and stuff. It is all cool though it was our secret but you can be in the group so you can know too. You are cool, and stuff, right?" Stephanie says while Crystal is now looking at me with what appears to be both awe and fear.

I cannot look her in the eyes. Suddenly, my body feels very strange and little noises like a popping is hitting my force shield. It feels like pebbles one would chuck into a fishpond. Her eyes feel like they are reaching into my mind looking to steal my work from my memory. I look away and down and up trying to see the pops as they collide with my shield. They are too fast, and I can never see one. I can only hear and feel it.

Stephanie starts giggling, "See! She is a psycho."

"Yes, seems so." Crystal giggles nervously back. "But is she dangerous? I mean the cops and all, and Kelly?" She has curiosity, but apprehension is in her voice.

I do not like them talking like I am not standing right fucking here. "Shut the fuck up," I say while looking toward the ground. I have to avoid their gazes or be overtaken.

"Nah, she is not dangerous! Are you Psycho? She only beats up people who mess with me. Like Kelly. So, as I said do not fuck with me and all will be fine," Stephanie assures Crystal.

I decide that I have had enough of this bullshit. Seeing that all the tables are empty, shit let them have this one. I cannot take all this chattering. I turn up my music and with my notebook I go to the furthest table in a huff from these two brain stems. No time for this nonsense. I have an equation to work on.

The popping keeps getting stronger even with the Sisters serenading me. I turn it to full blast but still the popping continues but it starts to keep the rhythm of the music. I sit down and start solving the equation again, but the rhythm is so hypnotic. My muscles are so tight I need to stretch them as they feel they are shrinking. I extend my arms and yawn, but it only helps till I relax them again.

This is a most horrible feeling as I begin to stretch my neck, my legs, my jaw, and my arms, over and over with no relief. It will just not stop. The rhythm is pounding as I find myself standing up. I begin to sway with the rhythm, I am suddenly dancing fast and furious trying to stop the muscles from tensing up.

I am not sure who is making me do this. I do not want to dance right now, I have shit to do, but I am like a puppet on a string unable to stop the puppet master. I close my eyes and it sweeps me away as I fly wildly around the picnic table in a fast, almost desperate stomping, pacing, and swaying. Still the feeling will not stop.

I open my eyes suddenly as the sensation of water collides with my face, neck, and chest. The sudden cold startles me out of my trance as I stop, whatever it was that I was doing. Beyond angry, I turn and see Stephanie with my jug. She stole my water jug I think wildly. She is trying to drug me again.

Feeling a rage overtake me, I plow into her grabbing her by the throat and squeezing trying to kill her with all I have. I hate this girl she has caused me nothing but grief. The laughter begins to spill from inside me as I see her frightened eyes and gasping mouth open to scream. She is so dead now. She is going limp ready to fall down, scratching at my hands as I growl at her.

"Let her go! Let her go," a girl's screams from behind me. "Stop sinner," she screams when I do not heed her first request.

This snaps me out of my murderous rage. "Oh, shit! What am I doing?"

I release Stephanie and back off her very confused as to why I was trying to kill her. Stephanie leans forward coughing and holding her throat but was not harmed too badly. I think Crystal said that, but how did she know to say Sinner?

Looking to my left I see it cannot have been Crystal, she is way over at the other table. So, who said that? I look all around there is no one else here. How can that be? I try to calm myself and remind me that this is all a delusion. This is going to happen as the real world sometimes slips through. I must have heard someone in the real world.

"It is all in the equation," I remind myself out loud, "just remember, this is normal!"

Stephanie walks over and grabs my water jug she had dropped during my attack. She looks at it then throws it at me. It bounces off my head and falls to the ground with a hollow sound. I turn off my mad box. It had not worked to stop the madness this time apparently. This is not good.

"Really! That is the thanks I get for trying to stop your fucking loony shit! I ask myself why I am still your friend every day. Stop hitting me every time I try to keep you out of trouble! You listening in there? Can you hear me? Stop it," she is turning red with the force of her words.

I cannot look her in the eyes but realize she is right. Something is not right with me. I cannot put my finger on it, but nothing is making sense and I think it did once. Maybe, I am going crazy? Maybe I am sick? I nod my head in shame letting her know I do understand her.

"I am sorry, Stephanie," I say softly, wanting to cry but I cannot. I reach deep inside but cannot find the sorrow to express it.

My feelings are like a memory from a dream I had once. I can almost remember, but they are too faded. Lately, I cannot feel any emotions, not the right ones anyway. They are all mixed up. I am so numb and cold inside most of the time. When I feel any emotion, it is so strong on the surface. It is like a waterspout that stirs the top of the water but below the surface is calm and void of movement. Nothing is reaching my heart anymore. Was I always like that?

Stephanie seems surprised I have apologized as she inquires, "Did you say you are sorry? You do know I am trying to help you, right," she is looking to see if I understand.

Signing I nod my head. I am going to need someone around I guess to keep me from doing whatever it is that I am doing to set her off like that. Now I was wet and that is not fun as the day is cold with a brisk wind. I shiver as it seems the cold is deeper inside me than it should be. My ears are ringing as a new headache begins in the back of my head between my ears. I rub the back of my head wishing I could just have things the way they used to be. If only I could remember what that was!

Stephanie motions me to re-join she and Crystal at their table. I grab my jug and papers and follow her. However, I am beginning to forget why I am following her. My memory feels like one of those old flip books where the artist makes the same drawing that is just slightly different on each page. As you flip the pages the figures become one, moving like an animation. There seem to be pauses with voids everywhere. It is getting very frustrating.

I sit down. Crystal is still staring at me. It feels like she is burning through me, so I again keep my gaze from hers. My head is really pounding now.

After a long silence the two girls begin to gossip about my condition. I listen and I know it is about me, but I cannot understand them. It is just not making sense. Stephanie is revealing my secrets and telling lies most likely. However, I cannot seem to grab my thoughts again as they are moving too fast and in the wrong directions. Random words catch my attention then echo and loop. I feel like I am on Thorazine again unable to do anything but stare and drool while waiting for this shit to wear off.

In my state of stupor, I watch in horror as a large group of teenagers come out of the cafeteria. They are a mix of male and female all laughing and horse playing. I cannot move as they see us and start coming for the table. The noise is deafening, but I still cannot move. They come up to gather around Stephanie and Crystal. I try to focus on their word exchanges, but it is all so messed up. Only bits and codes, I begin to see their words in the air. They appear as dark spots that hang in the air not unlike small holes in the tapestry of this delusional world.

Stephanie is looking at me concerned. She is standing up and no one is laughing or speaking anymore. Her mouth is moving as I watch the smoke begin to rise from the ground all around us. I smell fire.

"Something is on fire," this thought finally comes through loud and clear. Finally, I have broken my trance. I jump up excitedly.

"Idiots! Something is on fire! Run! I have to get out of here! Fuck this," I yell at the group of kids as I stand up and grab my jug and notes.

Everyone is looking in surprise at everyone else appearing unsure of what I just said. I do not bother to repeat myself. If they want to burn up, not my problem. I take off running not looking back. I keep running right off the school grounds. I am going home. I need some time to work this out, I have a mission to complete after all. I run till I am tired and then relax and walk the rest of the way.

There is too much noise at school for me to focus, that is all. Or that is what I am telling myself, talking out loud so I can hear the answer. I do not seem to be listening to me lately.

"I am unsure what your problem is, I know what is best for us. So, why will you not listen? Who is in control here," I say to myself? "Now we agreed we would focus and ignore the real world coming through. I thought we understood each other! Get with the program, asshole," I yell wishing I could kick my own ass to wake up.

A nagging feeling that something is very wrong keeps pricking me like needle. What is wrong with me? I bitch and threaten myself out loud all the way home to my cemetery hovel. Surely, this time we could keep this agreement. For now, I had the peace and quiet I needed to work on my equation. No more interruptions.

I lay my pad of paper out and settle in writing out the equation and working the formula without stopping for any reason till the sun sets too low to see any longer. Unable to write and all the paper covered in every clear spot anyway, I go to my outhouse and sit down still verbally working out the equation. I finally give that up, my memory is too poor to remember my place. After all that is why I have to write it down.

It is an overcast night threatening rain as I hear distant thunder. The ground rattles with it like an earthquake. I cannot sleep. I should be tired, and I am certainly thirsty, but I forgot to get water. No worries, the thirst will pass. My mad box had betrayed me earlier today, so I take it out of my hiding spot in my shirt and toss it into my supply box. It is as useless as the bible and psychiatric records so why not put it where it belongs, I think bitterly.

The outhouse usually calms me but tonight I feel I need more space. I walk out into the graveyard to watch the night sky as lightening splits the darkness with a loud crack. I feel the static pulsate in the ground beneath my feet.

"It is the answer for X," I yell out my smile spreading, "Static is the answer!" I could not believe I had forgotten that. "It is the static, I remember. I have solved for X."

The dark sky answers my telling her of my discovery by opening up her bosom. She releases her torrents of tears that I was finally free. I can hear God himself growling angrily as he sets the sky on fire. He realizes I had discovered the secret of this delusional world. I have my escape. The rain is freezing cold, but I look up closing my eyes as it runs down my face.

I begin laughing in the heavy rain at God and his useless anger. "You did not think I would find out, did you? Well, fuck you. I am not your puppet do you hear me! I am the sinner!" I laugh as I begin to dance in victory.

I am drenched to the core, but I do not care as I laugh and dance mocking God who was always too busy for me in his heaven.

"There you go, Stephanie! I am talking to God just like you wanted! And it's your guess as good as mine if I have pissed myself!" I cackle wildly spinning around and around like a top watching my shattered world merge into a single color of blackness.

The sun is weak as it attempts to find a way to reach out its life-giving rays through the blanket of rogue clouds lagging behind the storm of the night. I awaken on the ground with a busted lip and dried blood all over my clothing. I look to see there is blood all over the marker next to me. My forehead is tingling. I reach up and see fresh blood on my fingers. I have fallen and cracked my head on one of my roomies. It must have knocked me out. This makes me laugh. Silly me.

I am wet to my socks and covered in mud and my own blood. Unfortunately, I do not have any other clothes. Mary had taken them, I think saying she would wash them, but I cannot be sure that she did. I just cannot remember. One thing that was very clear as I dig frantically through my supplies, there are no other change of clothes.

"Shit! I have to get to school!" I grab my mirror and manage to use my sleeves to clean off my face mostly.

I cover it with my white make-up, but I am unsure why I look so odd. I do not look the way I remember but this must be me? The thought that someone has played such a trick bothers me, but despite my growing fear of this reflection looking wildly back at me I continue. The blood from a nasty cut just above the wig line in the top of the reflections head keeps oozing and mixing with the make-up. I give it up and add black to the eyes and lips. Now I stare at a ghoul with bloody lips and forehead as she stares back at me. It scares the hell out of me. I drop the mirror to the ground. I cannot look at this thing anymore. This mirror is apparently broken anyway as it does not work. I decide I will have to buy a new one.

I go to grab my jug and my notebook. My notebook is covered in the scribbling of my equation. Nothing else can be written on it. I look it over. The memory of discovery last night has already slipped away in my abyss of my disorganized mind.

"I know we solved X, but what was the answer again? Damn it, why you write it down, dummy," I yell to myself frustrated. Now we would have to start all over again.

Frustrated, with a nasty headache, muddy, wet and still bleeding, I take off towards the school. I need water again despite my apparent nap in a load of the stuff. I look at my old watch and see I will make it right on time. Still bitching at myself for not writing down the answer, I round the corner to the school.

Everyone now is staring at me babbling to myself, but I do not care. Let them look. They are not real anyway. I have control here. They are figments of my imagination and there is no God, or future. Nothing matters now that I have lost my answer again.

I go inside the school ignoring the sea of faces as I quickly make it to my first class. I sit down putting my jug next to me looking at my notebook hoping against hope that I did write it down but forgot like I tend to do. Stephanie walks by the classroom and sees me at my desk. The bell will not ring for another fifteen minutes so she come in excited at first but then I watch it melt away to a look of concern or is it fear?

"What the hell, Psycho! You look like a wet rat and your bleeding! What happened? Do you need a doctor?" She tried to touch my face, but I pull back fast almost falling out of my desk.

"Do no touch me," I growl quite irritated. This girl always brings bad news with her. "Go away and I mean it Stephanie! Leave me alone," I say gritting my teeth.

She stands there not knowing what to do. Finally, looking at the clock above the chalkboard she says, "Look it was funny for a minute, but you are seriously worrying me. You take off, dance, and hit people. Now this." She makes a motion of whole body at me. "I think you need help. I do not want to lose my friend, but I think you are going to die or hurt someone if you don't get help." She finishes appearing to really care.

I had to laugh at that, "Buzz off, Stephanie. No worries darling! If someone bothers you, just call on old psycho here and I will answer your call like a good little doggy! Until you need some killing done, so you can keep your hands clean, fuck off," my laughter is quite loud now.

Stephanie tears up and runs out of the room to my mocking laughter behind her. I watch her go with understanding for the first time in some time. She is useless as the rest of them. If I could get help, I would have gotten it by now. I already know that, and she should have too. Besides, she is not going to call anyone. No one cares about delusions. They are not real.

My mind wanders back to my equation issue as the class piles back into the room. The teacher approaches my desk and set a slip of paper on my desk. It is a note to Mary regarding my cutting detention yesterday. The teacher says I have to get Mary to sign it and bring it back.

"Or, what?" I ask setting my eyes on this old hag. I will all my hate into my gaze. I am letting her know fooling with me is not in her best interest.

She is startled by my response as waves of giggles break out among the class. She looks at the class with her own look of warning. The giggles quiet immediately. She looks back at me taking in the whole sight appearing disgusted. I can see she is resigned to let this go. Smart.

She goes to her daily lecture. I also let it go wadding up the note and dropping it on the floor. I heard the girl behind me gasp as it hit the floor. I rapidly turn in my seat mouthing silently 'shut the fuck up.' I give her the same hateful gaze as the teacher a moment ago. She looks alarmed.

I intimidate her with my eyes for a bit as I read her mind. She is thinking I am crazy, but I am not. She is the crazy one thinking that note mattered. She finally looks away to the floor and I turn back around.

Now, what was I doing again? I see the notebook and again pour over the notes trying to find the answer but without a place to write I cannot keep my thoughts in order. I look around and no paper but the wadded-up note. I am frustrated as I watch the teacher writing her nonsense lies on the board. Those equations are not the right ones.

I laugh to myself, "Fools all of them." Then it occurs to me. "The chalkboard is perfect! I could then write the proper equation and when I have used the space, I can just erase it and start over till we can solve for X!"

I stand up with only that chalkboard in my sight. The old bitch has the chalk I need. No matter, she is not real anyway. The class lets out a collective "Oh, my God" as I grab the old bags wrist and wrestle the chalk from her bony fingers. She did not see me coming as she was too busy spewing lies on the board when I got out of my seat.

She starts to complain, and I push her into the wall. "You are a liar" I say pointing at her, "That is not the equation to solve for X and you know it!" She stands there her eyes wide in disbelief at what was happening.

I turn toward the class and realize they are quite confused. Well of course they are, they did not know she was lying to them.

"Well. no worries, we are going to remedy that right here and now." I think to myself.

"Okay now class, calm down and I will show you the equation that solves for X. There is no need for all this bullshit lying. So, take notes it may be on the test." I lecture about twenty frightened student who have no idea what to do or what is going on.

I laugh at my threats of a test. I do not intend to give a test. I do not care if they get their solutions in fact, they are not real. I turn back to the board ignoring these false people as I begin to write down the equation that will solve for X. I babble on writing only stopping to wipe my eyes of the blood and sweat keeps pouring down my forehead. I am feeling fevered with the excitement that I am close to the answer. It is right there.

Oh, my Goth, beauties, looks like I am just about to solve the equation there doesn't it? Well, you will have to wait see if I find out the X that marks the spot! I am so happy you all are still on this trip with me as the roads are now getting a bit bumpy and no telling if we are even going in the right direction? Hummm, are we lost? No, promise I got you. I know the path like the back of my hand. Stick with me beauties, half the fun is in the getting there. Until the next chapter, don't forget your medications and keep your mad boxes charged!

Chapter 22: Riding the Lightening!

Greetings Beautiful People! Oh, my Goth! Who said that? Must have been the "voices" but no worries they are always right you know. Are we ready to solve for X? Great! For this chapter I would ask all of you to have plenty of electrical tape handy and do not forget to stay grounded, so you do not get fried by accident! I am right here next to you holding the lightning rod. I see the storm is coming so hang onto me tight. Let's get this shocking chapter started as we ride the lightning together. I promise you will feel so much better when it is over, just make sure you are not wearing any metal.

"Hell isn't merely paved with good intentions; it's walled and roofed with them. Yes, and furnished too."
- Aldous Huxley

"E is for electricity, which is the stuff the static is made of. X is unknown so with the coefficient of the shadows equal to S, and tools for escape equal to E to the 2nd degree. solve for X. The equation is E + E2 over S = X." I write in a loop all across the hijacked chalkboard babbling about the solving of X and answers to this equation.

My thinking is disorganized and shattered into bits. Nothing is making sense anymore. I cannot even understand my own existence. Reduced to the instinctual, I am holding on to the only thing I can remember. My lifeline to keep me from complete shutdown is this equation that must have been of some importance to me before the onset of the disease. Malfunctioned and wrongly recalled it is the only way I can call out for help. Deep down somewhere, unable to reach the surface, I am crying out for assistance. However, I am neither aware of it nor could I be. My insight is lost as badly as my organizations of thoughts. I do not know I am insane. In fact, I do not know anything anymore. I do not eat, sleep, bath, or care as these things no longer matter in the void of delusions and madness. Nothing is real, not even me. If help does not come soon, I will never have need for anything again.

My psychosis has been on-setting now for many months. Over that time, delusions of being drugged, attacked, and long periods of disorganized thinking with hallucinations has caused my weight to drop to an alarming low level. My symptoms are causing accidents such as jumping off bridges, smacking into headstones headfirst, vicious fighting, and body slamming. I do not feel pain, emotions, shame, social constraints, or hunger. Nor do I understand death or life. These are now hostages of my disease under lock and key. Those really are important to have, without them, no one lives long.

As the elderly teacher watches this bizarre scene in horror. She blinks hoping when she clears her eyes it will all go away. It does not. She painfully realizes this is not just typical smart-ass teenager behavior.

This kid is very sick and in a lot of trouble. She has seen this before as the demon Schizophrenia is no stranger to her family. She knows, because her older sister committed suicide when she was young child, because "God told her to." The wizened educator recalls this equation and the foul appearance with strange speech all too well. It has haunted her nightmares all her life. She still feels guilt. She believes she could have saved her big sister from the depths of this hell when she too began to do what she is witnessing here today.

"You can solve for X, no problem. The answer is static is answer for X. So, X is electricity." The old teacher says gently keeping her distance. She understands I cannot be touched.

I hear this answer. My thoughts grab it quickly. "Static is electricity!" That is the answer I think wildly. While dropping the chalk and stepping back from the chalkboard.

The equation glows with life seeming to come off the board right at me, all of it finally solved. Electricity is the answer. Now, to find the tools to fix the corruption of the electricity and I would be free of this hellish delusional world. Without even being aware of my fellow delusions I turn and wander out into the hall babbling about electricity and the "short circuit" that has caused a "power outage."

The old teacher has slipped past me quietly, careful not to move too quickly. She knows I cannot see her but does not want to call my attention by accident. She heads to the office and calls the psychiatric clinic, bypassing the guardian.

This teacher realizes this is not something that just happened. It has to have been going on a long time. Someone was not attending this child. She knew who that someone was. She watches the teen wander the halls confused, babbling almost appearing to be sleepwalking. Her physical appearance suggests she has been either in a fight or fall very recently. It also suggests the kid has been without any real attendance since she was taken from the school grounds last Thursday. She has been waiting on hold, but finally a voice answers her.

Dr. Scott is at the clinic filing case notes waiting for her next appointment, when her secretary informs her that a schoolteacher is on hold. The woman is calling with concern regarding what she thinks maybe an actively psychotic teen. Dr. Scott answers the phone. She listens to this very upset teacher repeat symptoms of a student who appears to be in danger due to spectacularly severe symptoms of mental illness, probably Schizophrenia says the teacher. Dr. Scott takes notes listening careful to the description and verifies this is either substance abuse or psychosis. The teacher insists this kid is in big trouble.

Sighing at being bothered with what is likely a teen tweaking from some designer drug, she asks for the student's name. Fear runs through her when she hears it. This kid was just here! She knew it! She tells the teacher to do her best to detain the teen without putting herself in danger and to call the police immediately. They will need to take emergency hold. Dr. Scott says she will meet them at the police station. She hangs up the phone and runs to her car telling her secretary she will be out all afternoon to cancel all appointments she is on her way to an emergency.

The old teacher watches the teen tearing up with painful memories of her older sister wandering the streets dirty and lost. Her parents had been embarrassed of her. When her sister got sick at just 17 years old her parents kicked her out to the cruel streets and left her to die. When she needed help, she was thrown away. Her heart is breaking as she wants to tell the student help is on the way, but she knows this girl is not there anymore. The teacher makes the call to Dennis and Boyd.

The same kid needs to be picked up on a hold and be ready in case she does not go quietly as some violent behavior was being demonstrated. She hangs up the phone looking Patty who is watching with interest as the kid is now pacing the hallway babbling.

"Tell Mr. Greene the police are on the way. Stay in this office with the door closed. Hold the bell for next class, and for goodness sake, mind your business and let the police handle this." the old teacher tells Patty with a look of this is serious on her face.

Patty nods and shuts off the bell alarm before entering Mr. Greene's office to inform him of this situation. Patty then calls Mary to inform her of her wards pending arrest. Mr. Greene comes out of his office to watch the teenager pace agitated cursing and appearing to become more upset with each passing moment. He hopes the police will arrive soon. This looks like trouble.

Dennis and Boyd are with Cathy bullshitting about the weather when the school calls about the same kid they just picked up a few days ago.

Cathy is irritated, "Why is she not in a hospital? She is obviously very sick! That does not go away in a few days, Jesus!" she yells at Dennis.

Dennis only shakes his head as he and Boyd head for the squad car ready to do the same job they had thought had already been done. A call from a Dr. Scott comes into the station. Cathy is informed a psychologist will be here for intake as the clinic has been alerted. She is also informed the patient may be violent.

Cathy hangs up and runs to the car and tells her fellow officers be careful. The Doctor is on the way.

The police officers jump into the car hitting the sirens blue and red. Now, begins a wild race to keep this kid from harming herself or someone else.

"Why didn't you listen to me! I told you the answer was a short circuit, but you are too stupid to listen to anyone. It is because you are a sinner, and sinners they are too stupid to do, to do, Oh! You are just not listening to me," I babble trying to recall where I am.

I feel angry and trapped but I do not know why. I pace trying to get rid of the tension, but it is not helping. My skin feels funny because it is not mine. Someone is playing a trick on me. They put a skin suit on me that does not fit. I begin to rip at my clothing trying to get the suit off. It is not working. There is a strange hole in my head, and it is letting to much air inside. That is it! The short circuit is in my head! Laughing erupts from my chest but it is not mine. It is coming from the walls all around me. I am so confused!

The delusion students are scared. I see them watching me, wondering too why my skin does not fit. They are hiding behind doors from the laughter. I would join them, but I have a mission to fix the power outage from the short circuit. The old teacher she thinks I did not see her slip back into that door and push those delusions inside like baby chickens. I did but they do not matter. They are not real. I am on a real mission and will deal with them later.

"Fix it the circuit is to be fixed, it is the X, is it is the answer to the power, the power is the answer to the fix," I babble as I see the tool I require to fix this outage.

Running full force into the lockers I bash my head into the metal door. It stuns me as blood pours down into my vision. I see the walls are bleeding and it is now raining, how odd? I laugh as I bash my head into the locker again harder. Stunned again, the world begins to spin as ringing like a million phones echo in my ears.

I stagger pacing still babbling and laughing. "It is the cure, you know, the cure is the circuit that is in the wait, what is that, no," I am suddenly aware I have to get out of here. The air is being pulled out and I will smoother if I do not run!

I see the door to the outside. Running like the wind I head for it slamming it so hard it comes off the hinges while ripping open. The light is blinding bright, but I ignore it and take off across the schoolyard not having any clue where I am running. Bleeding, ripped up sleeves, confused, laughing, and cracked I run for the woods.

A squad car and a station wagon pull into the school yard to the sight of an insane teenager laughing and running for the woods. The station wagon stops but the squad car chases behind the teen till catching up. It stops and out jumps the short but sturdy Dennis. He runs and jumps on the teenager's back. She is startled going down without a fight with dust flying everywhere as they hit the ground.

Dennis recovers quickly he picks the kid up she does not fight. To his horror the teen is incoherent and laughing while babbling nonsense. Blood is pouring down her ghoulish face and he wonders if he harmed her by accident while knocking her down. She does not appear to notice it.

He takes her gently by the upper arm and guides her into the squad car back seat. She is still giggling and babbling but offering no resistance. He closes the door and thanks God she is too far gone to fight. He had feared they might have to shoot this one in self-defense based on the call. He has great happiness it has ended without such a terrible result. He also has much sadness as this kid is obviously in a lot of pain. He is unsure if she can be helped, or if this is her future forever.

A woman is approaching him appearing concerned, or nosy is more like it. He knows this woman, Mary.

"What is the problem officer? Is my granddaughter, okay? What is going on?" She asks peering into the backseat at the now very quiet passenger.

"We will be in touch Ma'am. I am sure there will be some folks that would like to talk to you," he sneers.

Dennis knows Mary has let this happen and he intends to make her pay. "No one, not especially a child should be neglected like this," he thinks as he, still eyeing Mary, gets into the squad car.

Boyd and he speed off, sirens blaring, for the second time in less than five days over the same problem. Mary runs into the school ready with a story to spread to try to defend herself against the indefensible, realizing too late she should have made me take those medications.

The glorious peace of darkness has left me as my eyes open and the horrible unintelligible world comes into my focus. I do not know where I am. There is nothing but white I am wrapped in a tight-fitting jacket, but I have no arms. Someone cut them off. There is no bed, no commode, no anything. The world is spinning like a tilt a whirl and that makes me laugh. I do not bother to do more than sit up. This is a white jacket on me they must have made from the walls. It is strapped around the alien body I seem to be trapped inside of. My skin is too tight. So is this coat and I want out of both of them. I begin to struggle but I cannot even begin to unravel either of them.

They must have used super glue," I think, "but who is they?"

My head hurts when I try to think of who they are, but one thing that is clear, they are going to kill me for sure. I am in a slaughterhouse, which is what this is. They whoever they are, are not happy I have solved for X. They want to stop me. I need to figure out the plan and change it. I remember the LSD is in the food. They will try to make me take it for sure. I am not going to eat it even if they break out my teeth I decide. After all they already cut off my arms. Sliding to the furthest wall from the door I sit there watching.

Waiting with anticipation ready to fight them with all I have. I know what they want. I am not going to eat their poison. I am aware of their attempts to fool me into thinking this is real. I know I am a delusion, and nothing will take that knowledge from me, damn it.

The woman comes in the door finally. She has a plate of food with her on a tray (I told you) and she wants me to eat it. I know this woman. I saw her with Mary. She is in on it with Mary.

She puts some of the food on a spoon and wants me to put it in my mouth. I turn my head and refuse.

She sighs looking sad. "Good." I think, "she is realizing I am not going to give into her bullshit."

She looks at me, "Okay kiddo. We have not been able to get you to eat or speak since you arrived. If you can hear me, I want you to know I am your friend. You are sick, very sick. If you do not eat you will die do you hear me?" She is trying to see if I understand her.

I do, but I am not going to fall for the trick. I cannot die. I am already dead. Delusions do not need to eat.

She sees me glaring with hate at her and realizes I am never going to take that LSD. "Alright, have it your way. If the Thorazine is not going to wake you up, we have another way." She gets up and takes the tray of food.

She knocks on the door and a big woman in a white hospital outfit opens it and lets her out. They leave and I am relieved. They have given up trying to get me to believe them. That is great news. I could use some, these days. Everything has been so confusing but now I feel better. If only someone would just peel this damned wall coat off me. All would be fine.

Not long after that woman who is conspiring with Mary leaves, two big males in white coats come through the door. I realize this is not a good thing. They pick me up, as I have no arms, they have to grab my shoulders. They finally peel the wall coat off and

I have arms again. I am surprised as I thought they had been cut off. It was a nice surprise.

But they grab my new arms and force me from the white room into the hallway. The smell of rubbing alcohol and cotton fill the air. I hear crying and screaming in the distance. Oh, of course, this is the slaughterhouse after all, those are the ones they are killing. This scares me. I thought I was ready to die, but I think I have changed my mind. I begin to struggle but they are too strong, and I am being drug into a small room with a gurney bed. Next to the bed is a strange machine that looks like a CB radio transmitter box, but it has strange long wires attached to small bulbs. There is also a man wearing a surgical mask and hat with glasses in a blue surgery outfit.

"Oh, fuck this," I yell and really begin to fight. They are going to dissect me! "Fuck, fuck, fuck, let me go, I scream in full blow panic.

The men have me tight I am forced into the bed and strapped arms and legs as they start an IV in my arms. I am pleading with them to please not kill me, but they ignore me. The surgeon flips on the machine and it begins to whirl as the room seems to become warm. He starts putting suction cups all over my head that are attached to the CB machine. He then puts in a plastic mouth guard holding my jaw shut on it, as he injects something into the IV bag. My heart is pounding as one of the big men hold my head still. A sudden flash, darkness.

I open my eyes. A woman is there. She is holding up fingers asking me if I know 'how many fingers.' I do not even know what fingers are. I know I should, but this word is not making sense. I stare at her.

"Where am I?" I cannot remember. "What are fingers?" Fear fills me as I cannot remember who I am either. "Who am I?" I scream while trying to get up, but I am strapped down. This woman puts a needle into the bag attached to my arm. Darkness comes again.

I am back in the surgery bed strapped down. The whirling of the electricity machine is all I hear as the cold suction cups are placed on my head and guard in my mouth.

I am afraid, but so confused, "what is happening? Why do I remember this but not?" I think. The flash, darkness.

I awake again, the fingers question. "I do not know what...wait, two! I see two fingers," I say happy I can finally remember what fingers are. The woman smiles at me. This is the doctor. Dr. Scott that is her name, she told me once in a dream.

I smile back. I can understand again. "Where am I," I ask Dr. Scott.

"You were very sick. You are in the hospital," she says while a nurse takes my blood pressure. "A special hospital, a psychiatric hospital. Do you know what made you sick?"

I think on that. It was the LSD I remembered but something told me to keep that to myself. So, I shook my head no.

"You have Paranoid Schizophrenia. For some reason you were not taking your medication and you became severely psychotic with delusions. The medication was not working, and you refused to eat. We had no choice but to use Electroconvulsive Therapy to break your psychotic episode and give the medication something to work with. We only want you to be well. We are not your enemies please tell me you understand that" he said looking deep into my eyes to be sure I understood what she is saying.

"What is Electroconvulsive Therapy," I ask as the memories of whirling machines and scary surgeons make my spine tingle in fear.

She looks at the vitals monitor above my hospital bed, "you probably know it as shock therapy." Dr. Scott waits to see what I have to say about that.

I just look at her in disbelief, "She shocked me! What the fuck! Barbarians!" I wanted to cry but still that odd not being able to reach my emotions stubbornly holds on tight.

"I had solved for X. X was indeed electricity," I think bitterly. Shock therapy to be exact.

450 volts of electricity twice applied straight to my brain had awakened me from a complete disintegration or melt down caused by the ravages of my disease. I had just "ridden the lightening according to the other teenage inmates in the mental hospital there for various reason ranging from suicide attempt to "anger issues."

They were in awe of me. Not just because I was the only Schizophrenic there. It was also because I was the only one of them who had ridden the lightening. This treatment was a weapon of last resort. Dangerous at that time, it causes a severe Grand Mal seizure. The theory was that disruption of my disordered brain waves would force them to reset like a computer when you reboot it. People had broken bones, and even died when this treatment is used. Sometimes it did not work at all.

However, in my case it was the only thing left, I was going to die of starvation if nothing was done. I was already so close. So, they threw the kitchen sink at me. It had worked. As the days progressed, I became more organized and less psychotic.

Unfortunately, as I got better, I also got better at lying to them. Now that I was aware that certain admissions of symptoms would cause more medication, or even another trip to the "shock shop" I made sure to watch my mouth.

I learned that painfully when I admitted I thought I was a delusion resulted in a third ride. After that, I was never talking to anyone about that again

I was forced to interact with the other inmates, when all I wanted to do is be left alone. Not eating resulted in a trip to the "hole" in a straight jacket, as did talking back which I learned after my third trip to the hole to wear the one-armed coat. Medication was forced and refusal resulted in threats of the "shock shop." I had to go to group therapy but refused to speak which led to extra time in the hospital overall. If I tried to stay in my meager prison cell (room so they called it, bullshit) I was forced out and threatened with all the above. I was not allowed my clothing, other than a hospital outfit and socks. I was banned from razors, shoes, pencils/pens, the outside, or even any privacy with constant cameras, hospital staff and security guards.

The medications were forced into me at incredibly high doses. Despite the fact that I still knew I was not real and was certain they were giving me LSD, I did not tell them out of fear of worse treatments. I could do nothing but drool with horrible spontaneous muscle spasms as well as jaw grinding. I could often not sleep and found myself pacing and babbling. More meds were given to try to stop that with added side effects such as a shuffling walk, spontaneous sudden shouting/cussing, insomnia, urges to scream, uncontrollable stomping, hand/head shaking, sweats, headaches, and stomach aches as bad as the original poisoning from my mother.

Now, unlike the only mercy that my psychosis had provided me, I was very aware I was supposed to be a Schizophrenic. They had not only reorganized my thoughts, given me back my mind, but also my insight to just how bad this is. I knew they were wrong but the more I tried to make them understand I was not sick the more they treated me like I was.

Depression had begun to onset as the end of my first month of "incarceration" came to an end. As the new medications were added and they continued to tell me I was sick, I began to give up hope and felt suicidal. Another trip to the "shock shop" kept me from ever admitting that again.

I turned sixteen in the psychiatric hospital. I spent that day remembering Dr. Higgs telling me schizophrenics can have "Normal" lives. No one celebrated my sweet sixteenth. No one visited, no one cared. It passed like every other day of my life to this point, forgotten. Yep, this was certainly normal, my normal.

As the third month of hospitalization came to an end, I had become one bad ass ashtray maker, and had walked a rut into the hospital hallway that housed our "cells." I still did not interact with the other patients unless forced and then it was nothing more than a 'hi, yeah how are you.' I did not care how they were. I just wanted to go home to my cemetery and forget this ever happened.

Some of my symptoms had ceased such as "code breaking/automatic writing," disorganized thinking which had lack of recognition, and "the static with the death bug cicadas."

Other symptoms had improved, less auditory/visual hallucinations, cognitive slippage (memory loss), and inability to understand speech. However, some had deepened such as delusion that I was dead/delusion, being poisoned, and emotional coldness with inappropriate affect (laughing spontaneously).

I did not report them as I was capable of knowing that this was not what they wanted to hear. When the giggles hit me, I ran to the bathroom and stifled the noise till it passed. Thus I hid the symptom.

Three months and one week after my wandering the hallways mad as a hatter, I was finally released into the custody of Mary. She was most unhappy. She had to battle an investigation on her home for medical neglect. If she had hated me before she really hated me now.

They as always dropped the ball and the case was close unfounded, so it would appear all would go back to normal, my normal. With one exception, Mary insisted I take the medication, or she would force me to come back to her and Bob. She was going to check me every other day to see if I was "acting loony." I readily agreed to this seeing as how I was in no position to argue. I did not want to go back to her, and there was no way I was staying in this hospital.

With an understanding, I made this deal with my devil, even though I knew she was trying to poison me or drug me. I also did not believe a single one of them. I did not have Schizophrenia, they were wrong. This was just a conspiracy to keep me from the truth I had already discovered. I was dead and a delusion, and they are my killers.

Mary took me shopping for new clothing since all of mine had been ruined in my "drugged up haze" (had to be right?). I took great delight in spending as much money of hers as possible only because it pissed her off.

I bought an array of black outfits, many with punkish looks, long black jackets, chain jewelry, a pair of platform black punk boots, a black derby hat, and a long pretty blond wig. I also purchased a new mad box, and mirror since the other mirrors did not work.

I also bought many new artists cassette such as the Cure, Peter Murphy, Metallica, and the Cult. My final touch was white/black/red/grey make up and fake blood. Mary nearly fainted at both the items and of course the price. I informed her if I was going to be out there in the wild, I would have what I needed to stay "sane." No one wanted that to happen again. With such a threat even that dumbass could not refuse.

The delusional symptom had been allowed to fester unnoticed or unreported. Now it was all consuming as I was terminally infected with it. In fact, many of the re-emerging symptoms of my psychosis had gone on with almost no notice. This was sure to have future implications but without any real funds three months was all the agency was willing to pay for. So, with only a small patch on a tire with a huge leak, I was released back into the awaiting unprepared delusional world.

I had found my calling. I was a delusion. In my world I am the ruler. Neither alive nor all dead, that made me undead. I lived with both worlds, the real and unreal. My home is the graveyard, my friends are the dead. However, I walk above ground and must suffer the living.

My new look, much darker, more artistic and filled with deeper meanings had come from a vision I had while 'riding the lightening.'

A voice called out in the darkness of the lightening, "You are the bridge, between the worlds. Tell the suffering to beware, never become the bridge. The darkness is you." I understood this.

"I must help others stay away from the hellish world I was too stupid to avoid. I am the darkest nightmare they fear they will become. I knew how I got there, so I should be able to help others avoid it, right," was the thought in my head as Mary dropped me off at the cemetery.

She left without any words as I walked into my gate ready to embark on my "undeath" journey.

I know, my beauties, it is my shocking personality that helped you to get this far, but we really have just started, haven't we? Have you acquired a better understanding of the hellish nightmare of Schizophrenia from my story?

Next let me state that my memories are exactly as you are reading, because they are my memories, even if they seem strange to you. Where there are places with no explanation of how that happened, it is because I do not remember it due to psychosis, unconsciousness or medications. Where I have told this story in third person, I am using third party witness accounts and psychiatric records to tell you what I could never know due both to my own sickness and to the fact that their thoughts are their own (I stopped reading their minds long ago). Now all that explained, be so kind and research electroconvulsive therapy (ECT).

Chapter 23: The Mourning after Death, Because the Undead Cannot Cry

We shall continue on our dark path but please do not worry. WE ARE NOT ALONE. Do not mind the extra crowd tonight, they belong here, you just never noticed them before. Aren't you glad we found the shocking discovery that opened our eyes! That makes two of us, or more but who is counting? Okay, so throw away the medication, forget calling the cops, and start running because they really are after you. Don't worry about me, I am already at the finish line, and I have the evidence below...see you there.

"The schizophrenic mind is not so much split as shattered. I like to say schizophrenia is like a waking nightmare."
- Elyn Saks

"Can you breathe the filthy air, so tell me how it feels Can you learn to love someone if you can't see what is real. Can you feel the burning fear that tears you up inside And you don't sleep at night 'cause creatures disembowel all your dreams"
-Gothminister song Liar

Mary pulls away spinning out angry as I haul my many bags of new supplies through the cemetery gate. I smile to myself. I am glad she is pissed. For a moment I savor the sound of her revving motor as she speeds off down the old dirt road. I think that memory could hold me forever, she had caused me so much trouble with her tricks.

I got to my outhouse and despite being gone over three months no cobwebs and everything is as I left it. Odd, but then again time is not really in line here in this delusional world. It maybe had not really been three months here in my cemetery. This place was the portal to the real world that I could no longer reach.

I carefully, remove all my items and store them. I had also bought some canned food and a new jug full of water. I had decided I would never eat food from anyone else again. My water would be refreshed daily and as for that medication, well forget that, now that no one can force me to take their LSD tabs. I am not crazy, damn it, and they are not going to make me become that way.

After all my things are put away, I pop a tape in my mad box and go outside to check on my roomies. They had not fared as well as my outhouse. Clean up would have to be done. It would seem the outhouse is the portal and the grounds the rings, like on Saturn. I had seen a picture in a book about that once, so this makes sense as I think about it cleaning up the grounds.

Tomorrow I would return to school. The thought did not suit me well. Most of my trouble had come from that weak spot in my mission. Picking up fallen branches I contemplate a plan to get away from that distraction, when I hear a cough.

I look up and next to a head marker is a man. He is middle age and wizened by the sun. The man is so thin I can see his eye orbits and jaw bones. He is balding with a very pronounced Adam's apple, and old railroad clothes on. In his hand a hand rolled cigarette. He takes a drag and nods his head hello. It startles me. How long has he been here?

"Excuse me Mister, you are very rude Who are you," I demand ready to defend myself from this likely ragamuffin homeless weirdo.

He chuckles and drops the smoke to the ground crushing it out. "I live here just like you do, silly. I am Simon Brag. Don't you remember me?" He looks at me like we have known each other for years.

I realize he is obviously crazy. No one lives here but me and the rats. This must be a trick of Mary, or he is crazy. Either way I do not like this. "Okay psycho, how much did Mary pay you for this trick?" I ask him while looking about for a big enough branch to knock his ass out if he came any closer.

Simon starts to laugh. That is making me angrier. I do not like to be mocked. Finally, I spy a big stick and reach out and grab it ready to swing. However, I look up and Simon is gone.

"What the fuck?" I look around and no sight of the man. "He must have run away while I was grabbing the stick," I think.

I hear coughing again. I turn around and Simon is right there! I swing on him, but he catches my stick and holds it with incredible strength. He just stands there holding it with no effort staring at me with a smile.

"Let go and leave me alone, now," I yell at Simon.

"You already forgot? Well, that is to be expected. You are still sick from that poison you know. Stop taking it and you will remember me." He let go of my stick.

I do not know what to say. He has to have known me. He knows about the poison; how else could he know? I have not told anyone about it since riding the lightening. Telling anyone gets me punished.

"I am sorry, Simon," I say to him. I drop the stick.

"How could I try to hurt someone who was my friend," I think to myself.

He had to be because I would only tell someone I trust. Reaching deep as possible I try to feel bad for not remembering him and trying to hit him. However, try as I might the cold, dark unfeeling is there inside. No pain, no pleasure, no feeling at all. I look up at him to see if I can fake shame at least a bit panicked at this odd discovery.

He is laughing at me again. Now angry, that I could still feel. I am now sorry I dropped the stick.

"You are such a silly girl," he says still laughing, "You do not have to pretend to be ashamed you cannot remember me. I know it is the poison." He doubles over laughing harder with each word.

"Didn't anyone tell you reading my mind is rude," I said thoroughly disgusted at this Simon fellow. "Now, stop it. I am not trying to read yours. I know that is private."

Simon really started laughing at that and fell down on his back kicking his legs wildly howling.

"Oh, fuck you! I do not like to be mocked. Go away. I have had enough of this," I yell at him and storm off to my outhouse leaving him there laughing like a loon on the ground.

I get to the outhouse and Simon is already there, "what the hell?" I say looking back to where I left him laughing. "How did you do that," I demand to know.

"You know damned well how," Simon says in a mocking voice, "Now let's cut the shit shall we? You know where you are? Or did they fry that tiny pigeon brain of yours? Is your mission clear?" He is looking at me to see if I understand what he is driving at.

"Yes, I do know. I am on the mission. This is the portal to the real world and when I finish my mission,

I can go home to be real again," I say proud that I did remember after all. Sometimes I would forget things, but not this time.

Simon nods his head appearing proud I did remember it. So much had been foggy lately but now it was like the sun was finally rising, only for me it would be the moon as I knew I was darkness. This is my home here in the portal between the real and unreal. Here I am in control. All that matters now is my mission.

Simon rolls another cigarette and begins to ask me a lot of questions about my trip the 'loony bin.' He wanted to know what Dr. Scott said in particular. I answer the questions as well as I could. A lot of it I could not remember. He continued to ask about one thing in particular.

"What did Dr. Scott say about your giggling," he asked for the fourth time. I had already told him I could not remember any discussion about that.

"You sure? Try to remember," he urged.

I closed my eyes and the whirl of the machine echoed through my memory. Screams, rubbing alcohol, needles, pacing, but that is all that I can recall despite much effort to reach more information. This game was getting on my last nerve.

"Enough Simon. I do not want to talk about this anymore. Drop it. I am never going back, ever!" I finally open my eyes frustrated and ready to shut up his questions if need be.

"Oh my God! They did not fix you at all! You are psycho as ever," I hear a voice that sounds like Stephanie behind me.

I turn around quite surprised to see Stephanie standing there with a pad of paper and pen. She is wearing a blue shirt and brown skirt with worn out tennis shoes.

"This is not real," I say to myself as I stare at this delusion. I am sure is someone playing a trick on me. I am not going to fall for it. Not this time.

Stephanie never existed she was in my LSD riddled brain I keep telling myself. Now that I was going to stop them from drugging me, I will also get rid of this delusion once and for all.

"Go away, Stephanie," I say. Surely, since I am in control here, I can make the delusions go away anytime I want. I was in no mood for this one, or for Simon either.

"Who are you talking to psycho? There is only you and I here. I thought they fixed you in the hospital but here you are talking to no one just like before. Does Mary know," she says stomping her foot.

Now, that caught my attention, what does she mean does Mary know? I look at her suspiciously,

"How do you even know Mary, Stephanie?" In my heart though I always knew, she is in on this conspiracy.

She looks at me angrily, "Well, while you were gone, I came out here and protected your stuff till you got home. She came out here to hide your stuff in case anyone got wise with the law trying to get her and stuff. You know because, well because you are you and all. So, I got to know her, and she told me all about you and stuff. I helped her hide your stuff," she spewed.

"Sure, you did, liar," I growled back. "So, now go back and suck her ass some more, Judas."

Stephanie's anger turned to surprise then to tears. "Why are you so mean to me! I just want to be your friend and stuff! I was trying to help you and stuff! Look I even bought you a present because Mary said you had a birthday," she sobs while trying to hand me the pad and pen.

"She is mocking you of course," I hear Simon say behind me. "She is trying to trick you, watch out."

I nod my head because he is right. "Liar! You do not want to be a friend. You want to make me think I am crazy. I know the truth so cut the crap," I yell at her.

She drops the pad and pen and really starts sobbing putting her hands over her eyes. I don't care.

"Stupid delusion. Go away! Run back to your Mommy Mother May I Mary Mary May I!" I start to giggle at that.

"You are not better at all." Stephanie drops her hands and runs over to the gate. She sits down curls up and sobs loudly while rocking.

"I cannot believe this shit," I yell in disbelief. "This is a fucking insane asylum! I just want to be left alone! Why will no one leave me the fuck alone." I begin to pace feeling my skin is too tight. I really wish I could get this skin suit off.

As I pace, I consider what to do about this Stephanie delusion. She needs to go but she keeps showing up. I yell at her, hit her, but nothing works. She is like a nightmare that never ends. I can hear her sobbing like a goon over by the gate. It agitates me more. I am beginning to work into a frenzy. I go over to her 'present' and kick it. It lands a bit away, so I jump on it and grind it into the dirt. That made me feel better already. I giggled as I stomped the glossy paper covering into a dull memory of its former self.

I was having such a good time stomping it I did not realize Stephanie had gotten up and approached me again. I feel my shield enclosed and crushed as she grabs me from behind in a bear hug. It feels like I cannot breathe. With a yell I fall to my knees paralyzed by her touch.

Rapid memories of the straight jacket and white room with no furniture or windows flashes into my minds with the whirl of the lightening. Stephanie grips tighter and I begin to gasp sure that I will soon expire as no air can be pulled into my lungs. I am caught in a stupor of rapid flashing memories of the hospital and my mother burning me, hitting me, falling in a grave, I see the skeleton and blow pop all in one horrible flash.

"Please let me go," I manage to squeak out. I am gasping trying to will these memories to stop overwhelming me. My mind cannot process all this information so fast.

"No! I am hugging you until you stop being mean. You just need love is all. You are just hateful because nobody ever hugs you. I know because I need to be hugged too, I miss my mom! I miss being hugged and so do you. It will make you cry it out and all will be well," Stephanie says sobbing as she squeezes even tighter.

I know I cannot cry. I have tried, I can't anymore. I can't feel anything but anger, fear and sometimes pain. Simon had asked me what Dr. Scott said about my giggling. I now remember what she said.

I see her sitting there in her desk across from me, "You have Schizophrenia. Your emotions will be flat. That means you will often feel the wrong ones for a situation. Sometimes you will not feel any at all. The medication cannot fix that. It is called a negative symptom. Desire, motivation, lust all those things will never come back. Medication can only help positive symptoms like hearing things no one sees. This will make you appear cold and unfeeling to other people, and they will not like you because of it. You need to learn to follow the lead of others and show facial expression like them even if you do not feel it to function. Do you understand?" She is looking at me to see if this makes sense to me.

"I understand," I say gasping. "Please let me go Stephanie, I will stop being mean."

"Not till you cry it out," Stephanie sniffles back tightening more.

"I cannot cry, Stephanie, damn it. I am undead." I pull out all my strength and break free of her grip sending her sprawling to the ground.

I am ready to stomp her like the note pad but realize that may cause trouble. I have remembered something else Dr. Scott told me. That if I hit these delusions, they will send me back to the 'shock shop.' With all I have, I keep myself from bashing Stephanie's pretty blond head into the cemetery earth.

"Keep your fucking hands off me. Do not touch me ever again," pointing at her and making it clear to Stephanie, I mean it. I then reach down and pick up her note pad present. "Thank you!"

Stephanie is still sniffling and staring at me confused. "You said, thank you?" She is unsure, "You like it?"

I nod my head and smile hollowly at her. I cannot hit this delusion, it will not go away, so I may as well deal with it. All I can think is "I hate being undead."

Stephanie buys the bullshit and jumps up smiling with delight. She is so moody; I can barely stand her roller coaster ride. Stephanie the delusion was as wild in mood shifts as I was restricted in mine.

"So, we can be friends then," she says still smiling, appearing to have forgotten the whole crying thing in seconds.

"Yeah, whatever. Did you know you are a flake," I ask her very abruptly wondering if she was aware of how insane she really is. They say crazy people do not know they are crazy. I had heard once somewhere.

"Yeah, I do," she giggles. "But at least I am not a psycho. I am just very emotional you know and stuff. I see a counselor you know." She confesses to me.

"Huh?" Now this was interesting. "Why?"

She looks at the ground again I see her eyes about to break out into rain, "because when my momma died, I got really depressed and stuff. Tried to kill myself. Now I get depressed all the time. Sometimes, I feel all numb inside and hollow you know and stuff.

So, I cut on myself to feel something," she shows me her wrists with various healing superficial cuts on them.

I back up. "Oh, shit! This one is a nut," I think fearful I may catch the crazies from her. "No wonder she is always bothering me. She thinks I am one of them. Well, she has made a mistake. I am not like her. I am aware of the truth." It all made so much sense now.

"Yeah, they say I have this thing called a Borderline Personality Disorder and stuff. So, I totally know how you feel about going to the hospital. I had to go to the hospital for three whole days when I tried to cut my wrists and die. They gave me medication and talked to me and stuff. The medication does not work and stuff. I still feel like no one likes me and I am so afraid to be alone and stuff. Now though we have each other," Stephanie says smiling and appearing very happy the tears quickly drying up.

"Oh wow," I think to myself. "She is gone. Okay just think, maybe Simon will know what to do. This girl is going to hurt somebody. She is just one sandwich short of a picnic basket." I just smile at this crazy delusion. I did not want to upset her and set her off.

"Well now what? Want to just hang and talk about stuff? Oh, I have a ton of gossip and guess what? You are like a legend and stuff at school. I got to tell you breaking that locker with your head, the door and beating up Mrs. Wells like that was like brilliant and stuff! Everyone cannot wait to see you and stuff. I bet you could get me a boyfriend because that is what friends do." She babbled on and on and on.

I sat down on the ground and settled in. She would talk nonstop for hours, I knew that. I looked over at Simon watching from the outhouse from time to time. He would just laugh at me. I would just roll my eyes at him.

I know I would probably think it funny too had it been reversed. Trapped in my only sanctuary from the delusional world by a damned delusion crazier than anyone I had ever met. That was saying something as there were some really messed up delusional kids at the hospital but then again, none of that is really happened anyway. That was the LSD messing with me. The hospital is not any more real than the blathering Stephanie.

Finally, it got late, and she had to get home. I tried not to look so happy to see her go. It really was not too hard to fool her into thinking I cared. I watched her face when she laughed I smiled and chuckled. When she frowned I would too. By the time she was ready to go, I believe I had mastered this emotional shit. Just watch the face. Follow the cues. If only I could get this skin suit off, I thought all would be gravy from here. I can now navigate this insane delusional world I am trapped in till I can complete my mission and get the hell out of here.

I wave and smile at Stephanie as she leaves skipping down the road to her home. "Bye-bye nutball," I say under my breath still smiling.

I could barely wait to slam the gate and be done with this most uncomfortable interaction. I sighed and returned to my outhouse to get my blankets ready for sleep. The weather had warmed to Spring while I had been 'away' so no fire needed. That was a plus. I saw Simon waiting for me still hanging around. Damn! All this company, all I wanted was peace and quiet. I reached in to turn off my mad box.

I promised myself that from here on out I would always have my mad box music pumping at a low level in my ears. I took it out of my shirt and reminded myself if Stephanie comes back to turn it louder and drown her out.

Since there was no need to have the real-world distractions peeking through to interfere with my navigation of this delusional world. The music helped me to ignore the rips and tears in the tapestry I could see all the time. The delusional world is so weak and often will rip to reveal what is just underneath. Anything, that could help me stop focusing on these confusing sightings would be a plus. My mad box helped but could not keep it all out. I was still working on finding something else to supplement and solve this little issue. Noticing the rips upset the other delusions. I did not want to go back to the hospital.

I also need to figure out how to get out of this school business. It was a source of trouble. I also knew it was all lies. Mrs. Wells was wrong in those equations. I had solved it and X is electricity.

"But they are telling delusional truths you know," Simon says as I approach the outhouse.

"I am going to bed. I have had enough of this tonight so you should do the same," I say waving him back to, well wherever he came from. "Go home."

"I told you I live here too. I am the real and you are the delusion. You are the one who needs to go home. I am already home, stupid," he chuckles. "You should pay attention in their school and there you will find your answer on how to escape the world they put you in. You really are dumb not to know that already. You can learn their lies. It is lies that run the delusional world," he finishes looking very proud of himself.

I wanted to kick his ass, but he had a valid point. I could use their lies to find my way out. Then I could finish my mission once and for all. I just hoofed at that. No way I was going to let this smug bastard know he was on to something.

I also realized he very obviously knows more than I do. He is real and I am not. So, he had already found his escape. I decided to trust his judgement even if I though him a dickhead. I had already fucked up enough. Time to let someone else do the thinking here. So, I nodded that I would do that. As I drifted off to sleep, I promised to learn all their lies and finally get the hell out of here.

Simon shook me awake the next morning, early, very early. He looked scared.

"What the hell man," I groggily said.

"Mary is coming. She is bringing trouble. Watch out." He was looking toward the gate.

I look too and see the station wagon pulling in. "Shit! What is she doing here!"

Mary gets out of the car and I jump up to meet her at the gate. I do not want her near my things. Poisoning bitch.

She looks pissy as she and I meet. She is holding a paper and that so called medication.

"Here is your medication, sinner." She hands me the pills, several of them.

I take them from her hand as she holds them out in her palm. She has many bottles in her arms. I say I will take them in a minute. She frowns at that. "You had better. Do you know what this is?" She says bitterly waving the paper in her hand at me.

I nod my head no, of course not. I would never read her mind. It is too nasty to even consider!

"It is a court ordered counselor. You have to go every week and talk to this woman from here until you are eighteen. You have been more trouble than I could have ever imagined. You are even more insane than you mother ever thought to be. I told her to abort you," she says angrily.

"Wait, what," I ask sort of still asleep, halfway not understanding this crazy talk.

"They said your mom was a Schizophrenic too you know, but I knew the truth. She had fallen from the grace of God. You were begat in one of her drug hazes. She always did the demon alcohol and cocaine till it made her nuts. Mom and I tried to get her to abort you, but she would not listen. Now, I have to clean up her mess. Oh lord, why do you not just kill yourself and get it over with? Look what you have done, you put my daughter in prison, beat up a good Christian lady over a piece of chalk, cost Bob and me a fortune and our reputations, live like an animal, look like the demon you are, and now I have to take you thirty miles every week to see some counselor. Not like that would matter. You are hopeless and have no future. Why don't you just do everyone a favor? No one will ever love you and I understand you cannot love even if they could. The Doctor told me all about you. I know you have nothing inside you but evil. So just die." She threw the pill bottles at me.

I watched the bottles fly through the air and scatter hitting the ground at my feet.

"Just fucking die, sinner," she yells in my face tears streaming. "I hate you. Everyone hates you."

Having gotten her heart felt words of disgust out of her system she turned, walked to the car and looked back before she said, "I will be back at the end of the week to see if you are here for this counselor. Take my advice and just die." She gets into the car and spins out (as usual) rushing down the road.

"Well, that was unexpected," I say out loud as I pick up the pill bottles. "Looks like someone is riding the cotton pony there." That makes me giggle as I walk back the outhouse wondering why I need to see a counselor.

"Does that not bother you what she said," Simon asks me as I return to the outhouse with my bounty of pills. He had been hiding in here from Mary.

"What, bother me? That my mom was a nut? Duh. She did try to kill me, man. No surprise there. I saw her doing the drugs myself," I chuckled. Simon must be dense if he did not figure that one out.

"No, that everyone hates you. That you have no future? That you are supposed to die," he says now rolling another cigarette.

I had to think on that a minute, "Should it?" I ask rather confused as it seemed to me that Mary always hated me, again no surprise there. The feeling was mutual.

"Yeah, I think it should. What is wrong with you lately? Are you even human? I do not care who you are, that should have been upsetting. But here you sit like a fucking robot thinking about counselors," he stares at me intently. "If you don't even feel anything, why do you bother? Maybe she is right, and you should go die," he finishes and storms off angrily.

Now that was a surprise. Why should I care? Am I missing something here? I go out to ask him what his problem is. I see him over by his headstone looking at the ground. I approach full of questions, but Simon can read my mind and answers me before I can open my mouth.

"You can never have a future she is right. You cannot feel and when you do it is all messed up. No one can love you and you cannot love them back. You will never be able to enjoy life because you cannot even *enjoy,* that is an emotion stupid! Your delusion is malformed and an abomination. If you do take the pills at least, then you will have found your way out," he says not even looking up.

I had to think on that a bit. He was right. I had not felt anything lately, actually not in a long time, except fear and anger. I remembered what Dr. Scott said about that again. She called it flattening affect and blunting of mood. Should I be hurt at what Mary said, I wonder.

"Yes!" Simon reads my mind, "Damn it! You are sixteen years old; do you want a boyfriend? A girlfriend? Hey, how about a puppy? Think stupid! What do you want," he yells?

The realization that he is right is sinking in. "Oh no, I do not want those things. I do not want anything but to be left alone and to finish the mission so I can be..." I stall on it.

"Dead," Simon finishes the sentence for me.

"Yes, so I can be dead." I say thinking of the pills in the outhouse. "You think I should just take the pills then?" I want to be sure because Simon seems to know more than I do.

"Yes. It will give you peace, there is no future here. You are a pain to everyone, and you do not want to be here either stupid. What are you waiting for," he walks off again to the far cemetery wall to give me time to ponder what he is saying to me?

Now I am really confused. First, he says to go learn the lies and finish the mission. Now he says to take the pills and finish that way. I thought he was my friend but now I am not so sure he is not also working with Mary.

"Fuck you, Simon," I yell. "I don't need you. I don't need anyone! You are right I am a robot so guess what. I don't feel anything for you either go to hell."

I storm off to the outhouse and throw all the bottles into the old box with the bible, broken mirror, and useless mad box. I am sick to death of everyone trying to tell me what to do. Stephanie wants me to cry, Simon and Mary want me to die, and Dr. Scott wants me to be Schizophrenic.

"I just want to be left alone, damn it. That is all I want, Simon. Do you hear me? I do want something," I yell from my outhouse hoping he can hear me as I put on my new look shaking off this most irritating morning situation. "Everyone here is nuts," I shout when my make-up is done.

I put on my new wig and the black derby to help keep it from always being pulled forward or back too far. I grabbed my long black heavy coat even though it was not cold. Putting on my platforms I continued hurling loud curses at Simon. When I finished, I was looking at the darkest creature I had ever seen. Mary had called me a demon. Now I fit the part, all I needed was a pair of horns.

I stepped out of the outhouse and could see fog rising all around me. I knew it was just a tear in the tapestry, but it was super cool to watch as I walked through it to the gate. I had no fear this day, no pain, no well, anything, as I walked off toward the school, water jug in hand. I no longer looked like a frightened ghoulishly disorganized cemetery kid. I had become darkness herself: cold, dark, empty, and scary.

I am undead and the undead cannot cry. They are just delusions of a life that no longer matters, as it is over for me. Feelings are not a luxury I have anymore, they belong in a dream that I can never wake up from.

As I walk down the road, these thoughts are going through my mind. I begin to think Simon is right and I should give up the mission. Maybe it would be easier to just finish my mission like that. I would have run back and have taken them all right there had I been able to convince myself this was the correct route to go. For now, I am still very unsure. I will need more evidence.

I decided to work on that later and for today I will go to school, learn their lies, and maybe if Simon still thinks I should, I can take the pills later when I get back home. No hurry, I have all the time in the world. Because there is no world, I am a delusion.

CHAPTER 24: SIMON SAYS

Good day, Beautiful People. I hope you all skipped your meds today. Now, grab your radio transistors and rabbit ear antennas to be sure that I come in loud and clear. Call up your imaginary friends and tell them to bring lots of coffee. Time to head to outer space but no worries, I have the transporter warming up. If you get into trouble, just call me up through the chip in your back teeth and I will beam you up beauties.

"The pendulum of the mind alternates between sense and nonsense, not between right and wrong."
- Carl Jung

This time as I enter the schoolyard the stares are in awe. I could not exactly recall what had happened during my last school day months ago, but I had a sense things had gone from bad to worse in the popularity department. I based that upon the looks of the students faces as my undead form holding a water jug rounded the corner. I really did not blame them. Not every day you see that walking into your high school. It no longer bothered me. Inside I felt nothing at all. They were just figments of my imagination anyway, so I chose to ignore them.

As I walked into the school, I was stopped by Patty who looked like she may jump out of her skin if I made any sudden moves. I felt I should laugh at that, but no mirth was in me today as I seemed preoccupied with Simon's suggestion to finish the mission.

"Mr. Greene would like to speak to you before class. He is waiting for you in his office," she said trying not to make eye contact.

Probably afraid I would read her mind I thought. Silly woman, I thought her too stupid to waste my time. I just nodded and headed for the office to see old resting bitch-face Greene.

I walked to his office with a nervous Patty behind me the whole way ready to run. She knocked on his door as he was reading paperwork when we came to the door. He looked up with his same old look of having just eaten a lemon. Mr. Greene had apparently spilled coffee all over his white suit shirt. A large brown stain was over his belly making it appear like mud on a mountain top. I had to shake my head at that. If only Simon could see this, he would be howling in laughter.

He motioned me to sit down and shot Patty a look. "You may go and close the door on your way out," said looking stern.

Once she had left, he rubbed his face and sat back in his chair appearing unable to decide how to broach the subject he had called me into the office to discuss. I was getting rather bored waiting there but decided to just hang in there. I thought getting up and leaving may result in further trouble from these pesky delusions. I just stared at him trying to not think of my safe cemetery reminding myself that I needed to learn the lies they teach.

"Well, uhm, we have had a lot of trouble here in this school since your arrival," he said after clearing his throat, appearing a bit nervous. "I need to know you are going to stop starting trouble here. I have an agreement I had typed up. It basically says that you are aware that any further disruption will result in your automatic expulsion from school," he pushes the paper at me.

I look blankly at the agreement and recall the doctors telling me this is not my fault. They said it is a disease. However, this Mr. Greene wants me to sign an agreement I will not be sick anymore? I am completely confused now.

"Well, evidence you are not sick after all, silly." I hear Simon say.

I look behind me surprised. "How did he get here?" I think to myself.

Behind me stood my friend and he was rolling a smoke. I wanted to tell him to not do that, smoking is forbidden at school, but Mr. Greene was looking down at something he had dropped so maybe he did not see Simon come in, but what about Patty?

"They cannot see me silly. I am real and they are not. I am telling you this proves you are not sick. Just sign it and get to class and stop thinking so much," he says finishing his rolling job.

I forgot he could read my mind, so I just nodded. Made sense to me. I grabbed the pen and signed the contract. Mr. Greene retrieved his whatever he dropped off the floor and looked up to see me push the paper signed and back at him without argument. He looked at it suspiciously then smiled at me.

"God! He is even uglier when he smiles," laughed Simon behind me.

I wanted to tell Simon to cut that out, but I dare not call attention to him.

Mr. Greene then says, "Great, we understand each other. Now get to class and behave yourself you hear me? Or we both know what happens." He holds the paper up to show it to me.

"Or we get thrown out of Vietnam," Simon said laughing even harder at Mr. Greene's threat.

I stand up and leave quickly nearly knocking Patty over who was eavesdropping outside the door as I came flying out. Simon followed close behind laughing the whole way. I come out of the office and rush to class past all the delusions rushing themselves before they too would be late. That idiot Mr. Greene had made me late enough I would have to get to my desk with a full room. I hated that.

The room was packed as I feared so I took a breath as I kept my eyes on my desk and off the other students quickly walking to my desk. Mrs. Wells was not in yet which was a blessing or so I thought. She likely would still be holding a grudge over my taking over her chalkboard.

I sat down and put my jug to the side, just as the first note arrived on my desk. As usual, I ignored it. Several more followed. I did the same to them as the first one. I was knocking them off my desk into the floor wondering when they would realize I was not interested in anything anyone had to say, when Simon came through the door just ahead of Mrs. Wells.

My backside felt like it grabbed my seat as terror ran through me. I could not believe my eyes. He was smoking one of his horrid, rolled cigarettes as if he owned the place. Simon took a long drag blowing the smoke toward the ceiling as he came over and crouched near my desk. I looked around at the other students and Mrs. Wells to see if they could see him too. No one seemed to notice my friend there crouched like a hobo next to my desk, smoking and smiling.

"I told you they cannot see me; they are not real and I am. You need to get that through your head," he said again, looking a bit peeved while reading my mind.

I just nodded wide eyed in shock. Simon was a ghost in this delusional world. That knowledge truly frightened me. If I am seeing this much of the real world, I had to wonder exactly how dead I actually am. His suggestion to take the pills rushed into my mind again. Maybe, he is right. If I can already see him, then it would not take much to get me out of this delusion and back where I belong.

Thankfully, Mrs. Wells began her lesson without saying a word to me. I had been concerned she would mention her beef with me, but she was more of a lady than I had given her credit for. She was careful to not even look my direction. I was more than glad of that. Simon stayed crouched next to me the entire period as she droned on about the useless equation lies of delusion.

When the bell finally rung, everyone rushed out. I waited for everyone to leave unwilling to turn my back on any of these idiot delusions. Simon stood up to follow me out as I left when Mrs. Wells walked over and blocked the door. My heart pounded, as I assumed this was the moment, she had decided to retaliate for the wrongs she believed me to have done.

She was looking me right in the eyes, "How are you feeling," she appeared to be trying to read my mind.

Surprised that she had not struck me, I did my best to block her prying. "Fine," I replied flatly. But I began to wonder if she was toying around to be sure no one saw when she hit me.

I braced for it assuming any second, she would thump me. Instead, she stood there looking me over. She was definitely searching me for something. Of what, I had no clue.

She would not move. I stood there unsure what to do. Simon came up closer and whispered, "tell her you are feeling much better and say thank you, you stupid twit. Smile too."

I did not want to listen to his advice, but he must know more than me I decided. So, I did as he instructed.

Mrs. Wells appeared to relax when I said, "I am feeling much better, thank you." Then I faked a quick smile.

She looked at the floor, then to me and said, "I just don't want you to end up like Sissy. Please take your medication and if you ever need to talk, I am here to listen." She handed me a note not unlike the several I had already knocked to the floor.

"Take the note and smile," Simon whispered.

I blindly took the note faking another smile as Simon told me to do. Mrs. Wells seemed satisfied she had extended her best efforts and finally stepped out of the way. I rushed past her glad that mess was over.

As I entered my second period classroom, I stopped briefly to drop Mrs. Wells note into the garbage can. I did not care to even look at it. She thought she was helping me, but I already knew no one could. Only Simon seemed to understand everything in this very strange world and whether I liked it or not, he was sticking with me.

The second period class began as the first with notes being passed to my desk. I continued to knock them to the floor. I listened intently to the lesson of lies being preached by the delusional instructor with a focus I had never known before. Each lie spewed from her mouth seemed to build on the next as I began to build a foundation of understanding how these idiots worked. It was really a simple thing. I chuckled to myself recalling how I had struggled with this school business before, well before I discovered the truth of my existence. I had been like all the other students here buying into the lie that this was all real. Now with my newfound knowledge of the extent of the lie, I found school to be no problem at all. Each lie was written down in the stomped notebook Stephanie had given to me, but this time I had no real need to write it down. It seemed only truth would escape my memory. The lies preached in this delusional school were like flies in honey in my mind. Nothing escaped it.

By lunch time, I was ready to have Simon all to myself so we could discuss further his suggestion that I take the pills. I had begun to realize he did have a point. The more the "lessons" of the classes filled my brain the more I thought I did not want to remain in this delusional world long. It seemed to be a cold and rule ridden place. I felt no emotions myself, but this delusional world was even lower than that. The history class taught me that delusions were beyond awful to each other. It did make sense, if you are not real and there is no real punishment, why not? As the lunch bell rung, I left behind the charging student body mumbling to Simon about the idea that no one here had any consequences or at least did not appear to understand them.

Eventually we ended up at the picnic table in the cafeteria yard that had already been the site of so many other arguments. I had become very agitated at the idea that it seemed to me that in this delusional world the wicked get away with being wicked. I tell Simon that it seemed to me the victims have to suffer in secret or believe they are a type of hero for surviving the cruelty. They cannot just forget the cruel treatment, and some are dead over it. The victims have their lives destroyed in many ways never able to move on. In the end, the wicked never seem to pay nor do they have to believe anything. They just get away with it, period.

He laughed at me when I made that point. That made me very angry. Seemed as though his smart-ass behavior knew no bounds.

"But they don't Simon. They can get away with anything here and no one is punished at all!" I argued to his amusement.

"You are wrong there. You suffer do you not? You are a Sinner, remember. You never were very bright so not really your fault but still silly girl. I bet you even forgot who I am!" He said while trying to stifle his giggling taking a long drag of one of his smokes.

I thought on it, "You said you are Simon Bragg." I remembered his name.

That made him snort. "Not my name you little fool. I have told you and told you, you are my dream. I am real and you are not real. This is my world, and you are a part of my imagination. I was a Sinner too you know." he looked at me to make sure I understood. I nodded.

"So actually, you have to do what I say. If it were not for me, you would not even exist in any capacity." He laughed on that. "Do you remember that now or not? How much lightening did they give you anyway? I swear I still see smoke coming out of your ears," he put his smoke in his mouth and chuckled low.

I was angry he said that. I had decided that the hospital did not happen, and I did not like to talk about riding any lightening either. I did remember that I am a figment of his imagination. I did recall we are both Sinners but seemed to me that he had no right to go pushing my buttons. He knew I hated to be mocked. So, I reach out and knocked his cigarette out of his mouth.

"Shut the fuck up, Simon," I yelled at him. "I may have to do what you say, but I will not be abused by that toothless mouth of yours!"

I was livid and ready to beat the shit out of him if he said one more thing. "No wonder your wife left you, stupid drunk," I said now mocking him.

He just glared angrily at me. He had forgotten I could read his mind as easily as he could read mine. I rarely read other minds because it is truly rude. However, I had read his without any inhibition since Simon had not allowed me any privacy.

I could see his memories. Simon had been a shiftless man who loved his rotgut, bathtub bourbon. Always on the liquor in life he, was never sober even on his railroad job as a brakeman. His pretty wife Danielle with an Irish brogue and red hair suffered his alcohol induced rage with his beating her so often one day she could not take it anymore. Despite her deep Catholic belief about marriage, she had packed up her meager possessions and left him to wallow alone in the brown liquor mire he simply could not live without.

After Danielle left, he became despondent giving in completely to the demon alcohol. Simon's job on the trains of the late 1880's was a very dangerous job even when your rail worker was sober. Simon had met his demise thanks to a night of drowning in the bottle. In an error a sober brakeman would not have made he slipped and fell from a moving train while standing atop a car trying to apply the brakes to help slow the train. He was killed instantly as fell between the cars and was crushed. As I watched his story through my mind, in horror I began to wonder why I should ever take any advice from this idiot!

"Stay out of my mind, you hear me," Simon yelled in my face. He was visibly shaken I could read it in his eyes and see it in his mind.

I began to laugh at him. The tables had turned now. "The door swings both directions, darling. No secrets between friends, right? You are a toothless drunk. How dare you tell me how to live without sin when you could not do it yourself."

Simon got close to my laughing face and stared me right in my eyes, "I quit drinking. Yes, I was a drunk! Y.es, I paid dearly for it. But at least I could, and did, quit. I was a sinner but not anymore. At least I am not an incurable schizophrenic like you are. You are a sinner from birth itself. No redemption for you," he smiled smugly and chuckled.

Oh well, now that was simply uncalled for far as I was concerned. If Simon is my friend, then I would rather be alone.

I pushed him backward in his chest, "Fuck off, Simon. Leave and never come back, you hear me." I was yelling now at this drunken fool, as he fell to the ground from my shove.

"Jesus Christ! Do you ever have a moment of sanity?" I hear the horrid voice of Stephanie behind me as I reached down grabbing two small rocks from the ground to pelt Simon with if he decided to stick around.

I simply could not take another second of this crap. No matter where I would go, I could not get a second of peace and quiet or any privacy these days! Simon, or Stephanie, are everywhere. I turned and threw one of the small rocks without even aiming hoping to hit Stephanie in the head. The rock flew harmlessly missing as it landed with a thud behind her.

"What the hell, Psycho. You almost hit me. What are you doing and who the hell do you keep talking to? Did you take your medication? Does Mary know about this," she said looking at me as if I was a beaker of unknown fluid in a science experiment.

She was standing there with the Crystal girl. These two busybodies had come up on the argument I was having with Simon and no telling how long they had been standing there enjoying the show.

Now that, even more than hearing Mary's name or being asked about my medication, pissed me off. I took another of the rocks and this time aimed it right for her. It made a perfect connection with a whopping sound on her right collarbone. Stephanie let out a yelp and grabbed her shoulder. The look of surprise on her face made me start to giggle. By now, I was quite infamous for my infernal giggling episodes.

"Damn! You are a creep," yelled Crystal who was now assisting her bestie, Stephanie, as they examined the area where the rock had made a connection.

"Stephanie, just leave this insane bitch! She is going to kill you. When will you understand that?" Crystal shot me an evil look, "Leave her alone, Psycho."

Now that really made me howl! She wanted me to leave Stephanie   I wanted nothing more than to never see the girl ever again!

"Stop calling me Psycho you dumb bitch. That is not my name" I said, having to force the words through bouts of laughter, "or Stephanie will not be the only one I end up killing."

"Shut up, you fool," I hear Simon yell from behind me, "you cannot threaten them or the hospital, remember, you idiot. Take it back and be nice, damn you."

I look behind me to see Simon still sitting there holding his head and shaking his head as he says, "You had better apologize and be super sweet or 450 volts will make you be nice."

Damn, he was right, and I knew it which really pissed me off more. It just made no sense. These fools were upsetting me, calling me names, insulting me, and not listening to me, but I could not defend myself or they would send electricity through my head again. Now I would have to apologize and be nice to those who are not nice to me. How is this fair? There is simply no doubt I am a prisoner.

I now decided I was wrong in my argument with Simon earlier. The wicked do indeed get punished. I just wish I could remember what the hell I ever did that was so bad I deserved all this torment. I was sure it must have been awful, and likely I have it all coming but I really would like to know what I have done! I think the lightening probably erased the memory of these evil deeds. I realize I may never remember them. So, with a great deal of resignation at my helpless situation I take a deep breath and ready myself for a good healthy helping of bullshit. At least the damned giggling episode had stopped.

"I am sorry, Crystal, I did not mean that. I would never hurt anyone, I swear. Uhm, Stephanie I apologize for hitting you with the rock I was just, uhm, being, errrr, psycho, I guess. I am happy to see you both." I almost gagged as I said that. ECT was starting to look like an attractive alternative to this bullshit.

Much to my surprise the girls bought the false apology and they invited me to sit down at the table Steph and I had won the right to when we took on Kelly and her crew. I did not want to sit down but I did as asked in order to calm down the situation. Simon just sat on the ground rolling his horrid smokes and watching. It was like living under a microscope every move, every thought, every statement being criticized, and controlled by a dead brakeman. There was no doubt I had become a meat puppet.

The girls began to gossip about a new girl at the school who was fast making a name as a "slut," named Julie. They really seemed to hate this girl, talking in great detail about her latest conquests and foul unions with numerous boys about the town. I did not know this Julie, nor did I engage in gossip, so I just sat there pretending to be interested. I smile when they smiled and looked concerned when they did.

As a full-blown mirror to the delusions Crystal and Stephanie and a skin suit for Simon, what a life I had. Dr. Liar said I could live a normal life did he not?

Well, if this was normal, I was thinking maybe I would have to pass on it. The pills in the outhouse started to look like a very reasonable alternative to this hellish existence in a world of delusions.

I decided to take them all as soon as the final bell rung, and I was finished with the detention Mr. Greene had made sure I finished. He was unsympathetic to my "nervous breakdown", and I was told by Mary I was expected to complete it. At least Stephanie would not be there this time. She had finished her sentence many months ago while I was on "break." This time, there would also be no Mary to save me from my self-induced poisoning. It is what she wanted after all, it is what everyone wanted, and I finally understood that.

The rest of the day was uneventful with the monotony of whirling, bright lights, noises, and overblown sensory issues. I was starting to get used to the real world ripping through and often able to ignore it pretty well. It still bothered me a lot but I really was helpless to stop it, so I just took the pain of it all and tried not to look like it hurt. Simon followed me everywhere making sure I said all the right things and criticizing me when I made wrong moves. I was helpless against his orders too. If he said to do it, I did it or else he would nag me into submission of his will. I was already overloaded. I simply could not take his badgering too. By the time detention at the end of the day arrived I was so tired I felt I could sleep a week. I began a giggling episode as I entered the detention classroom with the thought that by nightfall, I would be sleeping a lot longer than a week.

I sat down at the same desk that I had so many months ago when a vision caught my attention. It was a girl with ginger colored hair wearing the most glorious purple outfit sitting in the back of the room. Other than she and I there were no other inmates this day in the detention hall. I noticed that Simon would not enter the room. He was afraid of this girl...well to be exact he is afraid of the color combo of ginger and purple.

He motioned for me to come speak to him but with a huge smile I picked up my water jug and books and got up moving to the back of the room selecting a desk right next to this lovely vision of a girl in purple. Simon was livid with anger. I had dared to deny him access to his commands. For a wonderful hour I would be free to think for myself without his influence, thanks to this girl. I now was very interested to get to know her. She was the first person I had been interested in knowing since Marie.

The pills, outhouse, Simon, and all the other nightmares were forgotten for the moment as I concentrated on the problem of trying to speak to this stranger without scaring the shit out of her. She is deeply involved in a magazine as I sit down and does not even look up and notice me. That is very unusual for this school's students. It seemed most of them are always on the lookout for other's business but not this one. I decide I already like her a lot.

I am at a loss on how to gain her attention so finally I just clear my throat and she looks up with surprise.

"Oh, shit! You scared me," the girl in purple said. "Holy shit! Why are you dressed like that? Now that is fucking cool. Hey, you must be that schizo...eh...girl everyone has been telling me about, the one who beat up a bunch of cops and looks like a gho...she is wearing a Halloween costume. Your name is Psycho, right," she says stuttering on some of her words.

I realize she is trying to be nice in her words, but she could call me anything she likes. I really like this girl and that is the end of that. I have already decided to be her friend, so she has no reason to hide anything from me. I smile in agreement as I nod to her, and she smiles back.

"I am Julie by the way," she says extending her hand to me to shake.

I look at her hand alarmed that I would have to touch her but for this killer of Simon's I would risk the shock of human touch. I take her hand and ignore the feelings of electricity. I smile even wider as I realize this is the Julie that Stephanie and Crystal also hate. This girl had everything I did not: beauty, intelligence, vigor, and more than anything else she was an anti-asshole device. She even liked me back I could instantly tell all of this by reading her mind. I knew it was rude, but I had to know if I was in for a heartbreak.

"So, Psycho, right? What do you do for fun around here? I hate this town. I used to live in Sacramento, California, but my parents moved back here to take care of my grandma because she is getting demented. You from here," she asked appearing truly interested.

"No. I uhm, was brought here against my will. Look can we just talk with our minds? I am not so good with speaking with my words. I don't want to make any errors," I said very excited with this possibility of a real friend, finally.

Julie looked at me oddly, "oh, so the rumors about you are true. How interesting. Well, my mind reading device is broken at the moment, so if it is okay can we just talk?" She is looking me over, with curiosity.

I confess I have no idea what she is talking about with regard to rumors, and I did not even know about any devices required to read a mind. Her purple dress was so calming to my agitation, and I just did not feel irritation at her strange statement. So, I just shrug letting her know I do not understand.

She lowers her voice, "You are a schizophrenic, right? Hey, it is okay if you are. I have been to a mental hospital, but it was because I was using marijuana to stop my panic attacks. My mom like freaked out and shit and sent me to rehab like weed is even a real drug! The other kids think you are like dangerous and stuff, but I met a manic depressive while I was in rehab, and she was totally cool. But she was not like you, I have to admit, she was well, more normal looking and acting." Julie started chuckling at that.

I chuckled too. I did not understand why she was talking about hospitals and telling me about phantom illnesses that never really existed, but I did not care what she said. Julie could have given the Gettysburg Address in its entirety, and I would have listened hanging on every word. I was captivated by her energy and mind. I so wished I could somehow escape my skin suit and switch with her. I was sure it would fit.

We had sat there the entire hour of detention as she talked of her life in the big city and how much she loathed these "small town hicks." Finally, to my greatest despair it was time for us to leave. I could have sat there the rest of my life happily listening to her words. I did not understand a lot of it but her voice and presence were so calming to me.

As we stood to leave, she followed me out. To my amusement I saw Simon running like hell trying to avoid being in the path of my companion Julie and her terror combo of ginger and purple. I started a giggling episode. Julie began to giggle too.

"What are we laughing at," she asked which surprised me. "Man, you are one weird chic!"

I just shrugged at her and kept laughing at my private joke. She cannot read my mind, so I need not scare her by talking of Simon. I really wanted this new situation to work out. In some dark cobwebbed corner of my now dead brain, I felt a stir of hope for some type of human contact.

I believed with all my black heart that my savior had arrived. How could I know the great one had come? Well, of course, the evidence was so clear; she was wearing the glorious of all colors purple and ginger!

I was not aware that I had begun to demonstrate the final symptom of my unraveled reality. One that would prove more difficult to manage than even my delusional fear of laced food and water. The assurance that my disease onset was finally complete was demonstrated by this symptom of delusional color symbolism that assured that the doctors' diagnosis of schizophrenia was indeed correct all along. Only schizophrenia produces delusional color symbolism where the schizophrenic "receives" messages from the colors seen during daily living. It may cause the schizophrenic to willfully wear certain colors due to delusional thinking that these colors will help out.

Chapter 25: Purple Haze All in My Brain

Morning, Beautiful Family. Yep, I am back, wait, am I? Are we ready to slip through the fabric of time and sneak a peek at what is hidden there in the folds? Great! Then just close your eyes, tap your purple slippers together three times and repeat after me...I can never go home...I can never go home, I can never go home! Now, you can be sure there is no one behind that curtain (I already checked the room three times) and you really do not need a heart, courage or even a brain for this trip! See everyone on the dark side of the rainbow below!

"Oh, and I certainly don't suffer from schizophrenia. I quite enjoy it. And so do I."
—Emilie Autumn

Julie and I left the schoolhouse through the very door only months ago I had ripped off the hinges with my wild fit of, well whatever happened there. Simon was already on the road watching but keeping a very safe distance from us. I shot a smile at him as I continued to bask in the captivating energy being emitted from my companion. There was no doubt Simon would make me pay for defying him, but I really did not care. Hanging out with Julie was worth anything he could dish out as far as I was concerned.

The bright light of a fading spring day blinded me as we walked out and without thinking I began to wince and try to block it from my aching eyes. Julie saw me acting like a vampire who had just accidentally left the coffin too early. She looked a bit disturbed by it.

"Light bugs you, does it? So why do you not just wear sunglasses? Oh, and what the hell is with that jug you carry," she said while watching my goofy display of displeasure at Mr. Sun's attempts to burn out my eyeballs.

"Huh? I asked still covering my eyes with my hands while looking at the ground. "I" had not thought of those, duh!" I started to chuckle again. I completely ignore her question about my water jug.

Julie stopped and for a moment she dug into her purse then to my utter amazement she handed me a gorgeous pair of black round lenses sunglasses. "Here you go, Psycho. That should help. I have an extra pair. I have a thing for sunglasses but, hey I like to smoke pot you know?" Now she was chuckling too.

I put the sunglasses on and immediately felt the relief. I admit I was beyond touched that she was showing me so much kindness. Really, I already thought she was awesome, gifts were unnecessary. However, this one was beyond appreciated.

I looked at Julie in her purple dress and thought to myself, "One more miracle from this person, well, then it is certain she is from Heaven itself. But wait, something is not right here."

My looping mind trailed off as apprehension fill me. I realized that this is simply too good to be real. Maybe, I was having one of those weird episodes again. I needed to be absolutely certain this was really happening. I could not be tricked again by some joke the shadows play. That was in my mind as I reached out and pushed her down hard with a sudden push to her chest. She let out a surprised cry as she fell to the ground taken completely off guard.

I stood over the now sitting Julie with my fists clenched. Lowering the sunglasses she gave me, so I could glare directly at her as I said, "Okay, stop fooling around. You trying to trick me? I will not tolerate it. Confess you are not real."

I was ready to beat this...well whatever the shadows are...to death if necessary. My muscles all tensed with what I was sure to be a fight to the end. Instead, Julie just stared at me appearing bewildered at my sudden aggression toward her. I could see she was shaking ever so slightly and seemed afraid. Now I was very confused by this. Somehow, I thought that the shadows could not show fear. How could this be?

"Okay, so Psycho, I have no fucking idea what you are talking about, but I am not trying to trick you at all. As for being real? I guess I am as real as you are. What does that even mean?" Julie was wide eyed in terror now as she could see my body language indicated I was not kidding around here.

Real as me she said. Now that made sense for a change. She had admitted she was indeed a delusion and not real. Julie is not a shadow but something else completely, a figment of some twisted creature's imagination, just like me. I smiled at that and offered my hand to her to help her up. Julie still looking completely freaked out took it as I endured the shock of her touch. She stood up but did not move. She only stared at me trying to read my mind I assumed.

"I thought your mind reading device was broken?" I said chuckling as I knew she could not read my mind. She already had said so. Why would she lie?

"Uhm...yeah it is. I told you that, didn't I," Julie chuckled nervously back but still kept her eyes on me as she began to brush off. "So, we good or what?"

I nodded yes while still smiling at her. I was really glad I did not have to kill this delusion. It seemed to me I had enough delusions on my hit list already without having to start today with this one. Besides, she was at least twice my size. It would have been quite bloody no doubt. I for one was tired of stitches, cuts, and bruises. Plus, I really did like her. Relief that she was indeed a real event and not some static joke filled me.

"So, I uhm, I need to get home now. See you tomorrow," she asked, still seeming a bit apprehensive about me.

I saw her wince and step back mildly startled as I pointed toward the road to my cemetery home, "I am headed that way. Yes, I will be here tomorrow unless I decide to finish the mission."

I had forgotten about my plan to take all the medication till just then. I was all caught up in the presence of Julie. Now that I was back to earth (okay so I thought I was) I remembered it suddenly. Without another word I left Julie standing there. I stopped briefly to fill up my water jug from the school hose. I did not even look back at her as I started my journey back to my boneyard home mumbling to myself about my "mission."

As I walked home my random thoughts were quite suddenly preoccupied (more like hijacked) with strange signals coming from some other plane of existence. I could clearly hear these signals telling me, by the use of imagery, the secrets of avoiding disaster. The codes were very clearly located in specific color combinations that were to be avoided at all costs. Other color combinations would predict good tidings and they too should be respected. Only the color black was neutral and therefore I should avoid tempting disaster or interfering with this delusional future by remaining in the middle and never wearing any other color than black until further information was sent. I understood this was not negotiable and agreed to follow the codes to the letter (or color in this case).

Julie was nearly forgotten by the time I reached the iron gates. Simon was in the cemetery already. I could tell even at a distance he was pouting as I entered. He could be such a baby sometimes.

"You are so stupid. What did you just do? Why are you talking to Julie! Are you going crazy again? That girl is trouble. You know better," he yelled at me even before I got close enough to see his eyes.

"Fuck off, Simon, you are just jealous. I can have other friends you know. Like one that is not a drunk wife beater, who will not leave me the fuck alone would be nice," I say walking right past him not feeling up for another argument. "Christ! Simon we are not married, and you are not my daddy so get off my ass."

Now this pissed Simon off more than I had calculated it would. He rushed at me and knocked me down. My water jug flew out of my arms. It hit the ground splitting the plastic as my precious water supply escaped into the greedy ground. I watched in horror as I realized I was now in need of a new jug which was not going to be easy to come by.

I turned beyond angry at Simon and plowed into him screaming, "Simon! You dirty bastard. What the fuck." I began to choke him wanting him to die

His eyes bugged as I squeezed harder. Then out of nowhere I was struck on the head with something hard. Knocked out of my senses (like I had any to begin with) I fell off Simon to the ground disoriented by this blow. What just happened? I rolled over on my back and saw Crystal standing there holding a now broken boom box. I had not seen one of those since the days of the denim brigade and for a moment I wondered if I had somehow slipped into a hole in time. Wait, what just happened?

I look to Simon who was now getting up and watched in utter terror as he slowly became Stephanie. I could not believe my eyes, he transformed into that nutball girl. How did he do that? I was so shocked at what I was seeing it had only just occurred to me that Crystal was now also in my sanctuary home. More like Grand Central Station lately.

Stephanie turned and looked at me still laying there on my back. "Stop hitting me, Psycho." She was crying as usual as she came at me and kicked me right in the stomach knocking the air out of my lungs and pee out of my bladder. And stop calling me Simon, you loon."

Crystal was staring at me writhing as I gasped for air, "Geez, Steph I told you she is going to try and kill you. And now look I broke the tape player on her head trying to save your life. My brother is going kick my ass when he finds out. She was getting pretty upset as she appeared unsure what to do now.

Stephanie who was as usual recomposing herself by turning off the waterworks went to Crystal to comfort the girl as they looked over the now damaged boom box. I lay there trying to recover from my most bizarre encounter wondering what the hell was happening. Everything was so mixed up. Somehow a boom box from years ago and another cemetery had found its way into the present and Simon can turn into Stephanie. This was just too much, even for me.

I finally got enough oxygen to stand up again and yelled at them both, "Get the fuck out. I cannot take this shit anymore. Do you hear me?"

I started looking for a rock, a stick, anything. These two were leaving and leaving if I had to beat them to death then throw their dead bodies over the wall. The agitation at these two being in my sanctuary was filing me to the point of explosion. I could not stop the onslaught of anxiety as I began to pace, wring my hands, and stomp about looking every bit the psycho Stephanie insisted I was. I could feel my senses becoming overwhelmed with light, noise, and movement. Despite my hidden mad box and newly acquired sunglasses, everything was too bright, too loud, and moving too fast. I was about to blow.

Stephanie looked up at me from the ailing boom box, finally realizing there was real trouble afoot. She motioned for Crystal to start to head for the gate which she did without a second prompt. It would have been smart has she done the same, but apparently Stephanie was not a brilliant girl. Instead, she decided she had not poked the beast enough already.

"Psycho, you are out of control. I got your medication out of your hiding place and notice you are not taking it because it is all unopened. I am going to have to tell Mary about this, you know. I think maybe I will just hold on to it and start making sure you take it on time, so you stop acting insane. You have a problem," Stephanie screams at me from what she thought was a safe distance.

My inner self shattered into a thousand pieces as her words hit my force shield like a carpet bombing on German factories during WWII. With an inhuman growl I stopped pacing. I removed my sunglasses dropping them to the ground. I glared at her with pure hatred. I stood there for a moment setting my sights on the cause of my irritation trying to wrap my broken mind around her lack of respect for my privacy. Stephanie clearly had finally overstepped her bounds; I began walking then running for her with every intention of ending her pathetic life. Murder was in my eyes, and this was not lost to Stephanie. Her look of indignation turns to fear as she turns trying to outrun me. She did have distance but if she tripped or could not outrun me, I would kill her, and this time I decided nothing would stop my intent.

Stephanie runs screaming for the gate where Crystal has been waiting just outside watching the entire scene unfold. She holds the iron bars open encouraging Stephanie to run faster. I am gaining on the dumb girl. I no longer can see anything but the color red. I easily hurtle jump the jagged headstones as Stephanie tries to lose me by zig zagging through my roomies final resting spots. Even in a pair of platforms I am very agile. She had to do better than that or she would be soon joining them.

"Run, damn it," Crystal yells as Stephanie finally reaches the gate barely ahead of my murderously raging form.

As Stephanie gets through it safely Crystal slams the heavy iron gate shut. I am running too fast to stop as I smack right into it with full force. Stunned and injured I stagger backward and fall hard, not even attempting to break my fall. I am on my back watching the sky with cotton clouds swirling into a mix of red and blue. Confusion as to what has happened fills my mind as the darkness of unconsciousness overtakes me.

I awaken and it is dark. At first, I am confused still unsure where I am. The moon illuminated my cemetery enough so that I finally am able to determine I am home, but what has happened exactly takes a bit longer to figure out. My head is killing me as I reach up and feel a large knot on my forehead. I remember running into the gate. I try to stand only to find I am still to dizzy yet. As I sit there in the dark, I recall chasing the Stephanie/Simon person, wanting her dead. She had said she took my pills and was going to tell Mary I was not taking medications. I feel angry again but only slightly as I am able to rise very slowly. I hurt all over. For now, I had to get back to the outhouse and see how much damage I have done to myself running into my gate. I would consider Stephanie's fate later. I was not feeling so well.

I staggered back to the outhouse. In the darkness I tripped several times, almost falling many times. My whole body seemed very heavy. My mouth was very dry. With a whimper I recalled my water jug was broken, nothing around to help that situation at all. It seemed so odd, I could not think very fast, as my inner self felt cold and distant. How hard had I hit my head? I wondered as I laid down on the ground in the outhouse and quickly fell to sleep.

I awoke in the morning to the face of Stephanie in mine. "Wake up, Psycho. Hey, we are going to be late if you don't get up." She was shaking me.

"Huh? What? Late? Where am I," I say groggy and feeling that same weird slowness in my body.

"School, stupid. Hey, you have been drooling everywhere. Look, I brought you some more of your medication. How are you feeling?" Stephanie was pushing some pills into my face.

I slapped her hand away. "Get out of here you bitch, and take your poison with you," I slurred as drool poured from my mouth. What the fuck is wrong with me. Confusion once again overtook me as I could not seem to move my lead encased limbs.

"Shit, Stephanie do you think we gave her too much of that stuff," I hear Crystal say from nowhere.

"I gave her two of everything, Crystal. She was acting stupid, it is medication. It is supposed to help her act normal. I think doubling up would work faster, don't you?" I hear Stephanie say to the invisible Crystal.

"Wait...you did what," I slur through drool as my very slow mind starts to realize in horror what has happened. "You gave me...a double dose of what?"

Stephanie smiles and gleefully says, "well, you were out cold, so Crystal and I gave you two pills from every bottle. It is your medication. Don't you feel better? You certainly are not angry anymore so it must be working."

"Oh shit!" I try to get up but fall backwards unable to get anything to move correctly. Drool pours from my mouth like a waterfall, "You stupid bitch. One pill a day is the dose. That is ALL, my medication there is two bottles of each of three prescriptions. What have you done? How many pills in all did you give me," I slurred realizing I have been overdosed on my own fucking antipsychotics by these two idiots. Well, I had wanted to finish the mission by overdosing on them, maybe now I may.

Stephanie laughs at that, "Oh come on, Psycho, I only gave you two of each of the three, a double dose is all. You think I am stupid? That is only like six pills. Right, Crystal?" She looks to see if she can get Crystal to verify her count.

"Oh uhm, no you gave her one extra of that Thorazine one, remember," Crystal said.

I wince at that. "Son of a bitch! You gave me a huge dose of the Thorazine, that is about 800 mg! I am fucked, Stephanie. I cannot function like this. What have you done?"

I would have cried if that had even been possible. Stephanie had just put me in a chemical straight jacket that could take many hours to wear off completely. I just laid back and stopped even trying to move. There was no point. I was not going anywhere for a bit, thanks to Stephanie's ignorance. I was not even sure I would not die from such a high dose of that shit. It was too late now; the medication was already coursing through my body locking up my mind in a cage. I was absolutely helpless at the mercy of this dumbass and her demonic friend.

I could hear Stephanie start to cry, "Will you die? Am I going to go to prison for murder now? I was only trying to help."

"Just fuck off, Stephanie. When will you realize I do not want you to do anything at all but just fuck off," I mumbled angrily staring at my outhouse ceiling feeling like a statue unable to move or even get that angry?

"We can't leave you here like this. You have to get up and get ready for school," Stephanie pleads, "plus Mary told me you have to see a counselor today or something. Oh my God if you do not get up, we are all in so much trouble."

I roll my eyes. Is she kidding? I had forgotten about the stupid counselor business. Things seem to just keep getting worse and worse. I knew as well as Stephanie that not going to the counselor would bring the authorities sniffing around. I could not have that any more than Mary wanted it. Sighing loudly, I willed myself to sit up. Drool poured from my mouth as my jaw felt numb and useless. Now this was going to be an issue. I asked Stephanie what the exact time was she forced that shit into my unconscious body (grrrrr). With a bit of work, I decided by the end of the school day I should be able to at least move more freely. The medication only lasted that heavy about twelve hours. I knew at such a high dose I would likely be this way several more hours.

"Okay you fool. Go to school. You will have to cut out your last hour today and come back here to help me get ready for the counselor. Tell Patty that I am sick and will not be in today. That will piss Mary off but better than trying to get through class like this. You had better come back I will need help! Otherwise, I may sleep through the whole fucking thing. You got me into this now you need to get me out!" I murmured trying to sound as angry as possible given the situation.

Stephanie nodded that she understood. She and Crystal left after we all agreed what would have to be done to bail us all out of this mess. As I watched them leave for school helplessly drooling sitting up against my outhouse wall, I suddenly realized I had no water. Nice. As usual, even in hell I could find a deeper level torment without even trying. I closed my eyes and drifted off to sleep thinking I would have to kill Stephanie now before the void killed me.

Stephanie did exactly as she had promised and at noon I was awakened by her abruptly. My mouth was so dry my lips had cracked. She offered me her own water bottle she had bought at school, but I refused. She had poisoned me one too many times for me to fall for that shit again.

With a lot of struggles, I managed to get my make up fixed from the torrent of drooling all night and day and found that the worst of the side effects had indeed passed. I could walk again, and that infernal drooling was much more controllable long as I was careful to wipe my mouth from time to time. I was still numb all over and my mind was foggy.

Stephanie in usual Stephanie fashion talked nonstop about all the gossip from school. She told me Patty believed the lie, and I had been excused. Mary had not been called thankfully. Finally, at least one break. Then Steph went into a long, nasty rumor about the new girl Julie. I realized she was trying to poison my feelings about Julie just as sure as she had poisoned my body with Thorazine. I really hated Stephanie above everyone but maybe Mary at this point. Every time I turned around; she was fucking up my already very fucked up life.

We waited at the cemetery for what seemed like eternity until it was time to walk to the school and catch the ride with Mary to this stupid counseling appointment. Stephanie talked the entire time and for the only time in my life I was glad I was on heavy meds. It sure helped keep me from throttling her till she shut up.

Mary was waiting in the parking lot as Stephanie and I blended in carefully appearing to be exiting the school building. Luckily, Mary was distracted reading a book and did not see us slip into the crowd. We walked to the station wagon, and I opened the passengers door to get in.

Mary looked up as Stephanie stood there waving goodbye to us. Mary smiled and waved back. I wanted to puke. Those two were worse nightmares than the schizophrenia ever thought to be. I did not wave but shot her a 'go to hell look' as I slammed the door.

"At least you have good taste in friends, Sinner," Mary said as we pulled out of the school yard. "I see you did not take my advice and end this stupidity by finally killing yourself. Too bad, I hope you will get around to it soon. I have better things to do then haul you around." She looked at me hatefully.

I did not even bother to respond to her insults. The Thorazine was doing its job well. I felt nothing at all but the cold void of the antipsychotic medications. Today, Mary could say whatever she wanted. I was not capable of being angry about it, vitamin T made sure of that.

She attempted a few more insults to get a rise out of me but nothing. So, the rest of the ride was uneventful. I think I was sleeping most of it. I hated the fatigue of medication, but today it too worked in my favor. If I was asleep, I did not have to look at nasty old Mar.

We arrived and Mary refused to go inside saying this was my "cross to bear. Whatever, I was glad to be free of her presence. In reality, I think she did not want to be seen in public with her insane Gothic creation. Oh well, I was not bothered by the looks as I entered the clinic. I seemed to recall this place from a dream somewhere as I signed in and sat down.

The other waiting clients stared at me with open mouths. I just yawned and wiped the drool that kept trying to escape my numb mouth. Nothing was bothering me today. Not even the feeling that I was a side show attraction for the masses. Really, they were there to see a counselor too, so judging me seemed silly, I thought.

Finally, I was called back to my "session." I was grateful to be getting this shit done and over. It really did seem so stupid to make me talk to someone about my so-called problems. In the hospital they had tried to make me do this, but I always kept my mouth shut. I had learned to not speak to anyone in authority about my so called "beliefs, visions, and thoughts." That only got me into trouble so I had already decided this counselor would also get the same treatment. I had nothing to say anyway.

I walked into the counselor's office and to my absolute horror I saw Dr. Scott look up from her desk. Shit! She had treated me in the hospital so keeping quiet would only go so far. She had helped to fuck me over in the first place with her ECT. She had constantly badgered me in the hospital, demanding I speak of so-called symptoms of some disease I did not have. In a word, I already had a deep hatred of the woman. She also was a smart one, so this was not going to be the cake walk I had hoped.

"Sit down and make yourself comfy! How have you been," Dr. Scott says smiling but not offering her hand to shake. She knew better.

I sat as directed. "Fine," I said flatly.

"You are looking thin, are you eating? Are you taking your medication as directed? Is your guardian helping with the reality testing exercises we gave her to help you with?" Dr. Scott began to machine gun fire her stupid questions.

I rolled my eyes, "Like a horse (lie), don't I look like I am taking the meds? (Only because I was tricked), and every morning just as you told her (lie)." I said in a monotone voice. I was already very bored with this.

She eyed me suspiciously, "are you still hearing Simon? or other voices? How about the static or cicadas? I see you are still dressing oddly, I thought we discussed your trying to drop this look for something more socially acceptable for a sixteen-year-old girl."

"Here we go," I think. Sighing loudly and with a yawn I responded, "Nope, Simon who? I see static on TV when the stations sign off where it belongs, and cicadas? Only in the summer like everyone else darling. As for my dressing, this is my artistic expression. Not illegal you know to dress this way. Is this America the land of the free or what?"

Dr. Scott slit her eyes appearing to know I was playing games with her. "We have discussed your denial of the seriousness of your Schizophrenia. Making light of your symptoms is not helpful to you or to me. Let's try a little honesty, shall we?" She picks up her pencil and starts writing.

Despite the Vitamin T this makes me feel uncomfortable. I do not like people talking about me where I cannot see what they are saying. I feel the paranoia seeping in like broken sewage line in my mind. I lean in a bit to see if I can see what she is writing down about me. Dr. Scott notices this very slight interest. Damn.

"Are you still worried I am out to destroy you," she says without looking up writing even faster.

I am sure she is fucking with me, and I hear Simon's voice say, "don't fall for it, she is baiting you."

I agree with Simon. This Dr. Scott is a tricky one. I just shake my head no, rather than respond verbally. I cannot trust my mouth to say the right things sometimes. This is not the time to blurt inappropriately.

Dr. Scott stops writing and looks up. I stare at her devoid of affect. She can try if she likes, I will not let her read my mind. I clear it best I can of any thoughts as I hum inside my head that "Girls just want to have Fun."

She stares hard, "any thoughts of harming yourself or others? Now answer honestly. How about the side effects of your medications any troubles you want to discuss with me about that?" I can see she is up to something, but what?

I shake my head no again, and stay emotionless still humming in my mind.

Dr. Scott sits back in her overstuffed office chair and glares at me, "I am not your enemy you know. I am trying to help you. Why won't you accept that? I did not cause your disease, but if you let me, I can help you learn to live with it. Don't you want a life worth living? Otherwise, you are going to continue to suffer these symptoms, maybe even hurt yourself or someone else. Is that what you want? To die? End up in prison? How about being a homeless person wandering mindlessly until someone rapes and murders you? How about that? That is the reality dear, you are sick. Until you accept help one of those is will be your future. That is the reality here. I know you are lying to me but if you don't let me help you, then I cannot do a thing but watch you slowly destroy yourself." She finishes her warning by throwing her pencil onto the desk. "So, what is it going to be?"

"You are saying you have a cure for this so-called disease, uhm, schizophrenia you said," I inquire trying to sound as smart assed as possible.

Dr. Scott huffs, "You know there is no cure. What are you…"?

"Then what the fuck are you bothering me for huh? You get a cure, and I will be happy to take it.

Otherwise keep your fucking snake oils and voodoo to yourself, witch doctor. And don't you fucking preach to me about my future you say you can predict, and then give me shock treatment for claiming the ability to do less! Hypocrite! Liar! Fake," I interrupt her angrily. "So, are we done here? I have more important shit to do than listen to this fantasy crap."

I stand up and start to head for the door. "Wait a minute, where do you think you are going, young lady." Dr. Scott says rising from her desk.

"Oh, now come on, you seem to know everything about me so why don't you just predict it. I can see you do not need my input there darling. Perhaps I will go get raped and murdered. You have a most blessed day." I leave her office slamming the door behind me.

I storm from the clinic rushing past the appointment desk without stopping. I have had enough of this happy horse shit. I find Mary reading a book waiting in the station wagon for me. I get in and tell her to take me home. I have already decided that Dr. Scott and I will not be friends. If I was going to have to do this every week till I was eighteen she had better take up a hobby. I was never going to comply with her program. The Thorazine had worn off and my ability to be angry was the first sign that finally that nightmare had come to an end. It was time to go back to my sanctuary to decide how to deal with

Stephanie. The Dr. Scott issue would have to wait for another day.

CHAPTER 26: THE PUPPET MASTERS:

Here we are again, and again, and again...wait are we stuck in a loop maybe? Hummm, no worries, I am sure that if we try just a bit harder, we can find the end to this circle...wait do circles have an end, I can't remember if they do? So, does everyone have their water jugs filled, backpacks, and mad boxes handy? Great because tonight we are going to be the entertainment! Now do not worry, you will feel a bit out of control and the strings take a bit of getting used to, but I have total faith you will learn to dance when you are told to dance! It may be funny to watch and a bit clumsy, but hey tonight you are the star of the puppet show! The smiles you put on the faces of everyone will totally be worth your pain and suffering...right? After all everyone wants to be a star right, even if it is against your will? Does it really matter that you don't remember going to the audition? Okay Beauties, Final Curtain Call! Let the show begin. See you at the intermission.

"My fault, my failure, is not in the passions I have, but in my lack of control of them."
-Jack Kerouac

Mary did not speak to me the whole way back to the cemetery. That was certainly fine by me. The last effects of the Thorazine were wearing off as I noticed the world was slowly returning to normal. I watched with relief as the fast-moving scenery speeding past the station wagon began to pulsate and glow in a way that I had become accustom too. I breathed a sigh of relief as I began to realize the straight jacket of my mind was about to be removed.

The sun had not set yet when we arrived at the iron gates of home. Mary finally decided to break the silence.

"So, I hope that next week I am making a trip here to your funeral. In fact, if you just finish this horror, I will even buy you a plot here so you can always be where you seem to love to be. How about that?" She smiled at me as she put the car in park.

I looked at her suspiciously. "What is her game," I thought, but out loud in typical smart-ass fashion I said, "Awe, really? You would do that for little old me? Gosh, you are just too good to me darling."

Mary's smile melted to a furrowed brow, "I mean it. Everyone really hates you. It is not just my opinion, ask anyone. How can you not feel ashamed being this...thing? I would have already killed myself months ago. What kind of a life can you ever have? You are lower than a cockroach, and fouler than a maggot. A real blight on the face of the earth." She looks to make sure I am listening. I was. "Tell you what, I will prove it and even show you that I purchased it. Just once in your life cannot you do something right? Something that is not just plain old selfish?"

I was thinking at this point who needs the demons and shadows. I could just hang out with Mary and get all the self-depreciating hate speech one could ever need. I frowned back at her wondering if she was really thinking I would ever do a damned thing she wanted.

I opened the door and got out, "Bet you are sorry you saved me back at Christmas, huh? Or from the suicide attempt? Well Ho Ho Ho, bitch. Santa's gift is one that keeps on giving you hell. You should have let me die but you were too worried about your god damned reputation. You had your chance, now reap what you sowed." I slammed the door hard and went into my gate.

She left without spinning out the tires this time. I listened never looking back assuming the lack of spin out was her calculating how she may try to change my mind when are forced together next week. Too bad for her. She just assured I would not kill myself. No way she was going to get control of this situation and now I was very aware my existence was a big pain in her ass, well, good

I would like to say I hated Mary but reality here is that I never loved her to begin with. She never let me. You cannot hate what you never loved. Those two emotions are forever in a dance with each other and cannot be found without the other. I now understood that because I had never known love. Therefore, try as I might, I could not truly hate anyone. I thought I could, but hate was a passion like love denied me.

Instead, it had become a wicked game of making her pay for what I was sure was all her fault. A game of revenge, not hate at all. I did not believe I was a schizophrenic. I had also decided I was not sick either, I was enlightened and normal. Everyone else was just well, evil is all.

I was simply misunderstood because of her. Also, because of Stephanie and Dr. Scott, maybe some others I had not discovered yet in this huge conspiracy to make me believe I was crazy. They were trying to discredit me. They all had certainly started lies, rumors, and stories that now they were trying to make me believe that actually happened.

I was on to the truth. None of that was real but they wanted me to believe in the hospital, weird experiences, and shock treatment. Nope, didn't really happen. I could see that clearly for the very first time. Now, I had decided to find out who all was involved in this plot and destroy them. Before they destroyed me.

I found Simon waiting for me in the outhouse. At first, I was unsure if he was not really Stephanie playing tricks but, finally I decided since there was no Crystal this was really my dear brakeman friend. My only real friend in fact. Simon was helping me get out of this mess, well usually.

"So, you were a bit nasty to Dr. Scott. You may want to tone that down just a notch. She can cause us a lot of trouble, you know," Simon said looking nervously at me. I could tell he was afraid of her a just a little, but I was unsure why.

I did not feel like fighting with Simon so I just nodded in agreement that I would try to stop acting like a horse's ass to Dr. Scott, for now.

"What about Stephanie? She poisoned us, Simon. She has to pay for that trick," I said bitterly.

Simon took a drag of his smoke and looked at the outhouse ceiling, "I think you let that go too for now. If you go knocking her teeth out, like she deserves, others will accuse you of being crazy again." He looked at me to see if I agreed.

I certainly did not! However, Simon was smarter than me, so I just nodded growling low in my throat. That void deserved to die was my only real thought.

Simon read my mind, "She does, and she will, I promise. But first we need to discover who is all involved in this conspiracy. We can then get them all at one time rather than picking them off one by one. That would get us caught and locked up. If we, do it all at once, we win." He smiled at me with his near toothless grin.

I chuckled, "Damn, you are ugly Simon." I said but he had a point, so I just let it go.

It would be hard not to kill Stephanie and for that matter Crystal for good measure. However, I would just let it go as Simon had said and focus on my mission. I sat down and with my stomped upon tablet I began to write out the names of those I suspected of being involved. I included the reasons they were suspected just in case I ever had one of my infamous "forgetting" moments again.

I fell asleep that night with visions of brutal homicide in my shattered mind. I thought of their terror when they realized I had figured it all out with a smile. I would make them all dearly pay; of that I had no doubt. The clock had run down and the much-needed anti-psychotics were wearing off. The beast was free again to seek her revenge as the senses once again began to tangle into a mess of confusion.

I could not have stopped the slippage if I had I wanted to. Stephanie had taken all my medication with her. She had forgotten to come back and return it to me, or had she kept it on purpose? Whatever the reason, that night the darkness brought with it a rebound of schizophrenic symptoms much stronger than the ones Stephanie had been trying to control.

Simon woke me in time to ready myself for school. As I readied myself, I received the transmission from "them." Today, I was to avoid the color orange at all costs and beware of the combo of green and yellow and all stripes, as those combos bore ill tidings.

I understood the communication and acknowledged I would do as they said. No information was given about my own color other than to remain in black and neutral. I was to stay out of the way and let "them" deal with matters. What matters, I did not know, but that is what "they" told me.

Simon and I walked to school together discussing the "plot" trying to decide who we could trust in a world that was fast becoming a war zone for me. Everyone was against me now. If I was not careful bad things were sure to happen. I had not eaten in days now. Dizzy spells would make me stagger from time to time. I was not worried, it would pass, it always does.

Simon was chuckling at my odd gait as I tried to "stomp" off the feeling that my skin was too tight. It sort of pissed me off but then I had to admit I likely did look the fool. If only I could get this skin suit off, all would be okay, kept looping through my mind. If only.

I made it through first period without much trouble. However, I noticed that Mrs. Wells was saying so much more with her lesson than I had initially thought. I wrote down feverishly the hidden messages she was conveying with her "equation lies" as I suddenly realized the answer to this plot was located there in her words. I just had to listen.

"So, Two Consecutive numbers have a sum of 91. What are the numbers? This *would be* stated as: x + (x + 1) = 91. *The Initial* Equation: x + (x + 1) = 91 can be *solved,* after *combining* like terms: 2x + 1=91 then, after subtracting 1 from each side: 2x=90. After *dividing* each *side* by 2 x = 45," Mrs. Wells said as I saw these words light up on the board and pulsate like the church window many months ago.

They meant something special. I needed to understand what she was really trying to tell me. I wrote down the words and worked them into my list. It suddenly made so much sense!

I was beginning to understand. The source would be Mary and Stephanie my initial difficulties with people both came consecutively, and now are combining sides to divide me from solving the problems of the mission. Mrs. Wells was providing me with the proof of the plot that I so dearly needed.

I would show this to Simon later. He had decided to wait outside at the picnic tables for lunch break. We had decided I would not speak to anyone today so he would not be needed until then. It seemed to be the lunch hour when all the previous trouble happens so it made perfect sense to me that he could wait there for me to help out.

Otherwise, the day was uneventful except the many codes and messages my teachers kept sending me on the chalkboards and in their lectures warning me of my impending doom at the hands of Stephanie, Mary, Patty, Dr. Scott, the Coach, and Mr. Greene. I was fast gaining a longer and longer hit list as more and more names kept coming across through the lessons.

When the lunch bell finally arrived, I had almost written a novel to show to Simon. I could hardly wait to show him with pride my latest "enlightenment" powers of reading between the lines and discovering the hidden messages in a person's conversation. I was sure this would please him a great deal. So, smiling and excited I headed out to talk with my best friend.

However, I was caught at the double doors by Julie. She was not wearing purple but today wearing an orange shirt with blue jeans. I recoiled at the sight of that color. I had been warned after all.

Julie noticed my sudden jump back as if I had been burned, "Whoa there, Psycho, what is up chic," She inquired trying to approach me.

I backed up further keeping her at a distance, "You're in orange. That is not okay," I flatly said looking for another way out, away from this color of doom.

Julie looked at me appearing confused then to her shirt. "Oh, this shirt you mean. Why do you not like orange?"

I knew she was teasing me, and I did not like that. Angrily I said back, "You know damned well that orange is not permitted today!" I do not like to be mocked.

Julie laughed at me, which really pissed me off, and then took off the shirt to reveal a black tank top under it. She rolled up the deadly orange shirt and stuffed it in her purse. "Okay Psycho, whatever you say. See the orange is all gone, poof!" She spread out her arms and demonstrated the lack of orange.

My anger quickly dissipated to calm as Julie had gone out of her way to remove the offending color. She had my loyalty once more and for whatever reason I believed I could trust her. I smiled and said, "thank you."

Too bad I had forgotten why "they" had warned me about orange in the first place. "Avoid at all costs," they had said.

"I am headed out to the picnic tables, you want to join me," she said holding open the double doors and motioning me to follow her.

I nodded forgetting about my "plot" for a moment. I did follow her out as she turned and asked me, "So, any other colors I should avoid?"

I was surprised she was interested to hear the truth. Now I was indeed interested in Julie. She seemed to understand, and best of all wanted to be enlightened. I could barely contain my need to tell her my information as I gushed out that ginger and purple scared Simon and green and yellow or stripes were not good.

She looked at me strangely, "Simon?" She saw me look at Simon sitting on the picnic table. He was not happy I could tell. He did not like Julie, no doubt.

"Yes, he is right there, see him?" I pointed at a now very pissed off Simo as he threw his smoke to the ground and stomped it while getting up from the now infamous picnic table we usually sat on.

Julie shielded her eyes from the sunlight and peered to where I was pointing and shook her head no. I was disappointed and did not try to hide that fact from her. I thought she was enlightened too. I was wrong if she could not even see Simon.

"Wait, hold a second, Julie said appearing to notice my sudden change in mood. She reached into her purse pulled out a pair of huge sunglasses and put them on and looked again, "Oh, wait Yes! There Simon is. Sorry, I was blinded by the sunlight," she apologized smiling at me.

That did make me feel better. She just could not see in the bright light. I had my sunglasses she gave me on already so it made sense or maybe I would not have seen him clearly either.

Julie and I walked to the picnic table together. Simon was so angry he started right away, "Damn it! Get rid of this girl. She is trouble, stupid." Simon was livid.

"Simon, shut up," I said back. I looked at Julie apologetically. Simon could be so rude.

Julie looked at Simon, "Yeah Simon, shut the fuck up. Me and Psycho got girl talk, no boys allowed, hear me," she said sternly.

Simon looked at Julie with pure hatred. "If you insist on allowing this interloper to sit with us, I am going home! Do you hear me? I am not going to help you anymore and you are on your own if you do not remove her now," he yelled at me.

I ignored him and sat down with Julie. Simon huffed and stormed off headed to the cemetery. "See you at home, Simon," I mocked in a sweet voice while laughing. I waved as he walked briskly not even looking back.

Julie just chuckled, "Didn't like the competition, I see," she looked hard at me.

I shrugged not understanding the statement. All I knew is Simon got on my nerves and Julie was like me, enlightened. She knew the truth. With Julie, I did not have to try to hide the realities of my strange new delusional world. After all, she could see them too.

I was so damned lonely for someone to talk to that was not trying to kill me, poison me, tell me what to do, or send me to a little cell with a one-armed jacket, that I would have had tea with even the devil had he made the time for it by now. Julie had come just in time to join me in the horror show that had become my life. There are no words that can describe how grateful I was to have someone understand me, when I had stopped understanding everyone else so long ago.

Julie reached into her purse and took out a rolled-up cigarette not unlike the ones Simon was always smoking. She looked around to be sure we were alone without prying eyes. When she was sure to my pure amazement, she lit it up and took a long drag and held it. I watched not saying a word in pure shock at the bravery she demonstrated knowing being caught smoking at school was automatic suspension.

She then tried to hand me the smoke, but I shook my head no. It had a smell unlike Simon's horrid home rolled cigs. "It smells like a skunk," I thought.

"I don't smoke," I said politely as possible out loud recalling her mind reading device was still broken.

"Seriously?" Julie looked at me appearing surprised. "I just assumed you smoked pot. So, no drugs at all? When did you quit them? When you went psycho right?"

Now that did make me angry. I stood up and grabbed her by the wrist of her hand holding the marijuana cigarette. "I never have done drugs, nor have I ever drunk alcohol. You are quite rude. I am sick to death of this lie you all keep trying to convince me of. I also am not psycho. Stop trying to say that I am," I yelled in her face.

Julie just looked at me stunned at my sudden aggression. Yet again she had not expected it. I glared at her waiting for her to move so I could excuse myself when I ripped her ginger head off its shoulders.

"I am so sorry, Psycho. I did not mean it! I just heard, well, I heard a rumor, but you are right they are all liars. How stupid of me to listen to them. They are all liars." Julie's eyes were tearing up as she tried not to break her gaze from our stare down.

I let go of her wrist and sat down. I had been tricked many times. Julie had just been tricked too is all. Now she could see that obviously. I was not one to judge after all. As long as she understood they are all liars, she was forgiven immediately. I smiled at her.

Julie was observably shaken but took a long drag of her smoke. She held her breath still staring at me sitting there smiling at her like nothing had just happened. I was as friendly as a puppy dog again. I really liked Julie a lot even if she did smoke pot at school.

She blew out the smoke slowly. After a nasty coughing fit, she put out the marijuana and looked at me, "Okay, so Simon does not like purple and ginger. The rumors are all lies. You are not psychotic. You can read minds and you get messages that some colors are not okay. Is there anything else I need to know," she said appearing interested in me again?

I did not understand what she was saying. I just shrugged again unable to grasp my thoughts about well anything. Julie seemed so calming and I just wanted to hear her talk even if I did not understand most of her weird comments. I did that sometimes too and no one could understand me either, so I could relate.

Julie did not like my not answering her strange question. I could read it in her mind. However, there was nothing I could do to make her feel better. I simply did not understand the question.

She suddenly looked toward the cafeteria doors and seemed disturbed, "Hey, your friend Stephanie and Crystal are coming I should probably get out of here you know. I don't think those two like me.

"They think you are slut," I said, matter of fact, still smiling. "I don't like them and soon enough will kill them both for poisoning me the other night."

Julie snapped her head back focusing on me intently, "they poisoned you? How," she seemed angry. I liked her even more for that.

"They knocked me out and slipped me a lot of anti-psychotic medication trying to kill me off. No problem. I have plans to end them. Just watch your food and water around those two," I said smiling again.

"Wait, they gave you anti-psychotic medication? Where did they get that?" She leaned in towards me as if the two monster girls were getting close enough, they may hear her question.

"It was mine. Dr. Scott is in on it too. She is trying to make me believe I have Schizophrenia. She is a dirty liar too. Dr. Scott gave it to Mary and Mary wants me to kill myself with it. Everyone wants me dead you see. They are all trying to kill me. It is self-defense you see," I said now leaning in too so Stephanie and Crystal would not hear me report that I knew all about them to my new friend.

This made Julies eyes go wide. "Wow, okay gotcha. Well tell you what, I will catch you after a bit. I have the munchies. Got to get a bite to eat. Catch you later, Psycho." She got up and flounced by Stephanie and Crystal who had just arrived at the table barely missing my confession.

The three girls shot each other hateful looks but nothing was said between them.

I waved, "Okay, Julie see you later." Smiling I was sure she would be back soon. Now it was time to play nice with these two nit wits.

Now I was suddenly very sorry I had sent Simon home. I was not sure I could keep my temper in check without him. I was really pissed at these two assholes.

"Psycho! What were you talking about with that girl," Stephanie demanded to know as she and Crystal sat down?

I shrugged. In truth, I had already forgotten anyway.

"You are so stupid! She is evil, you know. If you keep talking to her your reputation will be ruined," Stephanie said appearing to think that would snap me out of my adoration of Julie.

"My reputation? Stephanie now you are the stupid one. What the fuck do I care," I yelled already feeling my blood start to boil. I just knew I would not be able to keep from killing her right now, no matter what Simon has said.

Stephanie's brow furrowed for a second as she appeared angry at this comment but then quickly smoothed to that of the innocent girl (I so hated that look). She reached into her backpack and took out a small water bottle already filled with water with electrical tape around the cap.

"Okay, you talk to who you want, Psycho. Never mind that. Look I felt bad I broke your water jug the other day. I did not have a big one, but I got you a new one that is easier to carry. I know you do not like the water already in it but this one had tape around it already so you can trust the water is pure, you know," she said smiling while putting it in front of me.

I was horridly thirsty after not having a single drink in some time. I looked at the water and tried to decide if Stephanie was correct and the water good. I could have gone to the water fountain, but I had decided that they were contaminated by the mouths of foul students so could not bring myself to drink from them, or the bathroom faucet for the same reason.

I could just pour the water out and wait till the end of the day for the hose, but I was already dizzy from hunger and that Thorazine had done a number on me. Maybe she was right, with the tape. How could it be tainted?

I took the bottle of water. I carefully removed the tape and cap. I then rapidly drank almost the entire bottle desperate for relief from my horrid thirst. I had not realized how thirsty I was. Nor had I realized till the bottle was almost empty Stephanie and Crystal had watched me drink it silently smiling at me. My stomach whined a bit as anxiety filled me.

"Why are you smiling," I asked truly concerned that something was not right here.

"Just happy to be a friend," Stephanie said with a wink to Crystal. "So, after school Crystal and I are hanging out with you in the cemetery. I have some new tapes! You will love them," she said not even waiting for my response. She and Crystal began to gossip about the other students.

I just sat there watching these two brain stems wondering how anyone could talk so much. The entire rest of the lunch hour they talked non-stop as I pretended to listen. Secretly, I was watching the cafeteria doors to see if Julie would come back. I also was silently wishing Simon would come back. Neither of them did.

The lunch bell rung again, and I went to my next class disappointed that I had to spend the entire time without the ones who were really my friends. I went to class then smiled as I suddenly realized that Julie had detention with me for the whole week. I would have her all to myself without the horrible Stephanie. Maybe today would be a better day after all.

I could barely contain my excitement with every tick of the clock. However, besides the excitement at getting to see Julie again, I also had a building headache. It was in the back of my head. I figured out it was my jaw that seemed to insist on grinding against my will. It was causing a shit ton of tension.

I got up from my desk to head to my last class of the day and felt very lightheaded and strange. My mouth had gotten very dry and so had my eyes. Things seemed blurry, making it hard for me to catch all the secret messages from the teacher in my last class. I also began to feel very tired. I tried not to, but I fell asleep in the last twenty minutes of seeming to be in a trance I could not break. I finally awoke when the bell rung to end the school day. I got up to find my desk wet having drooled all over my papers and desk from a deep sleep. Yet, my mouth was so dry, how odd.

Julie was sitting in the back of detention as I staggered into the classroom, groggy, and with a raging headache. I was no longer excited to see her, so I did not bother to go sit next to her but grabbed the desk nearest to the door and laid my head down to sleep some more. I was not feeling well.

I felt a shock as a hand touched my back. I jerked up to the sight of a very startled Julie staring at me.

"Hey, Psycho, you alright? You look like shit man." She seemed concerned. I was too tired to care so I just looked at her groggily.

Julie just shook her head and took the desk next to mine up front. She looked at me again and with a quick glance at my nearly asleep eyes said, "If you want me to leave then say so."

I yawned and the yawn seemed to cause my entire head to spasm into a weird jerking movement. "No, you can sit where you like. Free country." I laid my head back down wondering what that odd jerking shit was about.

Julie began to talk but it sounded like she was far away. I drifted off to the sound of her voice asking me if I maybe had a fever.

I awoke to Julie again touching my back yet again with only a very mild shock this time. I lifted my head again to a river of drool from a deep slumber feeling even worse than before. Now my mind was so slow it took me several moments to even know who Julie was or where I was.

"I know you said you don't do drugs, but damn Psycho, I would not believe it if you had not said so. You were out cold! Are you sick or something?" She reached out and felt my forehead.

I tried to back away, but I was too slow and really to fatigued to care if she did touch me. I just wanted to sleep. To my surprise the touch did not shock me at all this time.

"I don't feel so good," I slurred, "Maybe I need more water?"

Julie looked around and saw my water bottle. "I will get you some wait here." She took it and left before I could stop her.

I laid my head back down. I really did not care what she did with what. All I could think of was rest. I was already asleep as she came back into the room with a full water bottle. She woke me again and gave it to me. I took it and drank deeply despite my fear of it being tainted. I knew I could trust Julie anyway. Besides, my mouth was dry as a desert despite my drooling everywhere.

Julie watched me drink like a starving calf from its mother. She did not seem to be in a hurry to get home.

"You know when I was in rehab with that Bipolar friend I told you about, she got this medication one time for cussing out one of the counselors. It made her all sleepy and she drooled like you are too. I can't remember the name of that stuff but man you sure are acting like she did. Did you take something maybe?" She was looking at me closely as if to discover some secret I may be hiding.

I shook my head no. "I have not even eaten anything for days. I do not take drugs I told you." I wanted to be angry but could not get the emotional response. I drank deeply again feeling that something was stuck in my throat as the dryness kept creeping further down my body. Nothing seemed to be helping.

Julie kept prying, "Have you drunk anything today? Damn, I have never seen anyone so thirsty."

I looked at her trying to focus on her most foggy form. My mind would not clear it seemed nor would my vision, "Only the water at lunch from this water bottle Stephanie gave me." I briefly showed the bottle to Julie, "She broke mine, so she gave me this new one."

A smile broke out on Julie's face. She sat back in her seat and put her hand over her eyes, "Okay, so you drank the water, right? And you said she has your anti-psychotic meds too, right? And she and Crystal poisoned you with these meds the other day, right?"

"I told you that already." I was too tired for this game. "Look, I am going home, okay? I will see you later." I stood up and felt dizzy.

After a few moments the dizziness passed, and I picked up my stuff and left Julie still sitting there with her hand over her eyes. I assumed maybe she was tired too. As for me I no longer cared about Julie. I just wanted to go home and get some rest.

The walk home was slow and somewhat painful, but each step seemed to help the terrible fatigue just a bit. I noticed the pulsating had stopped. I also noticed the scenery seemed a bit crisper. The trees and sky were not bleeding into each other as they usually do. That seemed very odd, but I would try to figure that out later. I really needed to talk with Simon.

I arrived home to find Stephanie and Crystal already rudely hanging out in my outhouse. I was not too happy about. I was quickly realizing I would not get the nap I so badly needed till I could get rid of my unwanted 'house guests.'

Stephanie saw me first and smiled running up to me trying to hug me. I ducked and she missed. "Back off, Stephanie," I growled. I was in no mood for her childishness.

Stephanie's smile did not diminish as she turned about recovering from her missed hug attempt, "Grouchy! So, Psycho, come listen to the tapes I brought for you. I have Duran Duran and Michael Jackson too!"

"Who," I said trying to get to keep my distance from her in case she tried to touch me again. "Do I care?"

Crystal and Stephanie laughed at that. They pulled out the boom box that Crystal had thought she broke over my head and popped in the King of Pop as they pretended to dance. I had to chuckle at their clumsy attempts. Seemed more like a standing seizure to me. As for the music, not interesting to me at all. It was campy at best.

As the two of them spazzed and gyrated, I looked around for Simon. He was nowhere to be found. Likely still pissed over the Julie thing I assumed.

"Maybe he's out drinking," I thought to myself.

I was still feeling strangely slow and numb but more than anything my mouth was too dry to even speak without a slur. I was constantly having to catch drool that wanted to slip out of my numbed mouth and my jaw would not stop grinding.

Finally giving up the search for Simon I sat down in front of Stephanie and Crystal watching them twirl and sing poorly with their crappy pop music. I seemed to be almost entranced unable to stop staring at them and though I felt like laughing I could not. Something seemed off but I could not think what it was. In fact, I could barely think at all.

Hours passed as I just sat there appearing struck dumb and unable to move. The sun was beginning to get low in the sky when Stephanie finally said to me, "Okay, Psycho, so I have decided you should not have to live in an outhouse, in a cemetery. That is just so gross. I packed up some of your things, so you are coming home with me tonight."

"What? Huh?" I was unsure if I was just dreaming or if this girl just said she was taking me to her house. Maybe I was indeed schizophrenic and now I was hearing voices like Dr. Scott kept trying to say I did.

"I said you are coming home with me so I can help watch you. I already talked to Mary about it, and she said it is okay. I can't let you stay in the house because my aunt thinks you are insane and a bad influence, but I have a tool shed outside. She will never even know you are there, and it is clean," she continued to babble on, but she had lost my attention as I sat there staring in disbelief at the audacity of this bitch.

However, try as I might I could not myself to get up and run her off. I watched almost helpless as she took my backpack and came over and with the aid of Crystal, they pulled me up. I stood there dumb founded until Stephanie began to push me ahead of her. I started walking unable to stop against her force. I did not want to go with her, but I just did not have the ability to fight her off and no energy to argue either.

All I could think is, "where is Simon?"

The two girls pulled and pushed me all the way back to town and Stephanie's house. With a bit of effort, she got me into her tool shed that was not any larger than my outhouse and without a privy. She had already set up a small cot in the corner that barely fit in as a rather large riding lawn mower took up most of the space in this tiny outbuilding. I saw the cot and realizing I was too tired to walk home I would just nap a bit and when Stephanie left sneak back home. This was incredible and I could not believe it was happening. Even in my strange world this had to be beyond weird. Stephanie as usual was babbling on and on about something but I did not hear a bit of it. I was asleep almost as soon as I laid down.

CHAPTER 27: Come One, Come All! Welcome to My Freakshow!

Did you grab a quick nap? Now suck down that coffee, shake off the last of the Sandman's kiss and get your rear ends to the stage. The Puppet Masters will not tolerate your being late! The show is about to begin, and the audience is ready to adore you! Are you nervous? No worries, just close your eye and remember, this is not real, you can wake up anytime you want unless of course, it is indeed it all real.

Well now, is or isn't it? Think hard if you can, try with all you have to remember, isn't it clear as molasses to you yet? No? What is wrong with you these days, the answers are so simple even a sixteen-year-old girl could figure it out. Not like it is brain science, right?

So, without further ado let's all get our flippers, scales, beards, and extra body parts out there for the public to inspect because it is showtime for the freakshow.

"The essential dilemma of my life is between my deep desire to belong and my suspicion of belonging."
-Jhumpa Lahiri

I am awakened by the sensation of water pouring down my throat in torrents. I choke as I try to open my eyes and clear my blurry vision struggling against the onslaught of forced liquid. I try to move but every part of my body is sluggish and slow to respond even with the danger that I am about to drown. I begin to swallow the water fast as possible unable to do anything else to keep from inhaling in the wet death being forced into my mouth.

The room is dark, and I have no idea where I am. I blink and blink but there is not enough light to see who is doing this. I have to keep swallowing the water. I notice someone or something is holding my head up slightly from my prone position. I am so confused. Is this a dream?

I am becoming desperate for this to stop, when my head is gently lowered, and the water stops flowing from, well wherever it is coming from. I lay there in the dark still trying to focus my sight to try to gain the slightest idea of what the hell is happening. It is just too dark, or I am only imagining my eyes are open. I feel the pull of the crushing fatigue as I fall back to the deepest realm of my own little slice of death called sleep. Slowly, I give in as the Sandman takes me into his loving embrace.

I do not know how much time has passed as again I awaken. This time no strange drowning in water, just a slow rise from my slumber. I look at the ceiling and realize this is not my outhouse, but where the hell am I? I look slowly about the room my vision still foggy and dull. I see a big riding lawn mower. Tools of all kinds hang on the walls. A very faint memory of a tool shed creep into my torpid mind.

There are two very small windows in this shed. The room is dimly lit with what appears to be the weakened sunlight of dawn or dusk? I am unsure of the time, the day, or even my exact location. I try to rise, and the dizziness is so bad the room spins wildly. I fall back to the cot again helpless and feeling as if I may puke. I am nauseous. My stomach is cramping painfully. My mind is very murky, but a memory of this feeling comes to me of a poisoning from long ago. I feel my skin, which is strangely very cold, prickle with slow terror. Have I been poisoned again?

I think briefly of Mary, did she finally get me? Then slowly I remember Stephanie. I suddenly recognize these odd symptoms. I am on heavy medication that is what this is. I have not been poisoned, well not really. Stephanie has tricked me again somehow, perhaps?

With much effort I attempt to recall the last memories before this moment. I seem to hear a pop song playing over and over. Something about leaving, wait no *Beat It* was the song. I was in my cemetery, but I was not alone. Yes, Stephanie was there and Crystal too. They were playing a boom box and dancing.

As I work hard pondering the events that led me to my present state, the door opens and in walks Stephanie. She is carrying a plate of something. She is smiling at me. I can do nothing but stare at her wondering what has happened here. How did she manage this?

"Good morning, Psycho! Wow, you must have been tired! I tried to wake you up all day yesterday and you just would not get up. I had to lie to Patty about your being at the doctors and cover for you. Thank goodness it is Saturday, and my aunt had to work today. I was starting to worry. She smiles and scoots past the lawnmower toward me.

I can smell food of some sort. Now my stomach really lurches. What has she done to me! I cannot move and there is no doubt in my mind she has managed to slip me either a high dose or an overdose of Thorazine again!

"Damn I must be the dumbest asshole on earth to fall for this twice," I think bitterly. I look at her trying to will anger in my gaze. My mouth is too numb to even attempt speech, or I would have told her what I intended to do to her soon as this shit wore off.

"I brought you some food! You are so skinny, so I made you eggs and bacon and even pancakes if you want them too." She looks at me smiling big and appearing proud of herself as she starts to put some of it on a fork.

My fear is so muted I feel it more like a tumbling numbness then as real anxiety. I can do nothing but stare at her, watching as she comes toward me with whatever nasty concoction she has on that fork. I hold my mouth shut refusing to eat it.

"Psycho! Open up, damn it!" Steph puts the plate on the lawn mower as she realizes I am not going to do this easy. She then grabs my mouth with her free hand forcing it open.

I taste the food but immediately spit it back at her. I could not have eaten that mess had I wanted to do so. My diet restrictions made it impossible to eat such things as eggs or bacon. This time the fear was able to break through loudly. If she forces this forbidden grease filled stuff into me, Thorazine would be the least of my issues.

"Stop," I slur spitting out her next attempt to force the breakfast in. "I cannot eat this kind of food." I try to rise up, and the dizziness hits hard as the room spins out of control.

Stephanie stops trying to force the food. Then looking at me confused says, "Why not? I am only trying to help you, Psycho!"

I just lay back and wish that I could die right there. Sighing at having to share such information with a brain stem like this (much less my obvious enemy), "ask Mary, I cannot have greasy or buttery food anymore. My stomach is messed up. I am sick," I mumble almost incoherently.

This makes Stephanie pause. She stood there thinking on what I had said appearing to realize if I did invoke the name of Mary, maybe I was being serious with her. She looks at the plate and to me. It seemed like forever before she decided she had better not try again.

"Okay, I am going to find out what you can eat and be back. You stay here," she chuckles at that knowing full damned well I could not get up to go anywhere.

I watched her leave helpless to do anything to fix this situation. Normally, Thorazine does not do this but in very high doses it can render the person almost useless in a slow catatonic like state. It is a powerful sedative antipsychotic, only used at this high a level to calm the worst of the psychotic fits. Only when harm is likely to the person or those around them would such a thing even be justified. There is nothing I can do until the levels in my blood stream lower. I am a trapped as Stephanie's prisoner for now, I realize with utter horror.

"Oh no! What if she forces more of Thorazine into me," the thought is too much to bear?

I try again to get up and the spinning sends me back to my prone position. I roll onto my side as drool pours out of my mouth in torrents.

"How much has she given me," I garble out loud utterly defeated. "Someone, please help." I then whimper but no one hears me. I am all alone. I am hostage to Stephanie and Thorazine.

To no one I call out for help for what seems like forever. I am so dry mouthed it is a horse and soft call. No one would have likely heard me even if they had been right outside the door.

I have not been able to scream since the attack so very long ago that landed me in a dumpster. Between my cotton mouth and scared vocal cords, I sound more like the croaking of a frog seeking a mate than a person making a desperate plea for assistance.

Stephanie had told me she would be back. My fearful thoughts that she would keep overdosing me until I died there in that tool shed kept me from falling back into the deep sedated sleep of vitamin T.

Stephanie finally did come back holding a bowl this time. Her innocent look made me want to retch. How had I not seen the devil hidden behind that sweet veneer I wondered. There was no doubt she was enjoying this caring" for her new acquisition. I glared at her groggily as she approached almost dropping the bowl she was holding on my head as she struggled past the lawn mower. The room was very small and not much space to maneuver much less house two kids and a cot.

"Okay so Mary said this is what you can eat, Psycho, so no arguments this time. Eat it," she said as she scooped up what to my horror was a big spoon of the most dreaded oatmeal.

Somehow, I already knew it would be oatmeal. After all Mary hates me, and she knows I hate oatmeal more than anything on earth. I look pleadingly at Stephanie as she holds open my mouth and forces the terror in. I try to spit it out, but she quickly holds my mouth shut. I struggle with her best I can. My limbs heavy and sluggish, useless to stop her. She staggers as she nearly drops the bowl.

"You have to eat, or you will die, Psycho," Stephanie yells turning red with effort to keep me from spitting out the oatmeal.

It suddenly occurs to me she is right. I am going to die if I keep on refusing to eat anything. I stop struggling and swallow the nasty crap. In my mind I clearly realize if she has indeed poisoned it at least I will be out of her fucking tool shed. If she has not, then I can get my strength back and whoop her ass for doing this to me. Either way, I win.

She notices that I have stopped struggling. A big smile comes across her pretty face as she watches me give in to her attempts to feed me.

"See! Told you I am the best cook. Now, there is no reason for all this fighting. I will help you eat till you feel better and hide you out too. I am your best friend and that is what best friends do," she said while scooping up another large spoonful and pushing it into my mouth.

I glare at her as she starts to blather on about our imaginary friendship while force feeding me like some bizarrely large baby. I want to call her a name or two but each time I open my mouth to cuss her out she shoves more oatmeal into it.

I am not worried about the horrid stomach cramping that usually comes with ingesting food. The hell of my situation is that oatmeal is one of the only foods that I can eat without pain. I had spent many hours since the poisoning and suicide attempt laughing at that weird twist of fate. One has to laugh at the horror. I could not cry but if I had cried about it, then it would drive me to madness.

She had made a lot of this horrid oatmeal but eventually the bowl was empty. The onslaught of forced spoon feeding stopped. I breathed deeply relieved that was finally over. However, in true Stephanie fashion she was not done torturing me just yet. Still yapping, she reached into her pocket and pulled out several pills.

"Okay so now, Psycho you need to take your medication now. No fighting me on this. You are sick and need your medication Mary told me." She tries to grab my head to open my mouth, but I twist it away clamping my mouth shut tight.

No way she was keeping me like this any longer.

Stephanie struggled for a moment as I now used all I had to lift up my deadened body. I was ready to beat her to death with my numb arms if need be. I was not taking that shit.

Stephanie dropped the bowl in the struggle, and it broke in the floor. She let out a furious yell, "Damn it, Psycho! Now look what you made me do. You take you medication now." She backed up surveying the mess of broken ceramic at her feet.

I saw my chance to try to talk some sense into this brain stem, "Look you are giving me too much Stephanie. That is too much. Let me see it and I will take the right amount." I was willing to do whatever needed to be done at this point to get out of there alive or whatever I was.

That made Stephanie pause, "You will take it?" She looked at me suspiciously.

"Yes," I slurred drool pouring out of my mouth. "Let me see it and I will take the amount I am supposed to take. I know what that is, and you do not. You are giving me too much," I insisted.

With a look of disbelief, she handed me the pills and I saw right away I was correct. She had way too many Thorazine tabs there. She was giving me more than they had even given at the hospital. No wonder I could not function.

I took one of Thorazine tabs, one of the Haldol and one of the benzos and said to her showing the pills I had selected, "This is the right dose, idiot. Are you trying to kill me?"

I took the three pills and put them into my mouth waiting for the water she surely brought, or did she expect me to swallow them dry? Not with this cotton mouth that was not happening.

She looked surprised and just stood there. I was sitting there too wondering where the water was. Finally, she figured out what I was waiting on and reached into her back pocket and handed me a tin foil pouch that said Capri Sun Apple on it. I looked at it bewildered, huh?

Stephanie then apologized, snatched it back. I watched fascinated. She took a small straw attached to it. She punctured the pouch with it then, handing it back she said, "here is some apple juice for the pills, sorry about that."

The pills were starting to dissolve in my mouth making the dry mouth taste even worse so without argument I sucked down the apple juice to wash out the taste and swallow the pills. I handed the extra six pills back to her while flashing her an angry look.

"Next time only those three, you hear me," I stammered between drinks of the liquid. I was so relieved to get something for my dry mouth I swear I would have drunk dog piss by then.

Stephanie looked at the pills and nodded she understood. "Are you very angry at me for slipping you the medication? I had to do it. You were going to hurt yourself again, she said doing one of her now infamous pouting looks.

Truth is I wanted to skin this girl alive and laugh while she screamed slowly dying. However, something told me that right now that was not the right way to respond to her question. I looked at the floor then, thinking of what to say to that. What does one say to someone who not only slipped an overdose of dangerous medication to you, but then holds you hostage in a tool shed like an animal? Bet hallmark doesn't even have a card for that kind of predicament.

"No, I guess not. But you should have just asked me, or at least told me," I said sighing.

Stephanie's face lit up like a Christmas tree, "I did try but you wouldn't listen! It is okay, I know you have that disease and all that stuff. So, we are still best friends, right?"

I nodded my head yes in surrender. There would be a time to get my revenge. I would have to wait till I could at least move at more than a turtle's pace. For now, better to keep this idiot placated so I could get out without further injury. Stephanie was one dangerous bitch. I had misjudged the threat she posed to my mission. I sat there listening to Stephanie again prattle on about how I needed a bath, and how I had pissed the cot.

That made me chuckle. "No kidding. You said I missed Friday, Stephanie. I have been here since Wednesday, and you know it. It was Wednesday when you pulled that little stunt, and if today is Saturday, of course I would have to pee eventually." I was laughing a bit harder now.

It was a wonder pissing myself is all I had done in two full days and nights. With some effort I questioned her about how many times she had "given" me that much medication and when the last overdose had been forced in. I found that she had skipped giving me the medication yesterday. She had become scared because I was not waking up anymore. Go figure, she overdoses someone and then gets scared when they don't wake up? Idiot.

With some calculations I assumed I should start to feel better very soon despite the recent dose I had taken on my own. I knew my medications. The hospital stay had made me an unwilling expert in the world of psychotic pharmacology. This knowledge helped to alleviate some of my fear. Soon, I would be well enough to get the hell out of here and back home.

"Can you get up? I think you need a shower, and my aunt is at work. I have your stuff. You could get cleaned up you know," Stephanie suggested.

I agreed. Maybe a shower and clean clothing would help to break my Thorazine trance. I nodded my head, "Yeah, but I may need your help to get up and I will be slow."

She reached over and between the two of us I was finally able to get up. We struggled past the lawn mower and once outside I did indeed feel a little better. I was still very dizzy but moving make me feel less statue like.

I was able to slowly take a shower in Stephanie's bathroom and dress myself in clean clothing. Stephanie took my soiled clothing to another room. She said she was going to wash them for me. She returned after hauling them off and stood there smiling assuming I would thank her for the kindness. In truth, I felt she owed me at least that much since it was her fault, I had befouled them in the first place. I ignored her attempts to get me to give her compliments. I was polite. If she really expected me to gush over her after what she had done, that was unrealistic to say the very least.

After a few hours, much soap and continuous dizzy spells I was finally looking like myself again. My make-up, wig, and signature black outfit all reset to freshness. Stephanie watched me applying the last of my make-up from behind me in the mirror.

"You are so damned beautiful Psycho. I wish I looked like you. It really is so sad you are crazy. You know every boy is in love with you, and every girl wants to be you at school. Everyone is talking about it." She said looking at me with what appeared to be a longing.

I snorted at that. I looked at the stranger in the mirror looking back at me. Her fierce blue eyes empty of a soul and fake blond hair flowing from under a black derby hat. I opened its mouth and watched a bit of drool drip in a long rivet from the corners into the sink below.

"You are more than welcome to trade places with me, Stephanie. Which part do you think they find beautiful? The drooling, the disease, the nightmarish visions, or the scars," I asked her while pointing at the thing looking back at me. I stood glaring at her reflection in the mirror to see if she understood what I was trying to tell her.

She frowned at that, "You do not think you are beautiful? Well, everyone sees it but you. Look at that figure. Why do you hide it? And your face is so pretty but you mess it up with all that make-up. Why! Then your eyes! Oh my God! I would kill to have your eyes," she said in a rush appearing to want to argue this very unimportant point.

I saw the thing in the mirror smile at that, "Well, get me a knife and you can have those eyes right now, Steph. I no longer want to see through them."

In a very sudden mood shift, I turned to glare at her hard, "If you ever pull that shit on me again, so help me, even the Devil will not be able to save you. Do you hear me? Keep your fucking hands off my things and off of me. Oh, and by the way, your cooking sucks," I said laughing wildly at my attempt to hurt her.

I saw the tears start to well in her eyes as she realized I was indeed very angry after all. Now that I was feeling better and able to move, I had no intentions of playing this bullshit game any longer.

"Cry all you like, Stephanie. Cry and cry and cry, no one cares. They pretend to care when there is something in it for them Now let me repay your kindness at helping me get well by giving you a bit of advice darling. In the end, they will throw you away just like me, especially Mary. Why don't you go and visit with her husband, Bob, and he will teach you that lesson? No matter what you do, no matter where you go, they will always pretend to care till you have nothing left for them to take. Then they will throw you away." Stephanie was crying harder now as I reached out and grabbed her by her throat and pushed her to the wall.

In a deep growling voice with a murderous smile, I said right into her ear while leaning in close to her so she could truly hear me, "Oh, and we are not friends, Stephanie. I hate you. If you ever come near me again, I will kill you. Crystal is right. I am going to kill you."

I let go of her throat and she slid down to the floor rolling up into one of her rocking, crying fits. She began wailing loudly.

I did not care. I turned and left the bathroom, continuing out her front door slamming it hard on the way out. I was going home. I had enough of this insanity. After all, I had a mission and Simon to get back to. Stephanie was now dead to me. I never wanted to see or hear her again, or I swore I would indeed kill her.

I walked home in the late afternoon sun feeling sluggish, but clearer than that morning. My mind went over the events of the last week as I wondered why Stephanie kept butting in on my life. Why did she care if I was sick or well? I knew there had to be a reason. No one cares about a stupid homeless rat like myself without a motive, I was sure of that. However, I simply could not find a reason that she would not go away other than wanting me dead. She had nearly killed me twice already. Why didn't she just kill me outright?

Perhaps she was enjoying torturing me. I know my mom loved it. My mother truly delighted in my torment, screams, and terror. I could still see her face smiling and laughing as she and others, well did what they did, all those years. The memory made me shutter a bit, so I shut that thinking down.

Whatever was going on with Stephanie was just going to have to stay a mystery. We (all of us including Simon) were forbidden to ever think of my mother, or any aspect of my life before this world came.

My mind was a no-man's land of land mines waiting to go off with every step. Picking at my memories would assure destruction of what few holds on reality I still had left (if there were any). Somewhere in my very sick mind I understood that one wrong step and I would shut down for good with a catatonic break. I could even become a human statue. I would be forever trapped staring from a shell without another thought again with my mind blown to oblivion. None of us wanted that.

"Think of something else," I hear Simon say.

I am startled out of my dark memories by the most welcomed sound of my best friend's voice. I turn around to see Simon standing behind me.

Before I could stop myself, I run to him. He puts his old sun chapped arms around me as I hold him tight, "I am so sorry, Simon! I did not mean it. Please, never leave me again!"

I would have cried to show I meant what I said, but Simon knows I cannot cry. He also can read my mind; he knows I am truly sorry for not listening to him.

He holds me for a few moments not saying anything smart assed, for a change. He knows I am at a breaking point. If he upset me right now, all would be lost. We just quietly hold each other, reaffirming our bond in the middle of the old dirt road not far from home. I needed the affection of someone who understood, and Simon understood me like no other ever could.

"It is okay. We have each other. You are young. In time this will get easier, I promise," Simon reassured me, still holding me tight. "Just hang in there, that stuff will wear off. You are just weak from it right now. Soon you will be right as rain again."

I nodded and let Simon go. He was right. Simon usually is right. The medication was fucking with me, messing with my head was all. How could I ever let Stephanie or ghosts of the past get to me like that. None of that mattered to the undead anyway. With a quick smile, Simon and I began our walk home again talking of the "plot" and plans for revenge.

The weekend passed peacefully for a change. Stephanie had been warned to stay away. For once she had done as she was told. Maybe she understood I meant it. I was going to kill her. No Mary visits either. I was free to just hang out with my beloved Simon as we talk of the world, argued about future plans, and enjoyed our dark music in the sanctuary of the cemetery.

Slowly, as the night came the onset of vitamin T side effects of jerking movements and involuntary spasms began to make me feel anxious. By Sunday mid-morning I was hit hard with them. I began to pace and jerk everywhere like a spastic asshole. Simon watched in horror. I panicked not being able to sit still becoming more and more frantic with the anxiety that it caused.

He finally could take no more. "Turn up your mad box and dance with me," he said while holding out his hands to take the lead.

At first, I felt silly dancing with this toothless old drunk all around the cemetery. I did not understand why he was doing this, but as the music swept me away, I really began to enjoy it. We danced together for hours. As a team, we worked out the ugly medication side effects in the elegant art form of dance.

By dark, I was beginning to feel almost like myself as the tapestry of the delusional world again began to blend together with the world of the real just below its surface. I had never been so grateful to see the trees pulsate and earth heave. Finally, everything was back to normal, my normal.

Monday morning brought a heavy Spring rain. I dug out the umbrella I had stored with my supplies.

Simon and I walked to school together in the torrential down pour. The thunder shook the earth as I made him promise not to leave my side this time. He swore that stormy morning to never leave my side again. We were a team now forever. It finally seemed like everything was going to be alright.

My day began without any troubles. I continued to receive secret codes from the lessons and chalkboards of which I dutifully recorded for further inspection later. I was in need of a new pad for writing. I had overheard Crystal tell Stephanie once that you could buy such items from Patty in the office.

When the bell rung before second period, I took my twenty dollars to Patty almost certain that I would be laughed at. I asked a very surprised Patty if I could buy a notebook. She seemed to be unhappy to see me but shook her head yes. Quickly she pulled several types of notebooks to choose from out of a drawer.

I immediately selected the one with a red cover. I had received my transmission earlier that morning from "they" and red was the color of information gathering tools. Now I would be able to hear every secret communication clearly with my color red amplifying the messages for me.

My delight at having been able to obtain such a precious item for "they" was not containable. Patty noticed my excitement. I could not help myself from petting the red colored notebook, totally enamored with it, while awaiting my substantial change from her.

She frowned at me, as she handed back the leftover money, "You taking your medication? You know Mary has been very worried about you. We all have." Patty was looking very closely at me.

I refused to make eye contact as I felt a hot rage at hearing again about this fucking medication and Mary in the same sentence. Not to mention the rest of that bullshit lie about anyone caring. I knew there was a secret message in her words. She was in on the plot. I was not going to tolerate this. Just before I could smack her right in her piggy face for insulting me, I felt Simon's hand on my shoulder.

"Let it go. She is a tool of those at the top. Do not blow it by showing her you know who she is. Just smile and leave, now," Simon whispered in my ear.

He was right even though it would have felt wonderful to bash in her stupid face. I just turned without a word and left back to the hallway already swollen with students rushing to class. Fuck Patty, she was not worth forfeiting the mission.

I had no further difficulties in my classes. My new red notebook worked beautifully as "they" had predicted, and the messages came faster and louder. I feverishly wrote all I could hear and see, recording all of them. The red was amazing! I almost felt like a winner for once. However, the dreaded lunch hour was coming. I barely could sit still worrying of what terrible situation awaited me as the lunch hour arrived. However, for a change nothing bad happened.

Suspiciously, maybe due to the ongoing rain, no Stephanie or Crystal. At lunch, Simon and I sat huddled at the picnic table refusing to go into the cafeteria even in this deluge of God's tears. We smiled at each other using our minds instead of voices to communicate jokes, stories, and information. Life was becoming comfortable for the first time in many years.

It did not bother me anymore that sometimes things did not appear to look as I recalled they should. I no longer cared that I could not always understand others. I also stopped getting nervous seeing things pulsate, breath, bleed, or disappear most of the time. It was time to just accept this as the way it was going to be.

My memory of the other reality was just a long, forgotten dream now. As long as it was just Simon and me, I could handle this odd delusional world I had fallen into. It was a place where almost everything made no sense most of the time.

The end of school day did not bring an end to the rain. I had to make up three days of detention from the week before thanks to Stephanie's little tricks. I did not mind since it meant an extra hour of not getting wet.

I walked into the detention hall to the horrific vision that made me suddenly feel I was trapped in a loop. Julie was there sitting in the back of the room, in a purple dress.

I looked back to my dear friend Simon in terror, but he was already running away. He could not tolerate that color combo. Julie knew that. This made me angry but there was nothing I could do about it. My blabber mouth had told her Simon's secret. I privately damned myself for it and sent an apology to Simon by mind for fucking this up so bad.

He did not respond. Simon was likely too far off to hear me.

I sat down in the front desk where so much trouble had already happened. My apprehension at that knowledge was hard to quell, but I was not going near this girl. Simon did not like her. No matter what I thought of Julie, Simon's will outweigh my own. He knew more than I did. Plus, I needed Simon to navigate this strange new reality. Without him I was surely lost.

"Hey, Psycho," I heard Julie yell to me.

I did not turn around but opened my notebook to examine the latest messages. Decoding them would keep me busy so I could ignore this temptation called

Julie. I began with deep concentration to work out the codes. I was so into my task that I did not even notice as Julie came up and sat down in the desk next to mine.

"Psycho! Hey are you deaf." Julie said loudly startling me out of my trance of code breaking.

I looked at her irritated that she could not take a hint. Obviously, I was not interested in her or anything she had to say. Everyone in this delusional world is beyond rude.

"Wow, so you on medication again? I was going to tell you that your friend Stephanie, well she slipped you something last week. When you did not come back to school the rest of the week, I felt terrible I did not say something about it." She was looking into my eyes.

I knew her mind reading device was broken so I decided to tell her off with my words, "Look, you should know I will deal with Stephanie in my own good time. Until then, stay out of this. If you did know, you should have stopped it. You are no friend of mine."

"Julie had known She did not tell me. What an asshole," I thought to myself as I went back to my code work. Simon was right about this one. He is usually right, damn me for being a fool!"

I could sense that Julie was confused and upset (good) as she shifted in her desk nervously.

"I did not see it to stop it! I only noticed it too late like you did, damn it," she yelled at me suddenly.

I nearly took off running in terror from the room as her sudden loud shouting startled me so badly. I had not expected her to yell. I stopped my task again and glared at her.

Julie decided to try to reason with me, Did Simon tell you I was involved? Or did Stephanie say I knew? I hate that girl and want her dead like you do Tell Simon to fuck off. He is not allowed here. I am in purple today and I have ginger too," she pointed at her red hair. "I am your friend, Psycho. I was scared to death they had hurt you bad," she finished in a huff.

I got up and went to the back of the room and sat down at another desk. Julie had mocked me and that was not permitted. Her pretending she cared is utter bullshit. I had not seen her there trying to save me in the tool shed. Nor had any police calls to report me missing been made. These delusions all love their lies. I am a delusion too, but I do not lie about caring when I clearly did not.

Julie got up and followed me to my dismay. She was not going to take a hint apparently.

"Psycho, look, I am really sorry. I should have told you. I should have tried to help. What can I do to make it up? Just tell me," she said before even sitting down in the desk next to mine.

"Fuck off is what you can do," I said not even looking up from my notebook. She was starting to bore me. What had I ever seen in this idiot?

Julie just huffed and sat there staring at me. I did not bother to look up but could feel her broken mind device trying to probe my mind for a way to calm my choice to ignore her forever. I focused harder on my codes to keep it from accidentally getting any information from me that perhaps I was not even aware of. My mind could not be trusted to keep its secrets. If I let down my guard maybe she could glean something from its vastness I did not want discovered even by the waking self.

"Okay, okay. You are right, I am a bitch. I admit that. Look give me another chance," Julie plead to my deaf ears.

It did not work. I continued to ignore her the entire hour no matter what she tried. On several occasions she attempted to tell a joke, a story, and once tried to cover up my codes with one of her fashion magazines. I just grabbed it and threw it to the floor without breaking my concentration on my task or looking up.

Her frustration was clearly felt by my force shield as a pushing sensation. She was trying to get inside my head. Too bad for her, I was not filled with the weakness of vitamin T today. She had no luck at all I was at full strength of enlightenment.

The hour finally came to an end. I quickly packed up my codes and took off headed to find Simon and get home where I belonged. The rain had ended. As I sped out of the double doors, I was grateful that I would not have to practically swim home at least.

I did not look back as I practically ran the entire way. I could barely wait to see the comfortable iron gates that would shut out the excess noise of a world I was no longer interested in.

Entering the cemetery, I felt a chill run up my spin, something was wrong. I looked around and did not see Simon as I expected. Inside of me I felt a rumbling. I felt cracks appear from within. I suddenly knew I was about to come apart into a thousand pieces and fly way. I dropped everything on the ground as the feeling deepened. Suddenly to my absolute horror I began to separate starting in the middle with sections of me flowing outward in every direction. I let out a yell as I fell to my knees trying to capture my essence before it flowed too far to be saved.

"What is happening," I yelled out in terror, unable to stop the pieces from flying away. "Simon help me, please."

Simon comes running up from behind and grabs me, helping me to stand back up. "Calm down, calm down You are hallucinating. It is okay, look at me. It is not real, okay? Do you understand me," he yells holding me up under my arms? "It is not real," he repeats.

I want to believe him, but I can see it. I yell out again and struggle trying to hold it together as I feel my head floating away now. Simon drags me through the cemetery grounds and helps me sit (what is left of me) on a bench. He begins to fan me and stoke my back, but how? My head floated off, didn't it?

"It is not real. Say it! This is not real! You are hallucinating," Simon says over and over in a loop to me.

I try to relax. Simon would never lie. "This can't be real, can it," I think as my shattered mind whirls and whines with the struggle of this experience. I can almost see the gears of my brain as they roll in all the wrong directions. I certainly can hear them!

Slowly and with much effort my pieces begin to be pulled back into the mainframe. At first the connection is very weak with many pieces short circuiting and fizzling in and out. Then finally, all parts are unified into a single unit of measurement again. I was so relieved I began to have a laughing fit. That had scared the shit out of me.

"Thank you, Simon," I said to my friend, "for helping me reconnect with my unit." I was really laughing now as I thought of the teasing he would do regarding this latest episode of weirdness.

"I told you to stop calling me Simon," Stephanie said from behind me.

I turned in surprise to see Stephanie standing there looking concerned and angry at the same time. "What the fuck," I yelled out trying to figure out how Simon had turned into Stephanie.

"You need your medication, Psycho. You are acting insane again. Now I have it with me. You did not come back to get it all weekend. You are sick again," he yelled while trying to push pills at my face.

I slapped her hand away angrily. "How did you turn into Simon like that," I demanded to know. I was really tired of her tricks, "I told you I would kill you if I ever saw you again." I stood up ready to keep my promise to her. I always keep my promises.

Stephanie began to back up realizing too late I had indeed meant what I had said. I was not a liar like she was. "Psycho, please take your medication. If you kill me, they will lock you up again."

Her plea fell on the ground, unheard, and without my interest. I continued to approach her with her death on my agenda. Stephanie whimpered and backed up only to trip and fall to her ass over a broken headstone. I jumped on her like a lion on a rabbit. Without any mercy, I began to hit her with my fists hard and fast.

Stephanie tried to fight back and hit me several times in her wild attempts. I did not even feel her blows. I was faster, more experienced, and determined to kill her. In fact, I would have killed her too. However, I had not looked behind me when I ran home. Julie had followed me from a distance. She arrived, having discovered my destination, just in time to see me beating Stephanie to a pulp.

"Whoa! Psycho, shit," Julie yelled as she dropped her stuff by the gate and ran over to pull me off the screaming Stephanie.

I roared as I struggled to free myself of Julies grip with only the thought of killing this pretty blond on my fucked-up mind. Julie was twice my size and stronger than me. I could not get free as she bear hugged me till I settled down from my blind rage. She did not say a word but just held on tight making sure Stephanie would not end up in a pine box that day.

Stephanie got up a bit bloody but mostly just bruised from her brief beating at the hands of the town psychotic. She stood up and looked at Julie and me, tears streaming down her cheeks.

"She can't help it, she is sick Julie," Stephanie blubbered to my captor. "Thank you for helping me. She needs to take her medication. Will you hold her so I can make her take it," she said rubbing her now bruising face.

My calm returned to rage immediately as I heard Stephanie's words, and I began to try to break free of Julie to finish my job again. "Who the fuck does she think she is," I think wildly. "I am going to kill her."

Julie held me tighter with my newest series of struggling. "She does not want the medication, stupid. Why are you sticking your nose into her business anyway? Leave her alone, asshole," Julie said back to Stephanie much to my surprise.

This made me stop trying to get away. Julie was on my side. I looked at Stephanie, who's jaw had now dropped. She was outnumbered. Julie was not her friend either.

"You are new, so you don't know but Psycho has the schizies for real. She needs her medication, or she will hurt herself," Stephanie pleads to Julie.

I hold my breath to see what Julie will decide now that Stephanie was telling lies on me again. Would she believe her? Everyone else seemed to.

"Fuck off, Stephanie. If she doesn't want that shit, then who are you to tell her better? She is not your sister; you are not her mother. Go home. Better yet, take that shit yourself," Julie laughed at that statement.

That made me laugh too as I thought of Stephanie drooling and helpless. Julie heard me laughing and immediately released her grasp to free me. I shook off her presence but never broke my suspicious gaze from Stephanie. She was too tricky to leave unattended even for a second. Plus, she could turn into Simon.

Stephanie looked from me to Julie then both of us again. She did not know what to do. Julie walked back to the gate and grabbed her things from where she had dropped them earlier. She reached into her purse and got one of her skunky smokes out. She lit it took a drag and returned to where she had left me and Stephanie staring at each other. Stephanie with fear, me with anger.

"Look, let's not fight, Steph. There is no reason for it. Psycho doesn't want the medication, okay? Just have a smoke with me and let's all make peace. Just think, the three of us good looking gals, could rule that school," Julie said as she approached Steph offering her a drag.

Stephanie took the marijuana and smiled at Julie appearing a bit unsure still, "Like seriously? You think that we could? I could live with that. But how?" She then took a drag and held it in while handing it back to Julie. "But you can't control Psycho if you don't get her to take that medication you know? She is really messed up, like seriously Norman Bates messed up."

"Oh, you leave that to me. I can get her under control. Watch me," Julie said as she too took a long drag and held it.

The weird event that had started this whole mess seemed suddenly like a minor incident compared to the bizarre scene and discussion I was now somehow involved in. I was stunned into silence. I felt like I had rooted to the spot as my essence began to flow outward and flowing away as it had earlier. This time, I said nothing as I struggled to stay as one unit of measurement. I was no longer in control of that I had no doubt. These two delusions had plans to do something that I simply could not understand. Somehow, they intended to use me in this plot, but how again I could not understand.

All I could do is try to hold my essence together as Julie and Stephanie began to prattle to each other about this evil new alliance while sharing a smoke. I could not find Simon; he was afraid of the ginger and purple combo. The sky darkened as the ground rumbled with foreboding thunder. I finally understood, that was the sound of God laughing at me.

Oh, my Goth, I am so proud the way you just stood your ground and accepted the taunts, jeers, and insults from a crowd of customers not so cursed as we have been. After all, in the real-world kicking others while they are down is just a healthy way for those who feel put upon to regain some control and feel better. Now don't you feel great knowing you have helped them get healthier, even though it did cost you all you had? Awe, see now you are truly understanding the way the world works. That can mean only one thing my beauties: You are ready to become full time members of the Greatest Freak Show on Earth, wait are we still on that planet, I forget? I hope you enjoyed your stint as the main attraction, but if you didn't too bad for you, because now that the public has tasted your talents, they will never be satisfied till they have eaten you alive! So, still want to continue this wild ride to Goth Queen?

CHAPTER 28: Seeing the World Through Psycho-delic Eyes

Are you scared yet? No! Well, that is just music to my eyes, errr, I mean mouth, errr, nose? I forget which sense deals with music, again? Oh, never mind all that, we do not have time to figure that out now do we! Why? Oh, I am so very glad you asked. Wait, what where we talking about? Now I know we are all gathered here for some reason but sadly my reason has just left the building. So perhaps, this time you will have to deal with it all alone. But you are never really alone, now, are you? Good thing too because without a lot of help you are going to be open to full on attack from, well everyone. Too bad you cannot tell who is here to help and who is here to hurt you, or who is really here at all. Now that you are good and confused, lets began shall we. Close your eyes, spin around several time and take off running fast as you can before they get you. Try not to trip even though you have no idea which way you are running! I will see you below, or is it above? I have already forgotten.

"Of course, I did not want the medication! They promised it would make this strange delusional world go away and bring me back to their reality. I had already been in their reality. I had the nightmares and scars to prove it. Why would I want to ever go back?"
-Alexandria Ausman, 1999

Julie and Stephanie shared the entire marijuana cigarette while they discussed their novel idea of creating a very special clique that would somehow move to the top of the high school pecking order. I stood there listening, not truly interested or even understanding most of what they said. My strange experience of flowing out of the unit of measurement floated through me like the racing dark clouds in the sky. To my absolute horror I could not find Simon. I needed him now more than ever. The enemies had broken through the gates of the castle. I needed his guidance badly. However, Julie had scared him away with her damned purple and ginger combo. No matter how hard I tried the guilt at having told his secret to this girl kept creeping into my brains making me feel very odd.

"You are a sinner," I hear the thunder say.

"Sinners deserve to suffer," it rumbled in the distance only moments after the first.

I could hear it clearly as I could hear Julie and Stephanie's gossiping voices right in front of me. I knew God was calling me out for all the evil I had done in my life. It did not matter that I could not remember what evil I had done. My memory lately was not my strong point. Surely, during some blank spot or weird episode I tended to have, I had done something so bad that God felt the need to tell me himself. It must have been bad indeed, since he never had bothered to answer when I was a kid. For him to finally take notice all I had to do was, well, whatever diabolical thing I had done. Now apparently, I had his attention.

I could recall once really wanting to hear from God, but never had I wanted to hear for this reason. My stomach knotted up and my knees felt wobbly. I was definitely scared. I searched my memory looking for something that may placate him, to calm his anger at me. My mind came up empty without any answers. No doubt, I will be damned for sure. I kept my eyes on the darkening stormy sky for any sign that God would indeed forgive me. Instead, I watched as lightening licked through the clouds reaching for the ground.

My memory of the ECT flashed like the lightening that now lit up the sky. I shuttered, realizing that too was the wrath of God. Mary had been right all along; I was a Sinner. Born to be a monster like my mother, like so many others.

Damnation was going to be too good for me, so God had decided to make a special type of punishment. He had put me into a delusional world where no one believed me, and no one cared either. To add salt to the wound he mixed up my senses, and then set everyone against me. Now I was trapped in a battle, where I could no longer tell who my enemy was and who is my friend. What I had done to deserve this suddenly became a moot point. All I knew is that I had been condemned to a level of hell that even Dante had not written about.

"Psycho! Come out of the storm idiot," Julie said grabbing my arm. She jerked me into the outhouse which woke me from my thoughts of, wait what was I thinking about?

I felt the shock as she grabbed me but did not fight her. She was stronger than I, so I just let her drag me along trying to recall what epiphany I had just had. I knew it was important but now I had lost it like so much other information lately. Damn my memory.

Stephanie was already in the outhouse now very crowded with three teenage girls. She grabbed my supply box and began to paw through it. I felt a flash of anger at her touching my things. I had told her to keep her hands off!

"Let my stuff alone," I yelled as I reached out to grab her.

Julie grabbed my arm, "Psycho, leave her alone. She is our friend. Friends share," She was staring at my eyes looking very stern.

I looked away. I did not want her to see into my soul. I knew she had said her mind reading device was broken but something was wrong here. I could feel her trying to take control somehow. This made me very nervous.

Julie appeared satisfied that I was not going to hit Stephanie and let go of my arm. I backed away still angry but unwilling to test Julies resolve to protect her. Stephanie pulled out my psychiatric records and handed them to Julie. My anger turned to terror as I watched Julie open the manila envelope.

"That is a lie." I tried to grab the records from Julie.

Julie pushed me hard as I reached for them. I fell backward into the wall, "Back off! I just want to see what they say Jeez, quit being a spaz," she said glaring at me again as she had before.

I stood there unable to challenge her. What was wrong with me? This idiot was invading my privacy. I was frozen in fear as I watched Julie go through the lies the doctors had written about my imaginary disease, I felt that same sense of crushing guilt with shame fill me as had earlier when God was voicing his anger. Julie's eyes were growing wider as she went through every single fable in that folder. She even looked at a few twice as I stood there useless holding up the wall. Stephanie was looking at herself in my old mirror that did not work anymore.

"See told you." Stephanie said while puckering up her lips to her reflection in the useless mirror. "Psycho is the real deal. Did you read the stuff about her mom?"

Julie closed the envelope and looked at me appearing bewildered. I looked away, upset that she was trying to get inside my head again.

"Jesus Christ," Julie yelled out suddenly making both Stephanie and I jump in unison. "What the fuck! Just what the fuck," she said now running her free hand through her ginger hair.

"Messed up, huh? Stephanie giggled still admiring herself in the mirror.

Julie looked at Stephanie angrily, "There is nothing funny about any of this, Steph! No wonder Psycho is well, psycho. Shit, who wouldn't be."

Stephanie paused her narcissistic adoration of her reflection at that, "Yeah, I know right? She is really badly fucked up and all. She has the schizies now and there is no fixing that. She needs to take the medications, Julie. If she doesn't, well you were not there that day. You did not see what she did. She broke her head into the lockers and then the police, oh never mind that, just she has to take the medications. She won't though."

Both girls were now looking at me. I did not need that medication. Normally, I would have been really pissed at the mere mention of it but at that moment I was too overtaken with overwhelming guilt and shame to even move. I could not even look at them. The outhouse seemed to be shrinking as my breathing seemed too shallow. I looked to the floor. Their silence as they stared at me make me want to run screaming into the raging storm outside. I could hear the wind picking up as the laughter of God shook the earth. I knew I did deserve this, all of this. I was a Sinner after all.

Julie finally spoke this time appearing very soft and gentle, "Okay...okay so now I get it. If you want to get well, Psycho, you need to take the medications. Stephanie is right. Haven't you been hurt enough?" She took a deep breath, "We are your friends. Please do this for us?"

Now my shame and guilt were replaced with utter contempt for this mocking bitch. She had fallen for the lies, just as I assumed she would. Damn her! Why had I ever thought she would believe me instead of these evil delusional people? Well, I had always been a fool, and here was more evidence to prove it. Once I had adored this idiot, but Simon was indeed right about her. She was dumb as all the rest of them.

"Fuck you both," I said through clenched teeth.

I stood up straight glaring at them and lifting my middle finger flipped them off. I turned leaving them there walking right into the tears of God without looking back. They wanted to live with lies so bad, let them. I could find another place to sleep. The cemetery was no longer my sanctuary. As I went through the iron gate, I thought of how fucked up one has to be to go out of their way to run a Psycho" "out of a shit house in the middle of a boneyard. I left down the road headed to the bridge not sure where I was going, but damned sure I was not taking any fucking medications for a bullshit disease that I did not have.

The storm continued to pour making my walk down the now very muddy road less than pleasant. I had not traveled far from the cemetery when I sighted Simon just ahead. I should have known he would never leave me. Despite the horror of the last few hours, I was able to shake off the bad feelings quickly as I saw my best friend. Everything would be alright as long as Simon and I were together. I waved to him smiling and he waved back.

I ran to him like a lost dog to his owner. I did not have a tail to wag but my smile worked just as well. Simon gave me a quick hug and threw his drenched jacket around my shoulders.

"Nice day for a stroll, my Lady," he joked while bowing. He started laughing.

"Indeed, kind Sir," I said with a quick curtsy. "However, I think we'd better get back to our castle." The storm was getting fiercer with wind gusting so bad it nearly knocked me off my feet.

"I agree, my Lady," Simon said as he turned me around headed back in the direction of the cemetery.

I recoiled and stopped dead, "Wait! We cannot go that way. Julie and Stephanie have hijacked our home, Simon. They are there now."

Simon stood in front of me. Even in the heavy rain I could tell he was crying. I had never seen him cry before, so I was stunned into awe at the sight.

"You have to go back. There is nowhere else to go. It pains me to send you back, but that is your home. If you stay out here, you will die. I don't want to lose my friend, so please for me go back. Just do your best to deal with these girls. Keep solving the code, the answer to this problem is there," Simon said looking at me with seemed to be pity.

I shook my head no in pure disbelief. Surely, he did not want me to be anywhere around Julie at least. He hated her. I tried to reason with him as the storm deepened, threatening to blow us both away.

Finally, I realized there was no other options. More storms would come. There was nowhere else to go as Simon had already pointed out. It was dangerous to be exposed to the elements and the chances of discovery would increase if I tried to carve out a new territory without careful planning. Simon was right, he usually is.

Simon walked me all the way to the cemetery gate before we both said a sad goodbye. The storm had slowed to a light mist by that time. I watched him walk away as we had already agreed. As long as Julie was around in that purple, he was unable to be at my side. For now, I would be alone at the mercy of these two brain stems.

I would try hard to remember what Simon had said on the way back. "No hitting them. No killing them either. Just try to play dumb and don't eat or drink anything they try to give you."

I took a deep breath before opening the gate to go inside. The rain had completely stopped as I got to the outhouse to find Julie and Stephanie still there huddled and smoking another of Julie's horrid cigarettes. They both looked up appearing sleepy as I walked inside.

"We knew you'd be back, Psycho. Nowhere else to go, huh?" Julie said while snickering.

Stephanie also chuckled at that. I just shot her a dirty look. "When are you leaving?" I inquired dryly.

"Oh, since the rain has stopped, real soon. Hey, but guess what? You are coming home with me tonight, Psycho. Steph and I decided you cannot live out here like a hobo. It is not right. She and I will take turns giving you a place to stay," Julie said while stretching her arms up in a yawn.

"Fuck you. Not interested." I said trying to quell the rising anger at the audacity of these two rats in my outhouse.

Julie really started laughing at that as did Stephanie. "Told you," Stephanie blurted out.

I watched them both laugh uncontrollably like a couple of loons. The whole building stunk worse than usual with that smoke. My stomach felt a bit queasy from it. I decided to step out and let them get control of themselves. They were completely insane no doubt. I stood outside listening to them wondering if maybe they should not be the ones taking medications.

It was not long before the laughter stopped, and I heard them gathering up their stuff to finally leave. I sighed with relief at the idea of Simon and I getting back to normal. my normal. I saw Julie come out first. She had all her stuff, and to my abject horror she had some of my things in her arms too. Stephanie came out behind her carrying more of my belongings.

"Hey! Put it back," I said while trying to grab my backpack from Julies overfilled arms.

She backed up and yelled, "Stop it, Psycho. You are coming with me, damn it You are wet, haven't eaten, and smell. You can't live in an outhouse. It is not decent," she was putting everything down.

I assumed she was putting it down to ready herself for a fight. "Fine by me," I thought as I got ready to battle her. I took my stance of aggression ready for her blows and ready to deliver a few of my own.

Julie looked at me appearing to know I meant business, "Look not going to fight about this, Psycho. You come with me tonight or I will personally call the cops myself and you can sleep in a hospital cell when they find you squatting in the cemetery." She glared, "You hear me in there? I am not kidding. Pick up your shit, and let's go before it gets dark!"

"Huh?" I said unable to understand what she had just threatened.

Stephanie walked up to me and held out her hand. I saw three pills in her palm. I stood there like a deer in the headlights looking at her hand then back to Julie. Somehow, these two had just gotten the upper hand. How can that be?

"Take them," Stephanie said while looking to Julie for back up.

"Take them, Psycho, now or else I swear I will call the cops," Julie said appearing irritated. "I mean it, stop dicking around. Things are about to change, and you had better get with the program or it can get ugly."

I shook my head no. I was not taking these pills. I was not going with Julie either. "Call them, I don't care, I finally said still somewhat dumbfounded.

"Have it your way, Psycho," Julie said to a now very upset Stephanie as she came over and demanded the pills from her.

Stephanie gave Julie the pills. "Come on, Stephanie, I have a phone call to make," she said while grabbing Steph and forcing her to walk with her past me and toward the gate.

I watched them leaving wondering what to do now. If Julie did call Dennis and Boyd, they would call Dr. Liar (okay, Dr. Huff) or Dr. Scott, and surely, I would go back to the hospital. Anxiety began to awaken and engulf me like a blanket, as I stressed on the idea of going back to the shock shop. Still, I was not going to take that poison they called medication or go with that evil bitch, Julie either. I simply did not know what to do.

Simon! Simon would know what to do and now with Julie and Stephanie leaving he would be here soon. I grabbed my supplies Julie had dropped on the wet ground and went inside the outhouse to wait for him. This would be okay, I just had to trust Simon to tell me what should be done now that we had been compromised.

I went to my old storage box to get the "false" psychiatric records. It had been stupid to keep those all this time. I decided to destroy them as I should have done in the first place. No one would ever see them again if I burned them up. However, as I dug through the pile of things, I had hoarded there over the last several months I could not find them. With horror I determined that Julie or Stephanie had stolen them. Now that made me beyond angry, how dare they.

I had my back to the door of the outhouse considering what I was going to do to get the records back when suddenly I was grabbed from behind and tossed out the door to the ground roughly. I did not even have time to recover before a large girl, I began to recognize as Julie was on top of me pinning me to the earth.

I struggled but she was twice as big as me and her weight was impossible to move even as I recovered from the shock of it all. "Let me up you bitch," I yelled still trying to lift her off me.

"You are a pain in the ass, Psycho I swear," Julie bellowed at me as she grabbed my face by my jaw. "Okay, Stephanie now."

Julie forced my mouth open as Stephanie came out of nowhere and pushed pills into it. I tried to spit them out, but Julie was ready. She quickly forced my mouth shut and held my jaw closed, as I struggled to knock her off by writhing. I then tried to break her grip on my head by shaking it. Neither worked. They tasted like shit, but I refused to swallow the pills.

Julie held on to me like a bucking bronco in the rodeo, never relenting for even a second. I relaxed trying to lull her into thinking I was done fighting, but she did not fall for that either.

"We can sit here all night. Swallow them or they can dissolve. You are taking your medication, damn it," she said red in the face with our struggling.

The dance of forced medication lasted some time as I continued to do all I could to get the shrinking medication out of my mouth before it made it to my blood stream. Eventually, there was no need left for me to fight, the pills were gone having slowly mingled with my saliva. Julie and Stephanie had won, this time.

Julie got off me sure that there was nothing left to spit out. She was winded but appeared satisfied with her little trick. Julie had not expected that I may be a bit pissed, about being forced to take such poison like that. Well, I was very pissed.

"Whoa you are strong for being so small, Psycho," Julie said bending over to catch her breath while chuckling a bit.

I stood up. Without giving two shits what Simon said, or saying a word, I walked over to Julie and punched her right in the face. She staggered backward from the force as I punched her in the gut. Julie let out a yelp as I then quickly swept her feet from under her with my right foot. She fell hard. I jumped on top of her this time. I grabbed her ginger hair in my left hand and with a right punched her in the face again.

Stephanie had been standing there trying to decide what to do. She decided to get involved by grabbing me from behind and lifting me off of Julie, knocking me to the ground. I grabbed Stephanie now and pulled her to the ground with me as she tried to scratch but I held her off.

Julie had recovered from my attack, so she returned to assist Stephanie by grabbing me by the collar of my shirt. She pulled me off the ground, breaking my grip on the struggling Stephanie.

We were face to face now as she let go of my collar and with a wicked right hook punched me in the jaw hard. I hit her back in the chest with my own punch as she hit me in the sternum knocking out my breath. We both backed off each other for a moment me out of breath, she appearing to need a quick rest.

I steadied myself still huffing trying to breath as I ran at Julie full force delivering another punch to her head. She groaned and hit me back, making contact with my left eye. Blinded I staggered back and was tripped by Stephanie who had gotten behind me. I fell backward hitting my head hard. The world spun out of control as I felt I needed to throw up.

I saw Julie standing over me. She reached down and pulled me to my feet again grabbing me by the collar of my shirt. The world was still whirling around me as I readied myself for the blow that she would deliver.

Instead, she pulled me close to her face, "Enough! Is this what you want? A fist fight every time someone tries to help you? Is that all you know? Are you even in there?"

"Get your fucking hands off me asshole." I spit my bloody saliva into her fast-swelling eyes.

Julie pushed me backward with all her strength and I fell to the ground hard again. I just laid there this time. I'd had enough for now. She was too strong to beat outright. No doubt we would have to kill each other to determine a winner. Besides, the damage was already done as I felt the medication 'head change' already beginning to take effect. My stomach had been empty a long time plus my heart beating rapidly from the vicious fighting. With the anti-psychotic trio pre-dissolved through my mouth, it was now clear to me that vitamin T had made me his bitch once again.

"Get up Psycho, get your stuff we are going home now. Don't make me hit you again," Julie said, now standing over me appearing to be very serious.

I shook my head no. I did not want to get up, but I also did not want to fight anymore, "Just leave me alone please. Why can't you just leave me alone?" I said covering my eyes with my hands to help stop the tilting of the world. I also did not want to look at her any longer.

I heard Julie's voice but did not uncover my eyes, "Steph, grab her shit. I guess I will be carrying her sorry ass. You hear me Psycho? I will drag you out kicking and screaming if need be. Up to you."

I just whimpered. This delusional world was so confusing. I just wanted to be left alone but no one cared, as usual. They all wanted to hurt me. Now, all I could do is hurt them back if I could. It was unclear when everyone had turned on me. Lately, I had been thinking maybe it was as far back as the day I was born. However, there was no real way to be sure. I felt Julie grab my arm and tug at me demanding I get up. I refused. I had already decided she would have to carry me as she had threatened. I was not going to make this easy for her when she was making life so hard for me.

Julie groaned and then reached down and grabbed me yet one more time by the collar and lifted me up to my feet quickly throwing me over her shoulder. That was too much. I struggled and knocked us both over to the ground growling and kicking her before she could recover. My boots made their mark in her ass and then in her back pushing her away from me.

"Leave me alone, damn it," I yelled as I kicked.

Stephanie had watched the whole scene go down holding my stuff. She already knew when I was not going to put up with it, there was no talking me out of it, "Julie, let's just go You got her to take the medication. Enough already before someone gets hurt. That is not going to get us anywhere."

I looked at Stephanie with a bit of respect. Finally, a voice that made some sense. She was right. Someone was going to be hurt.

Julie got up looking quite disheveled with blacking eyes, a busted lip and mud all over her purple dress. I had given her a run for her money. She may have gotten me to take the medication but getting me to go home with her was not going to happen.

"Okay, have it your way, Psycho! Just know tomorrow you will take that medication again. I know it takes a few weeks of taking it every day before it even works. I can wait. When you finally wake the fuck up from your psychotic shit you will be begging Steph and I to get you out of this shithole." She pointed at me, 'You will take the medication if I have to beat your ass the whole time, you dig?"

"Go fuck yourself, Julie," I said hatefully. She could try but I would not fall for this ever again. Now Julie was on my list of those to be destroyed.

I watched the two of them leave. The anger at their attack far outweighed the feeling of the vitamin T in my system. I was not worried though. Stephanie nor Julie had ever bothered to read the dose information on the bottles. I knew it would not last for long.

My prescription medication was a fierce customer. So much so that only a small dose every few hours was the standard. Stephanie had been overdosing me at hospital levels by giving several doses at once. The dose I had told her was correct. However, I neglected to tell her it was only enough to last about three to six hours. I was supposed to take that nasty shit at least three to four times a day. So, they had only managed only to piss me off, not treat any phantom disease of the brain they seemed to think I had. They had not even given me enough to cause serious side effects.

Chuckling at their stupidity, I got up and grabbed my things that Steph had once again dropped on the wet ground. Simon would be home soon and oh, what a story I had to tell him tonight.

Simon came home not long after the demonic duo had departed my sanctuary. He laughed as I told him of my fooling Stephanie regarding the correct dosage, but he seemed upset over the whole incident in general.

"They are getting more brash. Julie knows too much, and Stephanie has always been a problem. You have gotten in very deep. I think the best thing to do at this point is break the code so you can see what the message is for our mission," he said looking serious for a change.

I nodded my head. He was right. Somehow, I knew the answer out of all this was already in the secret coding I had been recording in the red covered notebook. Those teachers were speaking to me sideways as well as directly that had to be important.

Without further discussion I retrieved the notebook and a candle that Mary had brought in my last supplies. By candlelight, while sitting on the privy bench, I began to work out the coding one at a time careful to check my work with what I already knew instinctively about communication that is not verbal.

Simon watched me silently smoking his dreadful rolled tobacco while I tried to think clearly. Despite the growing fatigue cause by vitamin T, I had managed to get the first bits of the code deciphered. Blinking, and sure that I had misunderstood, I checked my work several times. I was correct. The messages where clearly stating that I had been chosen to serve a very important purpose. That I would be given special abilities to fulfill this function. The abilities were coming from a Power greater than God and older than time itself.

I looked at Simon so shocked I had dropped my pencil in the floor. "This cannot be correct."

"Why not? he asked smiling like a cat that had eaten the family bird. "Could you read minds, talk to the dead, or hear God before the static? How about "they", haven't you ever wondered why they warn you of the color coding?"

I had not thought of all that. Simon was right. I could remember a time when I could not do any of that stuff, but now I could. I could even escape the unit of measurement and flow out into the tapestry. I could see both the real and unreal world, but I never knew any of that existed before, before they said I was getting this schizophrenia crap.

"Come on, Simon. Why would this Higher Power select a foolish kid to do his bidding?" I asked truly thinking someone in the great void's human resources department had made a serious paperwork error. "That makes no sense!"

That made Simon laugh, "Oh, you think a Carpenter's son was an expected choice for God only begotten Son? So, the higher power chose a homeless bum. That is not so far-fetched when you think on it. Maybe they don't want your cover blown. Those who would stop the message would be looking for power, wealth, or fame. You don't even have a damned family or a life. No one would ever suspect you!"

Simon was making a lot of sense. However, I just could not bring myself to believe that something so ancient and powerful would bother with the likes of me other than to squash the life from my insignificant body. Still, I could not explain the sudden enlightenment" "easily either. This would have to be considered for a while. If were the truth, then surely the Higher Power would send me a sign that even my foolish ass could not miss.

Simon read my mind, "You will get a sign. The creators always send a prophet a sign. Remember, like Moses and the burning bush?" He looked at me with what I thought was pride.

"You really think the Higher Power would want a Sinner to spread his word, and what word am I spreading exactly?" I was getting too sleepy to break any more codes. Yawning, I laid down, falling asleep before I could hear Simon's response.

The next morning was clear and sunny. The numerous birds sung their frantic mating calls waking me from my deep medication induced slumber. I watched the various woodland animals running/flying/climbing about often shaking the excess of God's tears from the newly birthed flora and fauna of the rural landscape. It made me smile. All around me the sights and smells of new birth from a late Spring assaulted my senses. Today, I seemed to have less distortion of information going into my head. Smell came through my nose, sounds in my ears and sight, well except for my friend Simon that seemed a bit clearer as well. I almost had forgotten the latest discovery of the night before as I prepared for my school day. Until my chain-smoking friend reminded me.

"You had better watch closely for that sign from the Higher Power. It could come anytime, you know, from anywhere," he said stomping out the morning dew from his well-worn railroad boots.

"That is insane, Simon," I said finishing up my make-up while watching him in the mirror. "No Higher Power is going to fool with a nothing like me I already told you. I will recalculate my code decipher in detention. There has to be an error. My communication grid does malfunction from time to time after all. This is likely only a flaw of the unit of measurement."

Simon guffawed at that. "Whatever you say. Just don't be surprised when I am right and as usual you are wrong."

I grabbed my things ready to head to my school day. "My point exactly, Simon. I am wrong all the time. Not Higher Power prophet material there darling." I started to walk, "You are coming or not?"

Simon shrugged and followed me as we headed down the waterlogged road. He did not bring up the topic of Higher Power again. I had received my usual transmission from "they" earlier that morning and knew that today I was to watch for the color yellow with a quick follow of maroon that would signal trouble ahead. I stayed out of it in my usual black. No reason to get involved in the workings of things I did not understand than I already had.

I was looking at the mudslide that used to be a roadway talking of the morning transmission to Simon when I noticed he had stopped dead earlier and was now behind me a good distance.

"Simon? We are going to be late. What are you doing?" I turned and yelled at him only then noticing he was looking very frightened at something that was now unfortunately behind me.

I spun ready to run in terror to see the most unwelcome faces of Julie and Stephanie almost right on top of me. I almost fell backward in surprise.

"Who the fuck are you talking to Psycho," Julie demanded to know looking all around. She was again in purple. This was a different dress, but the color was not. "And transmissions? Christ! Does that medication do a fucking thing?"

Stephanie snorted, she talks to Simon all the time. Sometimes she calls me Simon too. It is so stupid. The medication only works if she takes it every day Mary told me." Stephanie seemed rather proud of herself that she knew something she thought important.

I walked quickly around them both not bothering to respond to their drivel. These pesky delusions were not going to set me off this morning. I had a mission to get to. Did it really matter what they believed about me? I decided it did not, as they already were a slave to lies. Let them have their false world. No way I was getting pulled into that madness.

Julie yelled out, "Psycho! You get back here and take your medication. I will tell..." she pauses likely looking at Stephanie for the name she could not remember, "Mary on you."

Without looking back, I flipped them the bird and walked faster. Let them tell Mary, not like that dumb bitch would do anything. After all she hoped I would kill myself not just take it as prescribed.

As I approached the school building, I rounded the corner and looked off to the left into the drainage ditch. I marveled at the trickling of a weak stream of water through it, having emptied its swell from yesterday's storms in the dark hours. To my utter amazement, I saw a small dog like creature shivering in the water. I stopped unsure if I was seeing a puppy, or if this was just an error of the unit measurement.

I listened and heard a faint whimpering from the small canine filthy with mud encased fur. I dropped everything and jumped into the deep ditch to save this poor creature that had somehow fallen in or been washed down the ditch.

It felt like I broke my knees as I landed. The ditch was deeper than it appeared from the top of the road.

After a quick wince against the pain, I rushed to the little animal and scooped it up into my arms. "There, there little one. I got you," I said to the very frightened pup.

It was very cold, so it did not try to fight me. I looked at it closely to see if it had any hidden injuries.

I was amazed to find I was holding a full-grown red fox not much bigger than a large breed dog pup. Had I any sense I would have been cautious as the fox is not a tame creature, and not a pet. They also can carry rabies. However, I did not think of any of those things. I only saw a life not so different from my own worth saving despite the danger.

I looked about and could not see a way to get us both out together. So, I lifted the fox above my head and put it on the ground furthest from the muddy road. It looked at me for a moment and then without a sound it gracefully slipped into the cover of the woods. I sighed a breath of relief. The fox would be okay. I got there in time to save him from the folly and selfishness of humankind. That drainage ditch ran through his home not the other way around.

Now, I had to figure out how to get myself out. I jumped up and grabbed the roadside of the ditch wall and began to try to pull myself out. My hands slipped and I slid back into the ditch almost falling on my ass. As I recovered, I nearly tripped over a black object I had not noticed in my hurry to save the fox. I stopped now curious to see what this was. I reached down and picked it up.

I blinked several times to see if this image in my hands would go away but it did not. I was holding Mary's bible. "How?"

My heart began to speed up with anxiety both because of the memories this object invoked and because I knew what this meant. I had gotten my sign from the Higher Power.

Are we all still here? I mean where exactly is here. If you do not know then I am afraid we are both lost. The GPS is broken, we took a wrong turn at Albuquerque and now your guess about the destination is as good as mine or is that the other way around? Oh well never mind, let's just keep going until we figure out where we are going or drive right off into the Grand Canyon Thema and Louise style! Sound like fun? More like funny farm, but who am I to say. No, really, who am I?

CHAPTER 29: CHAOS IS THE MOTHER OF THE CHOSEN ONE

Good day Beautiful Family! Okay despite some bumps in the road we are still rolling on! Where are we headed? Well, that is the nightmare of it all. We are well on our way to our destiny of utter destruction. It is too late now to back out. I really did not mean to fool you into this hellish road trip, I mean I did warn you several times to turn back did I not? I would tell you all that it is going to be okay, that all stories have happy endings, but now that would make me a liar, now wouldn't it? If you had any illusions that this is going to work out well, you may as well roll down the car window and throw it out now. Don't worry, here in the delusional world that is not littering. Here the road here is paved with shattered illusions/dreams. I for one am glad you are ready to lighten this load of all that useless baggage. We will need to travel light from here on out since our vehicle is already over the weight limit with things, we cannot fit out the windows or doors. It is getting way too cramped for comfort. So, if everyone is ready to get back on with our journey, then get started. I will as usual be laughing...errrr...driving the car.

"The psychotic drowns in the same waters in which the mystic swims with delight."
— Joseph Campbell

I am still staring in disbelief at the bible in my hands as Julie and Stephanie have finally caught up with me. They saw me jump into the ditch. From their vantage they had assumed I did it to harm myself. It was not their fault. No way they could have seen the sign granted me by the Higher Power from so far away. They were just regular delusions after all.

My shattered brain could not find a plausible reason for this bible to be here at this place under a half drowned red fox. It had to be the hand of the mystical.

Just why me? I had done nothing of any importance my entire life. In fact, I was not even worthy of a family or home (or sanity apparently). Yet, here was the proof of my divine mission in my now trembling hands. The sound of my heart pounding in my ears with absolute terror drowned out Stephanie and Julie's attempts to gain my attention for several minutes.

"Psycho. Hey, what the fuck are you doing? Psycho! Psycho! Earth is calling, Psycho." I finally heard Julie's voice as it broke through my paralysis of pure anxiety.

I looked up at her. Her face pulsated appear to shrink and grow at the same time. Till now, only things like trees or intense colors had done this and that one-time Stephanie had on the porch many months ago. Now, with amazement I looked at the girls. Both of them pulsated with a strange glow that flashed from time to time.

I knew immediately that could only mean one thing: My powers were getting stronger. I listened and could hear Julie wondering if I had lost my mind completely. It was loud and clear. Somehow, I thought I should be pleased at this sudden increase of my abilities. However, I shook in fear. Truth was I was beyond terrified. This just did not seem right, but I could not deny what I was experiencing so damned clearly. Simon had been right; the codes were deciphered correctly. I indeed had been chosen as a prophet for the Higher Power. This was a lot for anyone to accept much less for a troubled teenager.

"Give me your hand! We are going to be late idiot," Julie yelled down to me offering her hand to pull me up.

I ignored her. Instead, I quickly put the drenched bible into the back of my pants and jumped grabbing the lip of the ditch. This time I successfully climbed out. I did it without the aid of Julie.

After I was able to get to my feet and out of the ditch, I saw that Stephanie had picked up my backpack. She was standing there looking at me holding it like a baby in her arms. I walked to her abruptly and snatched it from her arms growling like an animal.

She was afraid I could hear it in her mind as she backed off wide eyed. The fight of only hours before had not left her memory yet. Stephanie more than anyone knew I had no problem with using brute force to get my way. She had witnessed and been a victim to it on more than a few occasions already. I could hear her think that she was in no hurry to add yet another fray with me to her already impressive number.

Stephanie looked frantically to Julie, "I think she is worse." She continued to back up giving me a wide birth as I headed right for the school.

I did not bother to see what Julie was doing. These two no longer mattered. I had to get to class to record my codes for deciphering. I had no idea what a 'prophet for the Higher Power' was supposed to do. That did not bother me too much as I already knew the answer would come to me as I looked at the delusional world through new and improved eyes.

All around me everything seemed to pulsate for a moment when I focused on it, then flash with a glow. I seemed to be able to hear every voice of the many students entering the schoolhouse. Their voices and their conversations melting together into a single song of unintelligible notes. Just above their sound was that of a metal roof catching all of it and reflecting it back as an echo. I felt as if I managed to enter into a vortex of unimaginable power.

I closed my eyes as I felt this 'power' welled up inside my chest threatening to blow it into smithereens. As it flowed through my veins with every heartbeat, I could sense a feeling of strength I had never known before. It felt awesome! I almost ran into the classroom door (which was closed) before opening my eyes to see it just in the nick of time.

In my mind I felt ten feet tall. I remembered reading a few comic books in my youth about Superman, well, I felt like that guy. There was nothing I was not able to do I smiled as I walked into the classroom truly enjoying this feeling with unequivocal pleasure. It had been a very long time since I had felt anything but fear or pain, but this was something beyond astounding. If this is what it meant to be a 'prophet of the Higher Power', well I was ready to sign the hell up.

I spotted a student that sat in the front row next to me leaning over a desk with a pretty girl sitting in it. He was busy carrying on a conversation with her. He wanted to fuck this girl. I knew that because I could hear his filthy thoughts. However, he was verbalizing to her deceptive small talk. His double speaks irritated me. I hate liars. So, as I walked by him on the way to my desk, I pushed him hard. He fell forward into the girl he was attempting to woo.

He let out a protest as did the girl. I turned and glared at them both, "Sinner. Rapist. You will burn in hell," I said coldly to the stunned couple.

Their mouths dropped open as did the mouths of most of the students within earshot of my very accusatory statement to the boy. I did not care. They were all doomed. It was not their fault, I knew that. Until they understood what the Higher Power had in store for them, it was only natural to think their bad behaviors had no eternal consequences. Thank goodness (well thank the Higher Power) I was about to help them find the path to "salvation."

Now, I just had to figure out what that path was exactly. I rapidly lost interest in the would-be rapist and went to my desk marveling at all the extraordinary new sights and sounds flowing into my head. It was frightening, confusing, and thrilling all at the same time. The only comparison I can offer here is that it felt like I was a race car with a powerful motor. The driver (who was not me) was putting the gas pedal to the floor revving then releasing over and over again. The inner feeling that I would blow up still came in spurts as Mrs. Wells came in and began the lesson.

Despite my overloading sensory input from the environmental stimulus, I was able to capture with ease each code Mrs. Wells wrote on the chalkboard. Each one lit up and pulsating and tracing across the board in a loop assuring I could not miss them if I had been half asleep. I wrote them all down for later decipher sometimes so fast I wrote them right off of the paper and on the desktop.

My focus was so intense to record all coding that when the bell rung to signal the end of class it sent me into a spasm of terror. I let out a yell while grabbed my ears knocking all my notebooks onto the floor and my pencil went flying across the room. Blind panic filled me as I could not understand where this horrible high-pitched sound was coming from.

"Oh, shit. There she goes again." I heard the boy in the desk next to mine say despite my ears being muffled by my clenched hands over them.

I could not understand what he was talking about. The loud bell continued to echo growing slightly weaker as I watched the students all get up and leave the classroom. All of them keeping a baleful eye on me. I clenched my teeth trying to will the hollow sound of that bell out of my ears.

My attention was so focused on my agony I did not notice Mrs. Wells had noticed me. She waited at the class door watching me. Finally, the echoing stopped, and I was able to lower my hands from my ears. I immediately set about to pick up my things and rush to the next class vaguely aware that bell was going to ring again soon. That was not going to be fun for sure if it sounded anything like the last one.

I heard Mrs. Wells close the door as the last student exited. I was retrieving my pencil but looked up startled. "Why did she do that," I wondered eyeing her suspiciously.

"Are you okay? Do you need any help," Mrs. Wells said walking toward me as I rushed to pack my backpack so I could leave with the rest of the students?

I looked at her nervously but did not respond. I grabbed the backpack and tried to get around her scurrying for the safety of the hallway with its mass of rushing bodies. She blocked my escape.

"Your behavior and look are declining. I think you may need to talk to someone. Are you hearing voices? Seeing things that are not there again? Are you taking your medication?" he looked hard into my face trying to capture my eyes with hers.

I looked to the floor. I knew this trick. She wanted to steal my powers. I would not let her get into my head. The medication was designed to poison my mind and confuse me from my mission. Everyone around me lately was hell bent on getting that mind controlling device into my body. It was infuriating.

I could hear her thinking I was crazy but that did not bother me. They thought Jesus Christ was crazy too. That did not mean he was not the one and only Son of God. I was a "prophet to the Higher Power" no matter what anyone thought or even if I wanted to be. That was not going to change just because this old bag did not agree with the truth.

"She is taking it Mrs. Wells," I heard Simon say from behind Mrs. Wells. "She has an appointment with her doctor after school too."

Mrs. Wells turned and looked surprised that she too could see Simon. "Ha!" I thought, "Simon is truly a friend to show himself to this meaningless old bat. Now, she will see how powerful I really am." I smiled as I saw my best friend wave at me from behind her.

I waved back. Simon was simply the best friend I could have ever hoped for to do this for me. Mrs. Wells was dangerous to the mission. Had he not stepped in, well who knows what she may have done to try and take possession of my powers.

"Oh, Okay. Well, then you had better get to your next class then," she said looking from the smiling Simon and then to me with bewilderment.

She apparently had never seen an old Brakeman before. That made me snicker. I quickly went around Mrs. Wells and followed Simon out the classroom door into the hallway. We walked together to the next class. Getting there was like being a salmon swimming upstream. With some effort we got the next classroom doorway when Simon turned around to me.

"Stop acting nuts, okay? I could hardly talk her out of calling someone there. I cannot follow you around all day keeping your crazy ass out of trouble. Now here take these, damn it!" Simon reached out his hand which to my surprise held three anti-psychotic pills in it.

I was pissed. "What is wrong with you, Simon, I thought you were on my side. You are no better than the liars!" I smacked his hand knocking all the pills into the floor.

"Christ, Psycho. What did you just do?" I watched stunned as Simon turned into Julie before my eyes, "and I am Julie, not Simon."

I shook my head in disbelief, "How did you do that? You liar. Fake. Sinner," I yelled back at Julie just as I punched her in the stomach.

She blew out all her wind with a rush as she grabbed her belly doubling over. I was livid. Faking that she was Simon was worse than anything she had done so far. If the next class was not about to start, I would have beaten her to an inch of her life.

However, the screaming bell sent me again into spasms. Once again grabbing my ears and clenching my teeth against the pain, I hurried into the classroom leaving Julie there nursing a stomachache.

I went to my desk and sat down noticing a dour Crystal shooting me a pissy look. She could go to hell and burn too I thought. The teacher came into the room and began her lesson. I again saw clearly the messages being sent to me by secret code as she prattled on about USA history.

There were so many messages coming at me all at once by the middle of class I could not keep up with them all. Anxiety at missing important information began a panic attack deep within me. I stretched and tapped my forehead trying to release the tension building inside me. It was of little help. My legs began to feel the inner agitation as I rocked in my desk and tapped my feet trying to relieve it.

By the time the bell rung, not only did the noise threaten to rip my head apart but the panic was sending me into a spastic fit. I needed to pace badly. So, instead of going to my next class, after I could uncover my ears from that horrible bell, I went out into the picnic area and began to pace. I wrung my hands together and paced in a straight line from picnic table to the next and then back trying to end this feeling of anxiety. I felt like I was unraveling when only a couple hours before I felt like a God! I feverishly tried to understand what had gone so terribly wrong to cause all this fear.

"You have to stop this now," I heard Simon say. I looked up to see him sitting on one of the picnic tables smoking and watching me pace. "They will call the cops on you. You know that?"

I nodded but quickly dropped my gaze back to the ground as I continued to pace. I wanted to stop but it was out of control. "I cannot stop it, Simon. It is not me Someone else is doing this to me can't you see," I said frantically hoping somehow, he could help me regain control of myself.

He got up and walked over to me. "Okay, then we need to get out of here. I know where we can get help. Come with me before someone sees us." He grabbed my upper arm pulling me to follow him.

I decided he was right. This was a lost cause. Staying any longer at school would compromise our mission. So, jerking free of his grip I grabbed my things and started to walk towards home. School was out for today no doubt.

Simon walked with me as I began to sweat heavily and mumbled to myself in a language that "they" seemed to be broadcasting into my head. This was scaring the shit out of me. Nothing like this had ever happened before. It seemed like I was nothing more than a tool for "the Higher Power" and an antenna for "they."

We got to the cemetery in record time as my stride was frantic. Nothing was helping this anxiety. I could not get it to settle down as my clothing became damp with lakes of my sweat.

Once inside the sanctuary I paced from wall to wall non-stop, mumbling and stretching out my arms trying to settle my feeling of my skin suit shrinking all around me. Fear continued to well from within. It was appearing to flow from an endless ocean that was churning with a powerful summer hurricane. I was so tired I wanted to fall over and sleep forever, but the anxiety kept me a slave to its will.

Throughout the many hours of pacing and sweat, I continued to receive transmissions from 'they' in an endless series of flashing color combinations, codes and even random words. I could hear, see, and taste them all at the same time. Confusion was not even the right word. All I could think among this wreckage that had once been my mind was "Please kill me."

By the earlier afternoon I was repeating that very phrase in the same endless loop as I could hear in my head. All around me I hear the whispering of those long dead as they laughed, talked, and disapproved of my moral character.

"Sinner. Creature. Go die loser. Why are you here? Please help me. Suicide swimmers. It was a fox that brought the rain. You have been chosen," and so many other words spun around my ears all in unison.

I had wrung my hands till the palms were bleeding. My legs threatened to collapse from hours of fast pacing. I looked as if I had stood in a pouring rainstorm drenched in sweat and far too many layers of clothing for the temperature must less this level of expense of kinetic energy.

Simon had sat quietly on one of the benches the entire time watching. He seemed very worried but did not dare to try and interfere. Simon knew I was on the brink of destruction. By now I did also.

Finally, after many hours, Simon stood up and approached my still agitated person, "We have to go back to the school. Mary will be coming for the counseling appointment. Please stop this now and come back to Earth," he finished dropping his rolled cigarette on the ground stomping it out not making eye contact.

I heard him. I had forgotten about the appointment with Dr. Scott. Now I was in real trouble. This was not something I could stop. Someone had hijacked my body and was making me do this. No way Dr. Scott was going to understand. Fresh panic filled me.

"I can't, I can't, I can't, I can't. Please kill me, Simon. Make this stop. Kill me," I said near frantic with frustration.

Simon stands there looking afraid, "No. I am not going to kill you. Look Mary may if we do not get back to the school and meet her soon though."

I suddenly got an idea, "Simon you can turn into Julie and into Stephanie, can't you just turn into the single unit of measurement and fool Dr. Scott like you do me all the time?"

I was desperate enough to ask my friend to take my place. I trusted him. It was a horrible nightmare I was asking him to do. I was painfully aware that being me for any length of time was like asking someone to eat maggots. However, at this point, I was hoping he did indeed love me enough to suffer such an indignity for the few hours I required to avoid detection by Mary and Dr. Scott.

Simon stared at me appearing very confused by my request. "I am not Simon. I am Julie. There is no Simon. I cannot turn into you or Stephanie or a dude that does not exist. Psycho, please listen to me There is no Simon. You need to take your medication to stop this."

This made me stop pacing. I looked again and as I watched Simon began to look more and more like Julie until he was her and she was he.

This confused me even more. She said there is no Simon, but I know she is wrong. I have seen him, hugged him, hit him, and lived with him fora long time. Julie is a liar. She hates Simon because he knows the truth about her. I stood there staring at her trying to think what to do with this lying idiot.

Julie shifts her weight from one leg to the other, "Psycho, you can hate me if you want. Simon is not real. I should not have told you he was and pretended to see him. That was wrong of me. I did not realize how sick you are. Look, if you do not take your medication the law will lock you away in a straight jacket in some padded cell forever. Do you understand that at least," she looked to see if I was listening?

I was, but she was just a liar. She actually had just admitted it. She never saw Simon. He is real, but she pretended to see him. Julie had lied about being enlightened. I began to laugh as I thought of how now she expects me to trust her after already telling so many lies. My laughter got harder and harder until I was nearly on the ground with it. Julie was a massive idiot. That and the idea I had actually liked this girl once seemed hilarious. Why? I had not a clue.

Just when it did not seem things could get any worse, I heard the familiar sound of the station wagon pulling into the cemetery drive. Mary had arrived to pick me up for the enforced counseling appointment. I could not stop laughing. Seeing Mary accompanied by Stephanie walking through the gate only caused me to nearly split a gut with howling laughter.

"Of course," I cackled almost mad with the hilarity of my predicament.

Mary looked at me with disgust. I was on my knees forced there by the hyena giggle episode.

"Girls, I will need your help. Grab her and get her into the back seat of the car. I need to get her to the doctor. This has happened before. Can you come with us," Mary said looking at Stephanie and Julie?

They nodded at Mary. Stephanie looked scared but Julie rolled up her sleeves as they both came at me lifting me by my arms dragging me to the awaiting car.

I would have struggled but I was still worn out from the hours of pacing and hand wringing. I did not fight as they stuffed me into the backseat. Stephanie took shotgun to Mary and Julie jumped in next to me. The laughing fit finally calmed as I sat there now sinking deep into my shattered mind trying to calm enough to get through this appointment without getting locked up again. Even in my deep psychotic state I was aware of the seriousness of this situation. If I could not get a grip, then I surely would be riding the lightening before the cock could crow.

No one spoke the entire ride. The tension could almost be felt in the stale air of Mary's old bible wagon. I sat there appearing calm and still. In truth I was trying to recover my strength. I had stopped sweating like a field hand and now I felt chilly as my damp clothes seemed to cling to me like a slimy film.

It was terrifying trapped there surrounded by my worst enemies. I used every last bit of strength I had to keep from freaking out again. Off and on I considered jumping from the moving car to be thrown to a quick death from the fast-moving vehicle. I was too afraid really to move. I knew these three intended to have me locked up in some hole in the ground. I would be forever forgotten in a prison cell where no one would hear me scream.

We arrived at the clinic. I quickly got out of the car and headed inside surprising the trio who had been lulled into believing I was near catatonic. They all tried to jump out, but I was too fast and made it through the doors for check in before they had even gotten out of their seat belts.

Once inside, I approached the check in attendant and signed the appointment pad. Smiling at the pretty lady sitting behind the glass I thought of something nice to say to show I was perfectly fine, "Where on Earth did you get that incredible pair of shoes," I asked pointing to her pair of Nike high tops. I certainly knew what those were.

The young woman smiled appeared flattered, "Oh they are having a sale at...." I did not hear where but nodded my head still smiling.

I really did not care about her shoes or her. Just that someone could back it up that I was normal and not crazy.

I heard the three Judas supporters come through the door as my new "friend" rattled on about the type of high-top shoes that are the best. I continued to appear interested smiling and nodding at her, not hearing even two words of the conversation. I was secretly watching my captors from my peripheral vision. I could see them standing in the waiting area looking in confusion to each other. Finally, they all took a seat.

The high-top lady finally had to answer the ringing phone thus ending my clever cover. She apologized and closed the appointment window glass as she took the call. I turned sighing. Now I would have to sit down and wait with these assholes breathing down my neck. I shot an evil smile of triumph at the three as I selected a seat nearest the door out and grabbed a magazine pretending to care about the latest article of Time. My sitting so close to the door certainly made them nervous. Mary had even started to get up to come after me, but Julie grabbed her arm and told her to calm down. Everyone needed to be calm and play nice. At least Julie understood my behavior.

When my name was finally called Mary got up and attempted to come with me. I stopped her cold, "Mind your business. I do not want you anywhere near me," I growled to her quietly so the nurse could not hear.

The nurse watched us and our little dance of dominance looking a bit suspicious. However, Mary decided not to start a battle in front of all the other "patients" as that would be undignified. I chucked as I walked back with the nurse. Mary was such a hypocrite. For once I was grateful. I could already feel the flow of the powers granted by "The Higher Power" starting to fill me again. I would need to hurry, or I would not be able to get through this little acting job without blowing up like a caged beast as I had earlier today.

I entered the room and Dr. Scott looked up from work she had been doing on her desk. She frowned at me as she motioned me to sit. The nurse closed the door.

She looked me up and down. This made me nervous, so I looked away and kept from making eye contact with her. I did not like it when people tried to read my mind. Especially, this person.

"How has it been going? Any symptoms of psychosis this week you would like to talk to me about," she said hollowly.

I shook my head no and faked a smile. "Everything is great."

Dr. Scott sat there silent for several moments. This made me very anxious, but I kept my cool, not giving in to the urge to run screaming from the room.

"Okay let's cut the crap, shall we? You look like shit. Are you taking your medication as prescribed," she finally said appearing to have figured out I was evading her attempts to control me with those pills?

I shifted nervously. My mind wanted to tell me she could read my thoughts, but I already knew she said she could not. She told me that in the hospital, so I ignored the nagging idea that she had learned to do it.

Otherwise, how has she known I was not taking them? No, that is a trick she is playing.

I look up right at her deep into her eyes suspiciously. I read her mind. I can see she is indeed fishing. She is trying to trip me up, but she does not know I am not taking them. This makes me smile. I have got this.

"I don't know what you mean. I just finished PE at school. I am thinking of taking up track. I take the meds four times a day just as the doctor ordered. I have yet to miss a dose," I said now setting my eyes on her with an evil grin.

This is a game, and I am ready to play.

"Any hallucinations? How about seeing," she asks me
hard, appearing unconvinced of my explanation for my disheveled appearance.

I lean back and stretch appearing uninterested. Truth is the anxiety was starting and the stretch was to cover my sudden urge to wring my hands and tap my forehead. "Simon is not real. Nope no hallucinating. No problems at all."

She sighs at that, "Sure. So, any side effects of the medications bothering you?"

Dr. Scott was now thinking I had figured her out. I heard her say it in her mind. She knew the game was lost. I was not talking.

I nodded my head no, still flashing my evil grin at her. Had I not been holding back a tsunami of hellish anxiety this could have maybe been fun tormenting her with lies. She certainly had it coming. I could not count the number of bits of information she had not only told me but said about me to everyone. Thanks to Dr. Scott everyone thinks I need medication and have a brain disease. She had truly fucked up my life in ways that had earned her top spot on my hit list. But for today, I was going to have to be satisfied with thwarting her by evading her questions. One day soon I would make her pay for her crimes against me though of that I had no doubt. My smile widened at that thought.

"You sure? Something tells me I should call your guardian in here and ask her about this. What do you think about that?" She smiled back at me.

Did she really think that scared me? Mary would die if anyone knew I was living in a cemetery outhouse not taking mind controlling medications or acting like a nut.

Leaning forward showing all my teeth I said, "Want me to go get her for you?"

This made Dr. Scott pause. She was out of ideas. I was not going to break. Then she remembered something and looked at me hard, "Do you have schizophrenia?"

Damn her. Okay, I still have this. Saying something does not make it so. "Yep. Sure do," I said trying to quell the anger I feel rising at her trying to make me lie like that.

"Oh no you don't. Admit to me and yourself that you have schizophrenia. I want to hear you say the words." She sat up straight looking at me hard.

Fuck!! Okay, I can do this, deep breath, doesn't mean anything, all just lies. "Yes, I have schizophrenia. There you happy? Can I go now," I said trying not to jump up and beat this asshole to a pulp at forcing me to say that bullshit lie.

She sits there looking at me for a bit. Dr. Scott does not want to let me go but I am not going to talk. Finally, she nods that I can go. I leave quickly without even saying "kiss my ass or have a nice day."

Mary, Stephanie, and Julie look up surprised as I briskly walk past them in the waiting room. I do not stop but go right out the clinic door and get into the station wagon back seat. I let out a long breath realizing with at least a tiny bit of relief I had made it through yet another dangerous game of chess with Dr. Scott.

This one had been the hardest meetings yet. I would have to work on getting through these with some kind of structured answers, but for now the anxiety was threatening to blow my rod through the block of my motor. I could hardly wait to get back home so I could pace and wring this horrible mess off.

The puppet masters finally come out to the car and get in. Mary drives us back to the rural town we all call home. You could have heard a mouse fart the silence was so complete. No one knew what to say or do. I had not gotten locked up as they assumed I would, and I had not had to be drug in kicking and screaming. I sat next to Julie smiling wide despite my growing agitation. I truly enjoyed their frustration at having lost their bid to punish me for not allowing them to control my mind.

Mary did not drive to the cemetery. She drove to Julie's house. As we pulled up, she looked in the review mirror to Julie.

"Okay make sure she takes it and if you have any trouble call me. I have given you the list of things she can eat. Good luck. You will need it." Mary was talking oddly.

Julie nodded then looked at me, "Okay, Psycho we are home now. Get out. I have your shit in the trunk. Help me unload it." She gets out of the car.

I watch in disbelief as Mary gets out too and goes back to the trunk opening it. I see my backpack and purse being handed to Julie.

Stephanie gets out too and goes back to help. I am furious. That is the final straw. I get out not bothering to close the car door.

"I am not staying here, God damn you all," I yell with great force, scaring the hell out of all three. They all jump, and Julie drops my backpack in her surprise.

"Psycho, now calm down. This is what is best for you. You are really sick. You need help. Since you seem to not be willing to let Mary do it, let me please," Julie said very softly appearing to mock me.

I look at Mary who is smiling with triumph. "You fucking liar. Sinner," I yell at Mary, who's smile quickly melts to fear.

Without another thought I run at her and plow right into that old bag of bones knocking us both to the ground. I immediately begin to slap and punch her in the mouth.

Julie and Stephanie initially stunned by my sudden aggression recover their senses and pull me off of Mary just as I am really putting the hurt on her head. I am yelling, cussing, and kicking incoherently at Mary with all I have but the girls hold me tight. I am too weak from the hours of pacing to break free.

Julie's father hears the chaos. He calls Cathy at the police station having looked out to see me beating the hell out of Mary in his front yard. For a change the rural police are there in short order having prior knowledge about this particular perpetrator.

I am still struggling with Stephanie and Julie when Dennis and Boyd pull up. Seeing the squad car really sends me into orbit as I bite Julie's arm and she releases me screaming. Before I can even get Stephanie to break her hold, Dennis and Boyd have me pinned to the ground. I am handcuffed and as so many more times to come, pushed into the back the police car to be hauled off to visit with Dr. Huff and a nice, padded jail cell.

To my dismay Dr. Huff had a new horror to add to my already overwhelming nightmare. Before morning I was going to be introduced to the dark villain, Prolixin.

Now was that not a trip? Aren't you thrilled you decided to ride shot gun on this one! Thank goodness we did not have a shot gun or things could have gotten ugly, eh? So, are you still up for this wild ride? What is that? Did you really think we were at our destination? Oh, Goth no! We still have miles to go and plenty of "accidents" and break downs to go! So, don't forget to buckle up next time.

CHAPTER 30: TAKING A BRIEF PAUSE FOR RE-MISSION

We have been on one wild ride for several chapters now. Are you all tired as I am? I think it is time to stop to stretch our legs, make a nature call, enjoy a smoke, and relax our sore bottoms. I don't know about you, but my ears are ringing from the endless whirl of the engine, and my back is killing me from all that baggage we have been carrying for some time now. Sound like a plan?

Just don't get too comfy, because this little peaceful rest will cost us time and we cannot be late. So, enjoy the sun on your face, peace and quiet while you can. Don't forget to ready yourself to pay double for the tiny pleasure. When I pull the crazy train whistle it is time to get back on to resume our nightmarish journey. Goth, I hope we don't derail right off the tracks this time. ALL ABOARD!

"Please hear this: There are not 'schizophrenics.' There are people with schizophrenia."
- Elyn Saks

I am not passive or calm this time for Dennis and Boyd. The laughing, non-aggressive teenager they had come to know in past incidents, has been replaced with a kicking, screaming, spitting, biting animal. The officers are surprised that this psychotic episode expression is so violent considering my previous expressions. Dennis is definitely suspicious that there is something driving this change in behavior from an otherwise relatively peaceful schizophrenic.

He tries to reason with me and gain information. He continues to ask why I am so angry once I am in the back of the squad car safely cuffed in my cage. I do not respond. I just glare at Boyd and him. His questions about what is happening between Mary and I result in my spitting at the back of his head. When that did not make me feel better, I kick the back of his seat. I verbally say nothing. I only growl and shout unintelligibly the entire ride to the station. I am beyond angry that they have interfered with my attempt to rid the world of the sinner Mary.

They struggle to get me into the jail house once we arrive at our destination. I am refusing to comply with all orders. They do not bother to do the formal intake process for the arrested. I am far too aggressive. I am taken straight back to the padded jail cell still yelling and kicking the whole way.

Cathy comes in with them. This time the cuffs are not removed. I try to attack her as well. I am not compliant for her no matter how much she tries to reason with me. Eventually, she realizes I am not going to listen, not even to her. Another female officer is called in just for the purpose of containing my raging person. The two of them work together against my violent struggling to strip me down. They are careful to check my entire body for concealed weapons or items I could harm myself or others with.

I had absolutely lost it. While they are working on getting me secured, I attempted to harm them any way I can. I was using any body part they did not hold tightly, including my head. When Cathy began to remove my shirt, I smashed my head into hers hard as I could. It about knocked us both out. After that, the ladies threw me to the floor and my clothing was removed by extreme force. I finally was contained as Cathy used her knee on my neck to hold me still. Her partner worked hard to get the incredibly filthy garments off my body.

Their body restraining did not stop my mouth from making threats, yelling, cussing, and babbling at them. This to me was an unfair indignity. How dare they take my things! What the hell were they trying to do to me, the perverts!

Getting the jail outfit on proved a bigger job than removing the many layers of soiled clothes. I was in a full fighting mood as both officers got their faces full of my saliva on several occasions. I had liked Cathy in the past meetings with her, but today everyone was my enemy. Everyone was trying to hurt me. I was aware I was acting like a hateful street thug, but in my shattered mind, I believed it was all in self-defense. They wanted to harm me, fine. I was going to do my best to take a chunk of these ladies to the hell I was now trapped in.

My intense and never-ending struggles led Cathy and the other lady officer, called Debra, to request a straight jacket. Cathy feared I was going to harm myself physically in such a state of irritation. Hearing that, I doubled my efforts to escape their hold. I had every intention of killing every one of them, if only I could get free to do it.

I had decided they should all die for picking on me like this. I had never gone to Mary's house and pulled her out, forcing her to live elsewhere. I had never gone to Julie's or Stephanie's house and rifled through their things. I had never forced pills into anyone I had never in my life ripped someone's clothing off, and forced restraining jackets on them, or put anyone in a cage.

No, I had always been pretty peaceful. I minded my business in my sanctuary home. These people had come and done this to me, not the other way around. My mind whirled with homicidal thoughts of how I would make them all suffer for doing this.

I thought to myself "Someday, we will get free, and that someday they will see us again. We will make sure that they rue that day," as I glared at the pair of officers as they finished getting me wrapped up in the straight jacket.

Once I was restrained in my one armed jacket, Cathy and Debra left the cell quickly locking me in. I looked at the yellow jail outfit and remembered my transmission from 'they' earlier that morning. There was no doubt I was doomed now. I had been warned to watch for yellow followed by the color maroon which would our signal doom.

I looked wildly around the room for that dreaded symbol. Everything was white and padded. Even the cot was bolted down. There was a toilet but not like I could use it wearing a straight jacket. I stood up and ran right for the door smacking into it full force growling with fury. This did hurt a lot. I was so frustrated I just needed to be sure I couldn't force the door open in some way to escape, so I ran slamming into it several times until I was sure I could not get out that way.

It was pretty obvious they had me locked up tight. I was not going anywhere, well not physically anyway. My mind whirled as I heard the sounds of the other prisoners in the jail talking to each other. The many voices spoke of plots to destroy me. Some, begged to be released from their cells. I was not sure why or how I could hear them, but I seemed capable of hearing through walls and reading minds even from inside my padded prison. For a very short time, this new power astounded me as I lay there on the floor spent from slamming the door. I quietly listened to the voices all talking and thinking at once. However, after a bit it was overwhelming and annoying. I could not get a moments peace even inside my own fucking head.

I stood up and began to pace again yelling at them to "shut the fuck up.

Fresh agitation began inside, as it had earlier that day in class. No matter what I did the prisoners voices and thoughts assaulted my ears speaking of horrid things they were all going to do to me. This made me both angry and afraid. The pacing became almost a run from one side of the cell to the other.

At some point during this mad marching, I noticed in the upper corner a camera. They were watching me. This sudden realization set off fear so deep I thought my bladder would explode as my knees turned to mush.

In my mind I suddenly knew it was true. They were out to get me and, damn it, they had gotten me. I whimpered as I did my best to stay out of the view of this camera eye watching like a silent God sitting in judgement.

"How could we have messed up so bad," I asked us as I paced trying to avoid the gaze of the camera. "What has happened? Where is the Higher Power? Where is Simon," I yelled out to no one.

My sense of time was so poor by now I have no idea how long I have been pacing and yelling before again the door opened. Dennis and Boyd came in and grab me, after I give them a run for their money. They had to work together as they ran around the padded cell in a silly chase. I was not getting away.

Once they had me, I was drug outside. I continued to fight them best as I could given the restraints.

We come out of the cell and two large male Ambulance Emergency Responders are waiting with a gurney. There was an IV bag attached to it. Dr. Huff is also there waiting.

I see him and spit his direction calling him a liar. He frowns at that as Dennis and Boyd assist the ER workers to remove my straight jacket and get me onto that gurney. There are too many of them for my efforts to be of much use. Within minutes I have very tight restraints on my wrists, ankles, waist, and chest. They make sure I will not get up and bolt from this most inhuman treatment. I continue to hurl insults and threats as I lay there tied down.

"I will fucking kill you. You hear me Dr. Liar. I will kill all of you. I am not crazy. Stop telling everyone I am crazy, you fuckers," I shout as I watch Dr. Huff filling a needle with something from a small vial.

One of the ER fellows forces an IV needle into my left arm and starts the saline bag. Fear fills me again as I watch Dr. Huff's activity. I barely feel the IV go into my body. I had suddenly realized they are going to poison me with hospital grade drugs. If they get those into me, I am lost for sure.

My threats now quickly became pleading for mercy, "Please no. Please do not put those drugs into me. I do not want to be my mother." I was nearly frantic trying with all I had to break free of the restraints.

In absolute horror I watched as Dr. Huff unmoved by my loud pathetic cries for mercy pushed his syringe of the deadly measured liquid into the IV lead. He looked into my eyes with what seemed to be pity. This did not help make me feel any better. Why would it? His regret at having to destroy me certainly was not stopping him from doing it anyway.

As the medication worked its way rapidly to my veins, I began to feel a spinning sensation in my head almost immediately. I could hear Dr. Huff giving medical orders to one of the ER workers who was writing down everything on a flat clipboard.

"Okay, I have injected 25 ml of Thorazine. In one hour inject another 50ml and then another 400 ml in another four hours. Continue at 400 ml intervals until she is controlled. No more than 800 ml daily. I will be out of town for the next few days but when I return, I will administer 37.5 ml of Prolixin to solve this apparent medication non-compliance issue. Do not remove the restraints until you are sure the patient is no longer violent or aggressive. It will take a few days to see the calming effects so make sure no visitors. Also, no stress in the environment," he said as he finished slowly injecting the Thorazine into the IV lead while barking orders to the worker.

I listened helplessly to Dr. Huff's words, as the dizziness began to make me feel I would throw up. I began to retch in response to it. One of the ER Responders grabbed my head and turned it to the side as I heaved. Nothing but air came out for my efforts. I had not eaten in some time so there was nothing to vomit up. Dr. Huff watches me briefly as I dry heave. He then reaches into his medication case that has sitting on the jail guards' table.

New terror fills me as I see Dr. Huff filling another syringe from yet another vial. "I am going to go ahead and administer a dose of 4.0 ml of Lorazepam to help sedate the patient's agitation and alleviate some of the side effects of the Thorazine." He barks to the worker as he injects this horror into my IV lead, "You can administrator this at six-hour intervals."

Within moments of his discussion of Lorazepam with the ER worker I feel suddenly very sleepy and have difficulty keeping my eyes open. Suddenly, I no longer want to hurt them all, nor am I afraid anymore. Instead, I want to close my eyes so I can be swept away, as I can feel the gentle call of the Sandman. I am aware that they are wheeling me from the jailhouse to a waiting ambulance, but I do not care.

It is dark and a cool breeze licks at my sweaty face making me shiver. I feel the gurney rolling along as I stare into the black star clad sky. I feel as if I will float away right into that void. This makes me feel a bit afraid, but the medications are doing the job they are designed to do. The fear is quickly restrained from within just as my body is from without.

The voices and lights that only moments before were overwhelming my senses now have dulled to a blurry mishmash of colors. I slip in and out of sleep as the ambulance speeds to wherever they are taking me.

I can hear the ER responder telling me it will be alright and to "hang in there." This does not really make any sense, but I smile at him and nod that I understand anyway. I feel that I am laying on a cloud of cotton as I notice this worker is wearing a maroon-colored scrub outfit.

The sight of the color makes me chuckle. "They" had been right. My doom was now assured. This was the last thought going through my mind as I finally drifted off to a much-needed rest far from the brutal assault on my senses.

I awake the next morning still restrained in a hospital room. A nurse has come to take my vital signs and administer my latest injection of Thorazine with a Lorazepam chaser. I am very groggy from the Lorazepam with a dry mouth and stomachache.

She asks me how I am feeling. I look at her with her long brown ponytail and happy dancing eyes. I want to hurt her and see the happiness in her eyes crushed to nothingness. There is nothing but hatred in my numb chest where my heart used to be. Her smile is abomination to my predicament. She finds all this funny I assume.

I try to lift up, but I am restrained. So, I turn my head and spit at her with what little liquid I have in my dry mouth. "Go fuck yourself," I say weakly.

The medication was keeping my beast caged. However, even if caged, it is still a beast. Of course, my meager spittle missed completely but she got my point. I enjoyed watching her smile fade as she quickly recorded my vitals and left. I smiled at that, good, I just wanted to be left alone.

The entire day I drifted from sleep to rude interruptions of hospital staff as they came in to check vitals, administer the medication or beg me to eat something. I refused all attempts at making me eat. I also did not speak to them. I would only hatefully glare or spit at them when they came in.

The Thorazine was not working very fast. My acute severe psychotic experiences were still painfully active. From my bed I could hear every single thought, conversation, and whirl of the machines in the entire building. The lights, and sounds threatened to split my head wide open. Thanks to the restraints I could not protect my eyes or ears from the painful, never-ending onslaught. I was trapped in a personal hell on earth.

The Lorazepam only kept me sleepy making my attempts at escape clumsy and unsuccessful. They would not even let me get out of the bed to use the bathroom. A bed pan was offered. The nurse's aide put a button where I could push it if I needed to go. I refused to call them even when my bladder could no longer take another second of its contents. I found the indignity of having someone watching me pee distasteful. It seemed to be truly uncalled for as a real invasion of my privacy.

I had been unable to outright punish them for such cruelty. In pure passive aggressive fashion, if I needed to pee (from the gallons of fluids they were pumping into me) I would just pee the bed. I admit I enjoyed the irritation it caused the staff that they had to come and change the sheets over and over again. Finally, fed up they put me into an adult diaper. There did not appear to be a limit to how much they intended to humiliate me.

The nurse's aide who put the diaper on me smiled after she had finished. She was laughing as she said, "well that will teach you to be a little brat. How do you like that missy?"

I looked at her with pure hatred then spit at her, "Go fuck yourself, you stupid meat puppet."

She snorted as she left appearing not to appreciate my heart felt appreciation for her attempts to make me feel disgraced.

I laid there suffering the effects of my disease in its cruelest form for the rest of the day. Nothing but hate, sensory overload, fear and medication side effects were there to keep me company. This continued into the next day and then the next.

On the fourth day, I awoke to a world that was calmer. It was not so loud and bright as the world I had become accustomed to. I was surprised, but pleasantly so. I listened hard as I could but could no longer heard the thousands of conversations all around the hospital ward. I also could tolerate the light better, as it too seemed to be a bit dimmer.

When the nurse's aide with the brown plait came in to offer me food, though I still refused it I actually smiled at her. The nurse smiled back appearing surprised. I was not feeling angry anymore. I finally understood I was in a hospital. I also knew suddenly that they are trying to help me find my way back from my nightmarish psychosis.

I looked at the nurse thinking, "They were not trying to kill me at all. This was a place to get well, not to be executed."

"Are you feeling any better today," the pretty nurse with the que asked me.

I nodded, "I think so. Hey, ma'am, I am sorry I spit at you and said those...uhm nasty things. I did not mean it," I said truly apologetic that I had behaved so badly to such a nice lady.

Her smile widened suddenly, "Welcome back sweetie. Don't you worry about all that. You were not yourself. I have already forgotten about it. Can you please eat something for me?" She offered the food again.

I shook my head no. I was not afraid of eating anymore, but I was so sick to my stomach I was not hungry at all.

She kept smiling appearing to know what the problem was, "tell you what if you promise not to act ugly and eat a little bit, I will let your arms out of the restraints. I will even sit here to visit if you like."

I really was not hungry, but the thought of having my arms free was enough to get me to agree to her deal. She removed the arm cuffs and sat me up. As she promised (likely to watch my crazy ass) she sat and made small talk as I ate the hospital food using my own hands. I decided I could get used to this freedom from restraints business.

I had just barely finished the hospital breakfast when Dr. Huff knocked on the door while walking in. He looked at me and seemed pleased.

"Well, you look better already. How are you feeling," he asked while grabbing my hospital chart to look over the recorded results of my slow recovery.

"Better, I think," I said unsure if I really was or if this was just another joke my mind seemed to be playing on me lately.

Dr. Huff excused the pretty nurse and came over to exam me himself. He looked into my eyes and asked a lot of questions like if I knew the day of the week, where I was, who I was, and who he was. I answered them to what appeared to be his satisfaction. He then pulled up a chair and sat down next to me with my chart.

"Okay, so you got yourself into some trouble. Your grandmother does not want to press charges, but the state is not going to let this incident go. I will not mince my words here. The state will not pursue criminal charges either but only under one condition, you have to comply with your psychiatric treatment for your schizophrenia," he said looking hard at me to see if I understood.

I actually did not understand. "I have been. I go to the counselor like I am supposed to. I see Dr. Scott every week," I argued.

This made Dr. Huff chuckle. "Yeah, I know she and I have spoken. I am talking about the medication. You have not been taking it have you." He was making a statement not asking a question here. He looked at me sternly, "This is not going to stop. You have to comply with your medication, or you will get psychotic again."

I looked away, now he did have me there. I may be a psychotic, possibly a sinner, maybe a prophet even, but I was not a liar. I shook my head no that I had not been taking the medication.

Dr. Huff let out a breath, "In order to get you out of this mess, I have recommended a long-acting antipsychotic medication that is given through a shot every three weeks. It is called Prolixin. If you agree to take this shot today and show the hospital staff you can behave yourself, you can be released by Monday. You can also go home to your guardian. Now, we can make you take the shot, but I would feel better if you agreed willingly. If you don't take this medication, then you will go back to jail. They can send you away for a year or so for what you did. Assault is a serious charge. Your lawyer has gotten the judge to agree to court ordered psychiatric treatment in lieu of jail time. Do you understand what I am saying?"

Now this had my attention. Lawyers? Judges? Jail sentences of a year? Shot of medications that last three weeks at a time? What the hell had I done? When did all this happen? So many questions were in my head, but I knew the answers really did not matter. I had no real choice. Take the shot or go to jail were my only options. That I did understand. I was just barely sixteen and already I was racking up a criminal record!

"Yes, I will take the shot," I said in complete terror.

Dr. Huff smiled as he got up and called for a nurse. She came quickly as he ordered the Prolixin shot to be administered right away. He also ordered the Thorazine be discontinued by IV. I could receive Lorazepam if needed in pill form but only if I got agitated again. He and the nurse left me alone briefly with my arms still unrestrained.

I looked at my hands which were shaking with the anxiety that was building inside. I must have been very frightened as the Lorazepam did nothing to alleviate this new feeling of terror. Fear had become my Master over the last many months. It seemed to me that even the drugs could keep it from making me its bitch.

I am unsure which scared me more, the idea of this medication wreaking havoc on my system or the idea of being locked in a cage for a year. I had already served so many years in various types of confinement of one kind or another. Including this latest nightmare called schizophrenia, which had made my very mind a torture chamber all its own. I could not even fathom spending time in a state-run jail cell.

The pretty nurse returned and removed my IV. She also released me from my restraints. Finally, I was permitted to use the restroom on my own as I took off the horrific adult diaper. When I returned from my call of nature, I found Dr. Huff waiting for me with the shot that would grant me both freedom and a new type of slavery at the same time.

I took it like a big girl and kept my opinion of this enforced medication captivity to myself. There was no doubt, this was going to happen. There was no reason to get myself in deeper by arguing subjects I clearly had lost. For now, I would have to play nice. I just reminded myself that once I was out and free again, I could then work on regaining control.

The hospital kept me until Sunday afternoon just as Dr. Huff said they would. Another week of lost school, lost time and enforced medication had interrupted my life. It seemed I was condemned to never be capable of just living without insane interference and weeks of recovery from it.

I tried hard to not think of that as I began to suffer the horrid side effects of Prolixin, which appeared to bring a new torture each day. My mouth was constantly dry, my stomach ached, my vision was often blurry, I could not stand without tripping from dizziness, and I was never hungry at all. By the second day I would constantly sweat, and my head often ached like it would split down the middle. However, by far the worst side effect of them all was the lethargy that kept me from even wanting to get out of the hospital bed to pee. I had no energy to even move most of the time.

My emotions and mind were just as tightly restrained by Prolixin as my body had been by the hospital bed cuffs when I had first arrived. Already, I was sorry I had not chosen to go to jail instead of allowing this all-encompassing discomfort called Prolixin.

Mary had come to pick me up from the hospital as I was released. To my humor she still was pretty bruised up from our scuffle the week before. She was not happy to see me, and I was far from happy to see her. I wondered if she was going to try and take me back to her home after all this.

Perhaps Dr. Huff had told her I was more complaint now and could be controlled. The thought sent fear down my spine. I was not strong enough to fight her with this medication controlling me. To my relief after I was loaded into the station wagon, and we were on our way she quickly made it clear she wanted me as far away from her as possible. The feeling was mutual.

"You are beyond redemption, demon. I want you out of my life, but you refused to take my advice and kill yourself. Now, I had to explain to Bob why our ward was in jail and then the hospital again. You have caused me so much trouble I have prayed for God to end you so many times. Yet, like any scourge you keep creeping back into my life," she said to me bitterly while driving a path I recognized would lead to the cemetery.

I was so grateful I would not have to fight her over our living arrangements I smiled despite her nasty comments. She never did like me anyway.

"Not a problem, Mary. Just take me home and we can go our separate ways. I will not bother you anymore," I said still smiling.

She looked at me and almost ran off the road, "Are you as stupid as you are crazy? They have court ordered to psychiatric treatment! Don't you even know what that means, idiot," she yelled at me while huffing.

Honestly, I did not so I shrugged. "I have to take a shot every three weeks or some shit."

This made Mary snort. "More than that, dummy. You have to see Dr. Scott, take the shots, and report to a probation officer every month! They are going to watch you like a hawk from now on. You are a wicked creature and even they know you will kill someone one day. I feel sorry for anyone dumb enough to get in your path. You fuck everything up." Well, she did have a point there. I do fuck everything up.

I was shocked, a probation officer? Wow, I had gotten myself in deep. "Oh well, so you have to drive me, and I have to stop getting angry that is all," I said somewhat dumbfounded.

This was not something I was familiar with, but it sure seemed to be upsetting Mary. That made me nervous. She was a dramatic bitch, but she was acting stranger than usual. I was now concerned there is something no one is telling me going on here. I wanted to ask her but decided to wait till we got to my home. I wanted to feel safe when I got whatever bad news she was surely holding back from me.

However, she did not go to the cemetery at all. She drove right to Julie's house. As we pulled into the driveway, I sat there blinking in disbelief. Was I having another acute psychotic episode? What is going on?

Mary put the car into park and turned looking at me with pure hate, "You are a demonic schizophrenic. The doctors have told me that you cannot look out for yourself, or you will keep getting into trouble, maybe even kill someone. You won't take the medication. You refused to kill yourself. God himself hated you so much he cursed you with a daft brain. Do you understand me?" I don't want you anywhere near Bob or me. Julie has agreed to look out for you, and her father has approved it. If you fight me on this, I will take you right back to the jail house or hospital and let them place you in some institution where I think you actually belong. She will look out for you. Why she would want to be is beyond me. I will take you to your appointments you sinning fool. Now get out."

Mary was still glaring at me waiting for my smartass response, for some kind of reason to take me back to the hell of the institutions. I just sat there looking at her in bewilderment. Somehow, my life had gotten out of control. Julie and Mary had taken it away from me!

"Get out, I said. Julie has your stuff. I will be back Tuesday after school to take you to your damned appointment with Dr. Scott, she yelled again louder, startling me out of my trance of dissociation. This just could not be happening!

Julie had come out to greet us. I was so busy reeling in disbelief of Mary's words I had missed her coming to my side of the car. She opened the door smiling big.

"Welcome home, Psycho. Oh wow. You are a foxy chick. I have never seen you without your make-up. Damn, girlfriend, no wonder the boys think you are the shit." She was looking me up and down. I just stared at her like a dumb cow. How could this be happening?

Cathy had been kind enough to wash my clothes she had removed during my stay at the jail. They had never taken away my wig which was the only kindness they had offered while in the hospital and jail. She had given my cleaned clothing to the hospital staff for me to wear home, well, to where I thought I was going anyway. I did not however, have my make-up. Because of my constant sweating from the Prolixin I had not put all the many layers back on. I was dressed simply in a black shirt, jeans, my platforms, and derby hat over my blond wig. Julie had never seen me without a heavy coat, and several shirts much less with a naked faced.

I did not like this kind of talk, so I jumped out of the car and slammed the door.

"You stay away from me, you fucking manipulating shithead," I said, glaring at Julie as her smile disappeared as she heard my words.

"Hey, is that anyway to treat a friend who just saved your ass from jail? Damn, Psycho, maybe you are more than crazy. I think I liked you better psychotic," Julie said back through clenched teeth.

I just stood there looking at this ginger haired menace. I could not figure out her game. Why was she so hell bent to control my life? I knew she had said she hated this boring town. Perhaps she viewed me as a form of entertainment. Whatever the reason I was sure that one way or another I was getting out of this situation and back home to my cemetery no matter what this manipulator or Mary did. The law could kiss my ass too.

As Julie and I glared each other in our battle of wills, Mary started the car and pulled out stranding me there in Julie's grip.

Trouble was I did not know this place. I did not know how to get home from this place. I was stuck here for now or I could risk getting lost trying to find the right road to get home. I decided rapidly to just wait till school the next day. I could find home from school. I would just have to deal with this asshole for the night is all. I could do that I was sure of it.

I turned and watched Mary speed away. I could almost hear her laughing. Suddenly, just across the street I noticed a chain link fence with a swing gate. Behind the chain to my relief, I saw the calming sight of several marble slabs standing proud and silent. A cemetery was only feet away from this newest nightmare situation. It was not my beloved sanctuary, but any port in a storm they say. On this day, I finally understood what that saying meant.

"You are stuck Psycho. You live with me now. Look I know this must be a bit stressful with a new situation and all you must have been through this last week. But hey you will love living here with me. Dad is an over the road trucker, so he is never home. He agreed having someone around to keep me company would be good for me. You should feel flattered. I like you so much that I asked him to let you be my roomie," she blathered on to my almost deaf ears. I was not listening.

I stared at the cemetery across the street as the feeling of peace filled me. I had never felt safe in the land of the living. Only in the world of the dead did I truly belong. Ignoring Julie, I walked across the street. I opened the gate and went inside letting the aura of that hallowed place fill me with the healing energy I was in need of so badly.

It was not very large, but it did have a few benches and a small outbuilding made of old brick. Not an outhouse but a storage building likely. To my dismay its door was sturdy and locked tight. However, it was a nice day so I would have no need of a roof anyway. I would only be staying one night. This cemetery was newer than my beloved homeland was. However, it was just as ill kept. Likely a family cemetery. Trees covered the entire boneyard just like at home so I decided for now it would do for a home away from home. Here I could figure out what to do about this mess without the distraction of Julie's nasty presence.

Julie had followed me to the cemetery, but I had not noticed spellbound by this new treasure.

"Psycho, what the fuck is it with you and filthy cemeteries? Look you want to hang out here, fine, but first you need to come inside and eat something. The doctors say you are dangerously underweight, and they think you need to gain some. Though I do not know why, you are fucking sexy as hell! I wish I had that figure." She was looking at me again in a way that made me very uncomfortable.

I was beginning to think Julie was interested in a special kind of entertainment with me. The way she kept looking at me, and her attention to my appearance was very creepy. This made me shutter. I needed to get out of here fast.

"Go fuck yourself, Julie. Where are my things? I want my things and then for you to leave me alone," I spit at her still looking over my temporary domain but keeping a watchful eye on this very scary girl.

"Psycho you can't live in a cemetery! Don't be so stupid," Julie yelled at me. "Look you come inside or else."

I turned glaring at her, "Or else what? What will you do Julie? Beat me up? I may be stuck here for now, but not forever. I do not think you want to make me any angrier than you already have. I am not kidding. Get my shit bring it to me, and then fuck off. Mess with me and I will show you what else." I clenched my fists. She did not want to push me. I really had nothing left to lose.

Julie looked at me then to the ground, "Look I am really sorry for what I did with the whole playing along with your seeing Simon and reading minds stuff. I thought you were like just messing around. But I sat there and watched you all day the day you go arrested. You really are very sick, Psycho. Mary and the doctors are right, you can't look after yourself. You will starve to death or kill yourself on accident doing that weird shit you do. Or worse, what if others find out a pretty young girl lives all alone unprotected? Haven't you had enough of the pain, Psycho?" She looked up to see if I was listening.

I was indeed, "I can take care of myself just fine. I don't need you, Mary or the doctors. Now for the last time I want my things,"

Julie decided to pull out the big guns, "I read your records, Psycho. I know all about the horrible things your mom and those awful people did to you all those years. I just can't even imagine; I just want to help you. I want to be your friend."

Julie's bringing up those "false psychiatric records" made my heart stop in my chest. I did not like to talk about the past. I had already decided that was not real as were most of the experiences in my life anymore. I simply could not believe the audacity of this brain stem to go so far as to try to say they were real.

"Shut up, Julie. I do not want to talk about this," I shouted angrily.

She paused and began to tear up, "You have suffered enough for a hundred lifetimes. I seriously don't blame you for deciding to go crazy rather than have memories like that. You were just a kid. No one was there for you. I can't even imagine how you survived."

"I said shut up. Give me my things and fuck off." I felt my mind start to whirl and a strange fear climbing up my spine like a lizard climbs a tree.

She kept going, ignoring me, "That is why you wear all those clothes isn't it and hide how pretty you really are. It wasn't your fault. Your mom and those people, they were sickos You don't have to be alone anymore! Plea.se let me help you," Julie was full on crying now.

Now, she had finally made me very angry despite the Prolixin and Lorazepam coursing in my veins, "Shut up, damn you. Those are all lies. I do not need you. I do not need anyone." I suddenly began to laugh wildly.

I had decided some time ago that all that horror in my childhood was just a bad dream. So, those records were all just a pack of lies. It is hilarious to me that she believes those 'false records'.

This startled Julie. She apparently had not expected that response. "Whoa, wait. Psycho, you mean you don't believe your own damned records. Those are official, Psycho, they are legit." She stares at me in disbelief.

I stop laughing while I shook my head no, "They are telling lies about me. None of that happened. They are trying to make me sound crazy and discredit me. Can't you see that or are you too stupid? This is a plot to ruin my life."

Julie came running at me. I tried to run but I was too slow (fucking Prolixin). She grabbed me by my shoulders. She held me tight as I struggled to get out of her grip.

"Seriously, Psycho, they have all the records about your childhood, even the court testimony is there. The doctors have pictures of your brain, and tests they gave you too. I have seen your insanity myself. Are you trying to say all those people from the case workers, the court records, to the doctors are lying? That I do not know what I saw with my own eyes That is insane. Listen to yourself. There is no conspiracy. You are schizophrenic and your childhood was a nightmare," she yelled right into my face.

I tried to get out of her grip, but the medication had made me too dizzy to have the strength to break her grip on me.

She began to shake me hard. "Listen to yourself. You are schizophrenic, damn it, and you need help."

I try to hit Julie, but she grabs my arm and holds it back, "say it, Psycho! Those records are true. You are schizophrenic."

"I am not. I can prove it." I was beginning to feel like the world was caving in on me, this had to stop and stop now.

"Yeah? Prove it, Psycho. I want to hear why you think you are not sick," Julie challenges me.

With a sudden rush of strength, I push Julie off me, "Everyone believe in God and say he is real. But none of you have never seen him. I have seen Simon, but you say he is not real because you cannot see him. If I am schizophrenic, then so is everyone who believes in a anything they have never seen."

The strange feeling of the world closing in had stopped. I felt vindicated having given my proof that I was not crazy at all. They are all wrong, I am not crazy, and that stuff in the records did not happen. I calmed down remembering just because someone says something does not make it true.

Julie starts to laugh at that. "Psycho, that is weak. I know you and have seen your psychotic shit. Trust me, you are schizophrenic. You can deny all you like but that is not going to make it go away. Now I am trying to be your friend and you act like an asshole. You are really just too much."

"What is so funny?" Stephanie, accompanied by Crystal and a new girl I did not know had walked up behind me during the argument with Julie. Their sudden appearance scared the hell out of me. However, for once I was glad to see her. This was one argument I never wanted to have again.

"What the fuck? Did you invite the whole fucking school to live with you Julie," I said while almost jumping out of my skin?

Stephanie laughed hard at that, "No silly. We are just here to welcome you back from the hospital, Psycho. Gosh you are so funny sometimes." She looked at the new girl standing next to her, "Oh this is Joni. Psycho you don't know her, but she is joining our group."

The new girl was a bleach blond with a very round face and pear-shaped body. She had very dark eyes and heavy black eyebrows indicating her very blond hair was not natural by any stretch of the imagination. Joni was dressed in a white button up shirt and jeans with tennis shoes. She was eyeing me with what appeared to be a tab bit of disgust. I immediately disliked her. Something told me the feeling was mutual.

"Howdy. So, you are the infamous, Psycho." She stuck her nose up at me.

"My name is not Psycho," I said to Joni, narrowing my eyes. Something told me this one was going to bring trouble. More of that, I simply did not need.

Joni scoffed, "Yeah, well I've seen you at school and I was there the day you flipped out in the hallway. You are indeed Psycho." She then started to laugh believing herself clever.

Julie, Crystal, and Stephanie started laughing too.

"Ain't that a fact," said Stephanie still snickering. "Hey, did they finally fix your brain this time? Or are you still all schizie or what?""

I'd had enough. Without a word, I turned and left the four snickering girls there made my way back across the street to Julie's house. If they wanted to be bitches, and talk shit, they could do it without me having to listen to it. If Julie did not want to go get my property for me, fine I would get it myself. The joke that once a long time ago I had wanted to have friends, was not lost on me. Now that I had them (these are friends?) I decided I had been wrong to want such a thing. If this was what having friends meant, I was not interested.

The medication was holding off the worst of my psychosis, so my understanding was unusually clear for a change. That was a lucky thing for that group of cruel teenaged girls. Had I been more "myself" they would have found out just how psycho I could be. I stormed through Julies front door ready to tear the place apart if needed to my things. I was not staying here. Tomorrow I would go home and figure out a way to take back my life from the doctors and from Julie.

Okay, beauties. The rest stop is almost over. Hope you got your coffee and smoke in because it will be many miles before we get to another place to stop and rest. This is your five-minute warning as the train is almost ready to pull out of the station. You would not want to get left behind now, would you? I hope everyone is still enjoying the trip but if not, well it is already too late. This train no longer has brakes, there is no stopping it now.

CHAPTER 31: THE PROPHET IS PSYCHO

Good day my most beloved and gorgeous Family. Well look at all of you, so adorable in your best clothing ready for this next leg of the journey! We must tell you all that we are more than proud you answered our call. However, we do wish you had selected your less than Sunday best for this religious experience. We can understand why you mistakenly assumed that when we said all of us are going to hear a sermon, you assumed it was going to be in the traditional church setting. But that was a miscommunication altogether. After all, in this world within a world nothing is as it seems. No, the pulpit in this sermon will be deep within the void of the darkness where only the damned will hear our choir singing songs of despair. Now it does not matter if you believe or not, this is not about the conventional or even understandable. This is a congregation of confusion and loss. So, with that in mind grab your holy books (whatever they be to you), mystic relics, and faith in things you cannot see but know have to be there somewhere and join use as we preach the rules of the insane.

"Believing that you are going crazy is a good clue that you are sane. When someone is developing or have psychosis from schizophrenia, they don't know it or even believe it. Part of 'crazy' is getting away from reality. They're not aware of the difference between a feeling and a fact. They will go through many periods of accepting and denial of the disease.

The truly insane do not know they are insane."
- Gerald Goodman, PhD, an emeritus professor of psychology at UCLA

I rush through the heavy oak door of Julie's house. Her home is an old schoolhouse that has been remodeled to the modern. The exterior is of a rock and grout, appearing to be very ancient. However, once inside, the visitor realizes they have been deceived because the floors are of high-grade hard wood. There was a roomy openness that screamed of expensive interior designer professionalism.

At first, even I was stunned enough by the contradiction to stand there staring in disbelief. I marveled at the smell of fresh air with overstuffed handsome leather living room furniture. Julie's father (or mother perhaps?) defiantly had fine taste in proper living space comfort. My interest in this amazing decor was quickly dashed as I realized I may have to tear this place apart looking for my meager possessions. There was a sense of excess wealth in the home. This fact, made a poor homeless kid like me shutter at the thought of even touching anything, much less pawing it to destruction.

I tip toed through the living room that was equipped with all sorts of modern devices such as a VCR and high-tech stereo. To the right I found a long hallway lined with pictures of a smiling Julie and her trucker father. The doors to all the rooms there were open, so I peered into each room. I found four bedrooms and two full bathrooms. I admit the idea of two bathrooms made me smile in delight. I had never seen such a thing in person. My life had always been one of intense poverty so to have a bathroom each was big stuff in my book.

Of the four bedrooms I discovered one had a waterbed with many pictures of half-naked males and band posters on the wall. I assumed rightly that this was Julie's room. I hoped she had put my things in here as I also assumed she would have been going through them. My hunch was. of course. correct. I found my purse and backpack emptied of their contents scattered about the floor next to that waterbed. Gathering my things. I cursed her creepy ass under my breath. Luckily, it was all there. I owned so little it only was a second of inventory to know I had at least not been robbed by this girl. She obviously had enough of the tangible without needing to steal from a nothing like me.

I was about to leave her room and start walking, well anywhere but here, when I recalled my records. Those records had caused me a lot of trouble. I needed to get my hands back on them so they could be destroyed. I truly believed this would end the spread of lies contained within them. I looked about the room hoping she had been as careless with their placement as she had my other items.

However, she had hidden them well. I could not find anything other than LPs, her stupid fashion magazines, and endless notebooks with bad poetry she had written. It was useless. I was never going to find my records in her mess of teenage angst knickknacks and sundry items.

Finally giving up, I left her room but was caught by Julie who stood at the living room end of the hallway blocking my escape.

"Psycho, I told the others to wait outside. We need to talk," she said putting her hands on her hips.

I noticed then she was dressed all in purple again. I groaned at that. She was still using my secret against me. Not that it mattered, I had not seen or heard Simon since the arrest.

"Move out of my way," I said dryly. I did not want to get into a scuffle here in this lovely home but if she did not let me pass, I was ready to do whatever it took to get free.

She narrowed her eyes at me, "Okay, I was nice. Now, you asked for it. You have to stay here and do what I say or else you go to jail. Staying with me was part of the agreement of your probation. You leave, I call the cops and off you go back to jail. I bet you understand that you stubborn fruit loop."

My eyes widened. "What? Wait, what? That is not true. You are a liar, Julie," I yelled infuriated that she would sink to such a level.

An evil gotcha smile spread across her face, "Oh yeah, you think? How about you call Mary? Or Dr. Huff and ask. Didn't they tell you all this? Ha! Well, let me get the phone and we can call them both." She stepped aside and pointed to a phone on a coffee table next to an overstuffed sofa. "There is the phone. I have the numbers here, including your probation officer."

Julie pulled out a wrinkled piece of paper from her front jeans pocket and read off the numbers and names. She again dared me to call any of them and ask.

I shook my head not able to wrap my mind around this horrible turn of events. "Is she telling the truth," I think, "Should I call and ask?"

"Go ahead, Psycho, call them. I want you to call them since you will not listen to me," she was yelling and pointing at the phone frantically.

I just dropped my shoulders in defeat. I did not want to talk to any of them. They had after all, sold me out to this insane idiot. What could I do? If I run, she will get me sent to jail and the hellish restraints. However, if I stay, surely I will go insane for real this time. I felt the hallway walls closing in on me, suddenly I could not breath. A full-on panic attack hit as I began to hyperventilate right there in front of my new found captor.

Julie saw my panic and smiled knowing she had won the argument. She walked down the hallway towards me as I felt my knees give way. I fell to the wooden floor appearing almost to be kneeling in front of the smiling Julie as she approached victorious. I could not catch my breath as the world started to spin.

"Stop acting like a nut, Psycho. This weird shit will stop, you hear me? Are you in there," she said bending down to stare into my gasping face? "Get up. Stop that. Calm down. All this drama over a shithouse? Really? Oh my God you are beyond crazy I swear."

I covered my head with my arms trying to shut out her voice. My heart was racing as the blood screamed in my ears. I could not deal with this information. I was sure I would blow into a million parts, and to be honest I was okay with that. Better to explode into nothingness than be Julie's slave.

Julie stood there silently watching my melt down appearing to not be willing to allow me even a moment's privacy to contemplate my pathetic existence in this new nightmare. I have no idea how much time passed before the sound of the front door opening signaled the other evil bitches have grown tired of waiting outside.

I was still silently quivering with my internal overload of terror when I heard Stephanie's voice.

"What the fuck, Julie? What did you do to Psycho?" She sounded concerned, but I knew she did not really care. No one did or they would have left me alone in the first place.

Julie responded, "nothing, just Psycho being Psycho, you know. Hey, order a pizza, will you? I am starving. Joni, you and Crystal find something worth watching on the tube."

I heard Stephanie pick up the phone and order the pizza. The sound of commercials and laughter filled the air from the television. Julie had not moved but was still standing over me like a shadow of death. Stephanie again returned to the pair of us in our silent stalemate of wills.

"Julie, I think Psycho is pretty upset. Maybe you should give her something to calm her down. Just saying and stuff." Stephanie again sounded concerned.

I could hear Julie shift her weight, "Yeah, you may be right. Go get that pill bottle out of my purse the Lorzie-something one. It is supposed to keep her from getting loopy like this."

I react immediately by spitting on her floor. I quickly stand up, forgetting my despair briefly. "Fuck you. I am not taking that shit."

My sudden movement startled the girls (likely still jumpy from my last attacks). Julie yelled, "God damn, Psycho you scared me," she grabbed her chest chuckling, "Okay no meds but you have to stop acting like a freak you hear me? Or so help me we will all beat your ass and make you take them."

I looked down the hall at Crystal, Joni, Stephanie, and of course Julie. My mind calculated I could not beat all four of them. That Lorazepam was horrible. No way I was going to take it. Despite my incredible anger and fear of this situation I just nodded I understood. I had decided there is always a solution to every problem. I now had a big problem. The Lorazepam would make my thoughts cloudier than they already were from the Prolixin. For now, I had no choice but to play submissive to Julie's delusion that I was going to live with her as her roomie.

"Now put your shit back into my room and come join us for some fun. You never have fun, do you," Julie said looking at me to see if I was going to give her further trouble.

I just shot her a dirty look. Without responding to her stupid question, I went into her room as she told me to and put my things carefully in the corner far as possible from her tainted items. She watched me from the door making sure that I did not run away or lock myself in. I came back out and started down the hallway to the living room Julie following behind.

She reached out and patted my back, "Good, Psycho. Now we understand each other."

I turned with as much speed as my Prolixin slowed body would allow feeling the shock of her touch strike my force shield, "Keep your fucking hands off me. Do not ever touch me again." Before I could think better of it, I pushed her backward.

Julie was angered as she recovered and started to come at me fists doubled, I did the same. Stephanie jumped between us putting her arms out, "Hey, hey, hey, cool it guys. Look Julie, Psycho, don't like to be touched and stuff. Come on let's all just hang out and get along, okay?"

Julie stopped and looked at Stephanie appearing to calm a bit. I however was still ready to beat her to a pulp. I realized it may result in jail, but I really did not care at that moment. I would not tolerate that filthy creature touching me.

"Okay, you are right. Let's all go sit down and play nice, shall we girls?" Julie looked at me to see if I wanted to push this issue further.

I was ready to push it as far as possible but not at that moment. This time I was in deep. The one thing I needed badly was time to consider a plan of escape. I dropped my aggressive stance turning without a word walking back into the living room. Joni and Crystal were sitting on the large sofa watching me walk in. I noticed Joni again looked as if she could smell something bad. My instincts told me to stay away from this one. Something was wrong here, but what it was would have to wait for now. I had much bigger fish to fry.

I sat down in the large recliner nearest to the front door. It was like the rest of the furniture overstuffed. I laughed out loud as I heard a man's voice say, "Overstuffed like the owners."

Julie and Stephanie were coming into the living room as I let out my chuckle. All the girls looked at me suspiciously. I stopped laughing immediately and looked at the television blankly as if it had not happened hoping they would just forget that little 'oopsy' moment.

I could feel Joni's eyes still on me. To my relief the other girls went back to their jabbering ignoring my outburst. I did not look at Joni but kept my eyes on the onslaught of images playing across the TV screen. However, I was not listening to the girls nor was I watching the TV really. I watched as Julie lit up one of her stinky home-rolled joints, passing it around to the other girls. I of course, did not join them.

I had to sit there while Julie laughed and told the others that 'I did not smoke weed because I was already high as a kite all the time.' The girls all laughed at her joke. That pissed me off, but I kept it to myself. It did appear I would have to pick my battles with these idiots carefully or I would do nothing but fight for the rest of my stay as Julie's hostage. Instead, I blocked them out of my attention while focusing on finding a solution to my current situation. The girls went back to their endless gossip and blathering.

I was so deep inside my scrambled thoughts that when the doorbell rang, I let out a yep as I jumped out of the chair. My wild attempts to flee the sudden unknown noise I knocked one of Julie's lamps off the coffee table. All of the girls in turn jumped as the lamp crashed to the floor. Julie recovered her wits first.

"Damn it, Psycho. You need to calm down. Christ, stop breaking shit, you are crazy bitch," she berated me as she went to the door to get the pizza that was being delivered.

Stephanie got up and picked up the lamp. As she replaced it, she turned it off and discovered it was in working order without any apparent damage. She smiled at me telling me not to worry, it was not broken. I shrugged at that. What did I care if it was? Not my lamp.

Julie came back with two large pizza boxes still eyeing me with disdain. She put them on the main coffee table and told the others to 'help themselves' never taking her eyes off me. The girls all began to rush in like hungry dogs talking of the 'munchies' and other things they liked to eat while 'getting high.' Julie noticed I was not joining the gorging frenzy.

"Psycho, you need to eat something. Remember, that is what Dr. Huff said. You have to start eating regularly." She was looking at me sternly. "Are you going to give me shit about this too?"

I looked at her with hate in my eyes, "You know damned well I can't eat pizza."

She laughed at that, "Oh yeah. Sorry now I am the one who is forgetting shit, huh? How funny of me." She got up and went to the kitchen.

The other girls looked at me quizzically as they gulped down their slices with gusto. I just glared back at them watching them eat a food I would never be able to eat again for the rest of my life. I had no one to blame for that but myself. Thanks to my stupidity last year food would forever be my enemy. I really hated them for making me watch them enjoy a pleasure I was now denied.

Julie returned from the kitchen with a plate full of baby food meat sticks. As if my total humiliation could not get more complete, she shoved the plate at me, "Mary said you can eat baby food without getting sick, so I had dad pick up a bunch of it. Now eat and no arguing I mean it."

I looked at Crystal and Joni who all had stopped eating now staring at me. The other girls sat there with dropped jaws at what Julie had said, well except Stephanie. She already knew I was reduced to only oatmeal, simple carbohydrates, and the horrid baby food diet due to a blown gastric system.

Joni spoke first, "Is this some kind of a joke? Seriously, baby food? How fucking insane are you?" Her disgust was no longer muted as she stared at the plate of baby food.

Crystal looked at it too with shock in her eyes, "no wonder you are so thin."

This made both Julie and Stephanie laugh out loud. They looked at each other knowingly as Julie took a seat on the couch next to her. "Nah, Psycho has a stomach problem. She can't eat regular food. It is a disease thing," Julie said still snickering.

Joni looked at Julie, "Well I would die if I had to eat that shit. Fuck that! Give me my tacos and pizza or give me death," she finished while taking a big bite of her pizza.

"Eat that, Psycho, I am not fucking around here. Want me to call Dr. Huff," Julie said ignoring Joni's comment still eyeing me.

I was not hungry, but I also was not willing to fight yet again. I did as Julie said trying not to think that maybe she had slip some of her weed into the food. I knew that was a bit paranoid but given the circumstances I was not sure at this point what she may be planning on doing to me. I also did not want her to call Dr. Huff and report I was non-compliant with treatment. Dr. Huff had used the horrid shot over such bullshit this time, who knew what they would do next time I got accused of that.

As I ate the bland substance slowly, I felt Joni watching me again. She was appearing to try to read my mind or figure me out or something. I could feel it even though, like the paranoid though about Julie's food, I knew that seemed impossible. I used to have powers but since the Prolixin, it appeared that I had lost many of them. I was sure at one time I could have read Joni's mind to see why she hated me, but since that shot, all I could do is see it in her eyes. It felt very uncomfortable all of the sudden as I ate. Looking up I saw every pair of eyes fixed on me looking me up and down.

"So, you were in the mental hospital a couple times huh? What they do to you there? I heard you got shock therapy. What was that like," Joni asked me, still looking me up and down?

I suddenly felt very sick to my stomach. For a moment I thought maybe Julie had poisoned the food, but deep down I knew it was not that. I did not like to think about the hospitals or shock treatment. I looked at the floor but did not answer.

Stephanie laughed, "Oh yeah, she got shock treatment. Didn't do any good though. Right after she got out of the hospital, I found her talking to imaginary people. The very day they let her out too.

You would think in three months they could at least fix that."

"I saw her dancing with no one, and she calls Stephanie, Simon all the time. She is always writing weird symbols too. Plus, she will attack you for no reason," Crystal chimes in trying to sound like she has mysterious information.

Julie laughs now, "Oh Christ Simon. I hate that guy. Stephanie is not the only one she calls Simon. Psycho has called me that too." She lit another joint.

As Julie passes it to the others as they continue to talk about my 'odd behaviors' and 'crazy shit.'

Joni adds, "Well I saw her bust headfirst into that locker. They had to replace the door it was so dented. You should have been there. She was fucking babbling and running into shit. The cops had to drag her off kicking and screaming."

Stephanie's turn again, Oh yeah? You missed last week. She attacked Mary, the cops, hell everyone, spitting and biting even herself," She took a long drag of the joint and held her breath.

I wanted to scream at them all to shut up. But I just kept looking at the floor while trying to will myself to go deaf. I could not beat all four of them up, could I? They were acting like I was not sitting right there.

"Bet it is pure hell to be schizophrenic. I had a great aunt they said had it. She killed herself jumping off a building. They said she thought she could fly. What a crazy bitch, huh? Well, she couldn't, so she went splat." Joni made a squishy sound, which made the group laugh wildly.

I thought of my bridge swan dive. I did not think it funny that someone jumped off a building. She obviously was in a lot of pain. These girls were evil, pure and simple, to laugh at the death of poor tortured soul like that.

Julie stopped laughing, "Psycho, tell us what is it like to be, well, psycho? Do you see like ghosts and shit? Or hear voices? Is it scary?" Julie was staring right through me.

The others stopped laughing waiting for me to answer. I could feel their curiosity like needles all through my body. I could not take another second of this.

"I am not psycho, damn it. I have never been in a mental hospital, and I have never had shock treatment. Stop telling lies, Julie." I stood up and threw the plate of half-eaten slop at Julie, like a frisbee.

It hit her in the stomach sending the baby food flying as the plate bounced off her and hit the floor. It did not break but spun briefly like a top finally settling with a hollow sound.

Everyone looked at Julie who was now staring at me hard, ignoring the mess I had just made of her clothes and furniture.

"You are schizophrenic, Psycho, everyone here knows it. We have all seen it. You are crazy. The only liar her is you," she yelled at me through clenched teeth.

"Is she serious," said Joni appearing surprised.

Joni looks right at me, "Are you serious? You stand there and deny you are fucking insane? Holy shit. What is in this weed, Julie? I think I am hallucinating myself. No fucking way you did not know you are a fucking nutball."

Julie looks at Joni briefly nodding. She then glares back to me, "Psycho knows it is true. She just won't admit it! She seems to think that if she says she is not crazy then she is not crazy. Well, that is stupid."

"Stop calling me Psycho, Julie," I yelled back really starting to lose it. I felt the agitation rising in me.

Not even the Prolixin could stop my waking demon. These girls were stressing me out and pushing all my buttons. Suddenly, everything seemed very bright as the sounds of cicada began to call to out my name. My powers were returning like a waterfall across my senses.

Stephanie joined in this attempt to drive me crazy, "Jesus, Psycho. Surely, even you can see you are sick. Just admit you are schizophrenic and stop acting crazy just once in your life. Or do you have to get Simon's permission to say it and stuff?"

Stephanie's joke about my dear Simon made all the girls start to laugh. Crystal even gave her a high five saying "good one!"

"Stop mocking me, you bitches," I screamed frantically fighting off the urge to kill them all with my bare hands.

I turned and ran out the front door with the sounds of their howls of amusement hounding me. I went straight to the cemetery across the street from her house. I was so upset I did not look before crossing the road and was nearly hit by a speeding pickup truck. The near miss at becoming roadkill did not even pick up my heart rate. My mind was suddenly alive and whirling as I had become so accustomed to all these many months. For the first time since the day before my arrest, I was feeling back to old self. Whoever that was?

All I could think is I needed peace. If these girls insisted on telling lies, mocking me, and making fun of Simon, I did not have to sit there and listen. No one said I had to put up with Julie, just stay in her house. As for the other monster females, no one said I even had to speak to them much less tolerate their persons.

Once inside the cemetery I began to pace from one side to the other side of its fence. I was mumbling to myself about how bad I had fucked up my life by losing my temper with Mary. I made promises to myself I would make them all pay. I berated myself while arguing with me about which was worse, Julie or jail.

I really needed help from Simon now but still I had not been able to find my friend in a week. This was all Julie's doing! She had gone out of her way to come between me and my best friend. Now Simon, like me, had even become the butt of their cruel jokes.

My frantic pacing was suddenly halted by a transmission from none other than the Higher Power itself. I was stunned to idiocy as images, voices and coding ripped through my head. The sensation actually made me piss my pants as I was pulled to the ground on my knees by a magnetic force. I had my eyes wide open as the landscape of the cemetery warped into a strange vision of lights, fog, and pulsing colors. I tried blinking to make it clear, but each blink made the sights ever more confused.

In my ears The Higher Power told me of the perversion of all humankind. The Higher Power said my mission had been in error. I was not to find my killers at all. I was to warn the cruel of their folly and repair the wrongs of the evil treatment of all lifeforms as within my abilities. To my terror I was told my powers would be turned up to full volume so that the Higher Power could communicate orders and carry them out adequately. I was told that if I refused to follow the commands it would result in my utter destruction in the most heinous of ways.

I tried to call out for help, or beg for mercy, but my vocal cords were frozen. All I could do is listen to the commands from The Higher Power helpless to escape. The vision/episode ended almost as abruptly as it had begun, leaving me breathless and fatigued. As it faded, I collapsed onto the ground unable to maintain my body weight on my knees. I rolled up into a ball and closed my eyes shaking from the terror I had just endured.

Then, to my horror I felt the chaos begin in my mind as the overloaded synapses cried out for relief. I whimpered helpless to stop the oncoming Grand Mal seizure. I could hear the whirl of the shock machine just as I saw 'the flash.'

I was still in this position when Julie found me unconscious a few moments later. A quick check told her I was breathing but not responsive to her attempts to wake me. A decent person would have called for an ambulance. However, not this girl. She was worried they would come take her latest toy away. So instead, she called the girls to help her haul me back inside to her bed.

I awoke four hours later groggy and confused. Julie was sitting next to me in a chair she had pulled up next to her bed. Her worried face is the first thing I was able to recognize. Someone had removed my clothing as the next thing I noticed is I was in a white bathrobe that was not mine. This upset me badly. I did not like to be in clothing that did not keep me neutral. White was a powerful color, not meant for a nothing like me. I quickly began to tear at the terry cloth garment feeling as if it was burning my skin.

"Hold up, Psycho. Stop that, what are you doing?" Julie grabbed my hands. I was still too groggy to stop her.

Get it off! Get it off. It is burning," I cried out feeling desperate for relief of the pain.

Julie realized I mean the robe finally after struggling with my attempts to rip the thing off for several minutes. Okay, okay. Let me help you, damn it!" She said grabbing my arm to help me from the now violently rocking waterbed. "Can you stand up?"

I nodded that I could stand. She assisted me to my feet as I tore the robe from my body not giving a damn that she was there staring at me like I had lost my mind. As suspected, I was naked under the robe which further upset me as I slowly came back to my senses (whatever that may be). I turned to her angry as hell that some pervert had taken my clothes to replace them with this atrocity. What else had the person done to me? I wanted answers and I wanted them immediately.

Where are my clothes? Who took them? Why am I naked? Who did this," I yelled at the very startled Julie?

She looked at me dumbfounded at my anger, "Uh, Psycho, you were out cold. You pissed your pants for some reason. I had to strip you down so I could put them in the washer. I covered you with my robe for decency. The girls helped me. Why are you so angry? We were helping you, damn it," she spewed at me.

"Give me my clothes," I demanded, approaching Julie who was now backing up.

Julie was clearly terrified of my naked person coming at her with such aggression. She did not want this fight. "Okay, back off Psycho. I will go get them. Just calm down."

She left the room to retrieve my neutral armor. I was worked up into a lather of pure tension. As I stood there furious at this latest indignity, I decided to kill this girl and do it soon. I no longer cared about jail or shots or even if I would survive another day. I had heard my orders clearly from the Higher Power. My life was over. It was never really about me anyway, so giving in to what was expected of my pathetic self would be no difficulty. At least, I finally had a purpose.

Julie returned pretty quickly with my clothing in her hands fresh washed and still mildly damp from a poor drying job. I snatched them from her hand and demanded she leave me be as I dressed. She did not argue for a change and closed the door behind her. As I got back into my covering of the neutral color a mild feeling of calm came over me. I did not like to be without my armor. The feeling of vulnerability caused by nakedness had always been a serious issue for as long as I could remember. To have this monster touching my clothing much less my unit of measurement really set me into spasms of disgust.

Once I had redressed, I also reapplied my make-up. Despite the Prolixin, I was feeling more myself suddenly. The stress of my situation was allowing me the power to beat its attempts to control my inner beast. I thought this a good thing as this Julie was a problem. I would need all my wits and powers to beat her at this strange game she was playing with my life.

The sun had set, and the darkness settled in for her reign as I left Julie's bedroom. I walked into the living room to find Joni, Stephanie, and Crystal asleep on the furniture. Julie was sitting in the easy chair I had not long ago claimed myself. She looked up to see me standing there glaring at her. Pure hatred was in my gaze.

"Well, you look more like the old Psycho I have come to adore already." She smiled at me.

I wanted to puke looking at this ginger haired freak. I had passed out and could not be stirred and was out cold for four hours. She had not called the cops, nor Dr. Huff, not even Mary. I was clever. Julie had made a mistake. She did not call and should have because I could have been in real danger. I had figured why she did not. She was afraid they would come take away her new plaything. This meant she would not call anyone if there was a threat I would be taken away from her control. So, I calculated as long as I behaved like a carrot in front of a jackass, she would never dare to call on me. This did not free me of her completely, but it did give me room to negotiate the comfort of my captivity.

I held back my desire to retch, "I am going to sleep across the street in the cemetery. You can call whoever you want Julie. I do not care. I am never sleeping in this house, or in your bed or with you." I had set my challenge. Now, I waited to see if I was indeed correct about my assumption that she would not call on me.

Her smile faded, "You head out that door and I will call," she said trying to bluff me.

An evil smile spread across my corpse like face, "Go ahead. I will see you in the morning for school out front. Good night, Julie, sleep tight. I hope the bed bug's bite."

I began heading for the door with that little polite statement of my desire she had a good night's rest. She stood up as I reached it and for a moment with anger flashing in her eyes it appeared that she may try to fight me. I waited. I was ready to attack back. However, she knew I had discovered her truth. If she and I got into fisticuffs, there would be blood, bruises, and broken furniture. She would have to explain that to Dr. Scott at tomorrow's appointment or maybe to this fucking probation officer I was hearing so much about. Julie backed off as I had suspected she would.

I opened the door and briskly walked to my temporary new home. She watched me go from her doorway. I turned and looked at the monster Julie as I opened the chain fence gate. I smiled hoping she like me could see in the darkness. I flipped her off and went inside to find my own bed for the rest I would surely need in the coming days. The battle to win back my freedom was about to begin. I would need all the strength I had, and so much more.

Wow. That did not go well did it, beauties? Guess we had not prepared properly for this sermon, so things have gotten a bit out of hand. No worries. We will brush up on our 'verses' and study our 'cannon' hard so next time we will have a more invigorating service.

CHAPTER 32: CONTAGION RAG'EN OF THE VIOLET VIOLENCE

I am sorry you all startled us there, Beautiful Family! Sorry, we are a bit distracted these days, but that is to be expected given the circumstances. Tell us, do you see IT too? It is okay to say no, but we have to tell you just because you do not see it does not mean IT isn't coming for us. Trust us on this one, your only hope of survival is to take our hand and run with us like the devil is coming, because she is. Whatever you do, don't trip! Once she has you it is all over. Usually, we tell you it will be okay, but not this time. We are not kidding, run like hell. I mean run from hell. See you all whenever we have escaped, if we escape that is.

HOW TO CALM DOWN A SCHIZOPHRENIC DURING A SEVERE PSYCHOTIC EVENT:

"Be respectful, kind, and supportive, and call the doctor if needed. If the person is acting out hallucinations, stay calm, call 911, and tell the dispatcher he/she has schizophrenia. While you wait for paramedics, don't argue, shout, criticize, threaten, block the doorway, touch him/her, or stand over him/her- Though schizophrenia isn't as common as other major mental illnesses, it is the most chronic and disabling. Schizophrenia can be a difficult illness—for everyone. During episodes of psychosis, your loved one is experiencing frightening sensations that you can't understand."

-Mayo Clinic: *"My loved one has Schizophrenia, how can I help?"* pamphlet given to my court ordered guardian, 1990.

I slept well in the center of that family cemetery on the ground. I was not unaccustomed to this type of rough living, so finding the ground soft, it did not take long for the land of dreams to find me. I awoke to the rising sun and chirps of the birds that called the trees in this place home.

At first, I was a bit confused. It looked like my own boneyard but not quite. Then the memory of the last week flooded back like a broken sewage pipe in my brain. The stink of it made me wrinkle up my nose. I could smell my memory sometimes. It was one of my many powers. This one was not one of my favorites as often my memories smelled like what they are, shit.

I looked across the street to Julie's house of lies. She had done something to trap me here but what I exactly I still did not know. It was very common for those around me to make decisions about my pathetic life without consulting or telling me. It had become very annoying. These delusional beings all wanted to call me a schizophrenic. They wanted me to believe I was insane. That was not true, and I knew it. No, I am enlightened. As I considered that fact, I suddenly realized I had powers and they do not. Why had I not been using them to defeat these brain stems all this time? The thought of my idiocy brought on a laughing episode.

Julie had crossed the street, but I did not notice it because I was too busy with my giggling. She found me sitting in the middle of cemetery laughing my ass off at my folly thus far in thwarting these insignificant delusions.

"Jesus Psycho, really," she said startling me out of my humor immediately. "Stop acting crazy please."

"Fuck off, Julie. In fact, never speak to me after you tell me which way to school," I said while raising and grabbing my things.

Julie got agitated at that, "Psycho, for the last fucking time you had better start listening to me. I am not going to put up with this crazy talking, laughing, and fighting. We are waiting for the others and then we will all go together. You live here with me now." She was glaring to see if I was listening to her.

This time I wasn't, not completely. The transmissions were coming in from 'they.' I heard 'they' loud and clear, today "beware the violet. It is coming for you."

This message scared me. I was very tired of running. It seemed that at every turn, things would go terribly wrong. I never seemed to get messages from 'they' telling me that 'good' things would happen but 'they' had never been so damned specific about the target. It had appeared I was the target with Julie's orange, and the yellow jail outfit and maroon scrubs but 'they' just said those things were to be avoided or signaled trouble. I had missed the warning signs, or they came after the trouble was already done. This time, it was personal. Something was coming for me.

Julie was watching as I finished my communications with 'they.' She had stopped talking to me at some point realizing I had not been responding to her threats. Her look of distaste told me she could tell I was more than just ignoring her.

"What the fuck was that all about? What are you hearing," she said leaning closer to see if she could hear whatever I was listening to?

I did not respond. I just looked at her blankly. This was not her business. I would not speak to anyone about 'they.' Especially the likes of this girl. I made a mental note that she was in purple yet again. Simon would not be having a happy reunion with me today unless I could get home and lose this bitch.

Julie stood there for a bit trying to wait me out. She thought I would break the silence. I did not of course. Silence was not a luxury I enjoyed anymore anyway. I could hear the birds, the clouds moving above me, the traffic far away, even the thunderous heartbeat of the earth below my feet. Most of all I could hear Julie's thoughts. She was thinking I was hiding something. She was right but since she did not have this power, I only smiled knowingly at her. As I knew it would from her thoughts, the smile made her angry.

"Stop that now. I know you are pulling shit Psycho. Stop listening to voices. The voices are in your head stupid. None of that is real." She was getting angrier by the minute.

I shrugged still smiling silently. She sighed out loud in frustration at my refusal to listen to her. "Fine, be crazy. But you mess up they will lock you up, Psycho. Then, you will wish you had listened to me and stopped all this nonsense." She turned and walked to the gate, "Come on you idiot. We have to get to school."

I followed her out to the road. We waited for the other three girls silently. Julie's thoughts were coming at me loudly. She believed I could stop being enlightened any time I liked. She was sure the medication was going to fix the "problem." Julie also believed I was going to learn that she was the boss. I started laughing again as I listened to her thoughts.

I heard her say in her mind, "Psycho, you will do what I say or else."

I shot a defiant look at her, "Julie, you are a fool. Say whatever you want. Threaten me all you like. I am not going to do what you say."

Julie's eyes widened, "Where in the Sam Hill did that shit come from? I didn't say anything." She backed away from me a bit.

The other girls arrived just as Julie was about to say something derogatory about my alleged "crazy shit" (I know because I read her mind). They looked at the two of us as we were about to square off yet again.

As usual Stephanie broke in, "Hey, what the fuck you two. Cool it. Stop all this fighting all the time and stuff." She got between us as she had the day before.

I pushed Stephanie hard. She fell to the ground. I then went for Julie grabbing her collar like she liked to grab mine. Her fright from my sudden aggression was evident in her eyes.

I pulled her close before she could recover, "I will be going home tonight or I will kill you in your fucking waterbed, pervert."

Julie reached up and slapped my hands off her collar. "Fuck Psycho. I swear to God, stop this crazy shit now. I will tell Dr. Scott today if you keep on listening to voices and threatening me," her face was red from the force of her yelling at me.

Joni helped Stephanie off the ground. "Fuck this shit. Call the cops and send her back to the fucking hospital, Julie! She will kill someone for real," Joni said glaring at me.

I really did not like this girl. I felt my anger overwhelm my fear of another lock up, as I began rapidly approaching Joni. She had pissed me off one too many times. I had decided I would personally shut that foul mouth of hers up. I could see the terror in her face as she tried to back up. I started laughing again at her fear. She had realized too late I would only tolerate so much of her sticking her nose where it did not belong.

However, I was grabbed from behind by a now recovered Julie.

The shock of her touch ripped through my mind. I was wild with anger now. I turned blind from the pain to hit her. Julie had already been made aware I did not like to be touched. She was ready for me. She hit me before I could even raise my fist. The blow connected with my right temple. It was so hard it sent me sprawling to my knees from the force.

As I reeled from the blow, I was suddenly very confused. "What was going on? Why did Julie hit me," I thought as I looked up at her holding my now throbbing head with both hands.

Julie stood over me. I cowered as she raised her arm as if to punch me again. I was suddenly very afraid. My brain whirled as I tried to understand why she was doing this.

"Stop Julie. Please don't." I was now shaking in utter terror of her.

My pleas fell on deaf ears as she hit me again this time in my chest. I doubled over into a ball on my knees while my chest felt like it caved in. I just moaned not even daring to try to escape further injury. I now assumed she had lost her mind. This crazy bitch was trying to kill me. I thought it best to stay down till she calmed. You should never upset a psychotic. Someone told me that once I remembered. I was as still as I could be, till she stopped hallucinating or whatever the fuck insane people do.

I heard Stephanie speak first (as usual), "Julie enough! She isn't fighting, damn it!"

Crystal and Joni said nothing, but I could hear Julie back off to give me room. I still did not move just in case Julie was still in a bad way.

"Get up, Psycho. We are going to be late," Julie finally said after what seemed like forever.

I looked up still covering my head just in case this was a trick. The girls were looking at me and each other all of them appearing unsure. "Probably afraid Julie will get them next," I thought as I cautiously got back to my feet.

Julie took a step toward me and this time I backed away, "You act up again I will beat the sane back in you understand me?" She was pointing and very angry.

I nodded not wanting to argue with this schizophrenic wacko. I was unsure why I had not realized she was ill before. As the group of us started down the road walking to school I thought of the weed she smoked. That had to be it. She went insane from that shit. I had heard once that drugs caused schizophrenia. I could not recall where I had heard that, but apparently it was true. That sent a chill down my spine. I had suddenly realized the whole damned group of them were likely cuckoo. They all smoked weed.

The Higher Power had warned me about the perversions of humankind and the punishment they would suffer for it. I could think of nothing worse than schizophrenia. Julie and the others were getting punished for being evil. Now I would have to be careful not to get in the way of their lashing out from their torment. It made perfect sense. That is why Julie, and the others, were accusing me of being sick. They are the sick ones. It was a shared delusion designed to defend themselves from their own horrible situations.

These delusional idiots were trying to make me look like the crazy one. I stifled a chuckle as I realized the whole truth. I was never crazy, these people are. Mary was sick too. Hell, the whole town was related, maybe they all had it.

I defiantly felt relieved to realize I was not sick, but I was also very upset that I had been mistakenly treated like one of them. I resolved to talk to Dr. Scott and get this misunderstanding cleared up right after school.

I would explain to her the terrible mistake she and others had made. I would tell Dr. Scott that I was not angry, hell people make mistakes, right? No harm done. Then finally, she would let me go home to Simon. All would be well, and I would never go near these psychos again.

For the first time in a long time, I was not afraid. Finally, an answer that not only made perfect sense, but assured I would not be misunderstood anymore. I could not suppress the smile at the thought of this nightmare coming to an end so I could get back on with my life!

I walked as far behind this group of whack jobs as possible, never taking my eyes off a one of them. My chest and head still ached from Julies little psychotic outburst earlier. I rubbed the sore spots wishing I had not said whatever I said to set Julie off like that. Once in a while she would look back to make sure that I was still following. I of course smiled nervously at her. I did not want her to know I knew her diagnosis. She might get upset and hit me again.

We all arrived at the school after a brisk thirty-minute walk down several dirt back roads that led from Julie's house to town. She did not live that far away but that morning it seemed like we marched forever. I knew that was only because I was anxious to be close to my cemetery home. I wished to see my best friend Simon who would be waiting to greet me after the appointment that would clear my name.

The girls all started to file into the schoolhouse promising to meet up lunch time at 'the table.' Julie hung back and as I tried to go past her; she grabbed my upper arm roughly. I bit back the terror of the shocking sensation as she pulled me closer.

Whispering in my ear she said, "I mean it Psycho, you act up I swear I will make you very sorry. I will be watching you."

I was scared by this threat. I was not sure what she meant by that, but I nodded anyway. She released my arm and I hurried to class. As the bell rung, I had a bit of trouble hearing the codes in Mrs. Wells lecture. I was sure that it was the strange warning Julie had issued distracting me from my purpose. No matter how hard I tried I could not shake it off.

"What did she mean she was watching me? How? And how would she make me sorry," I thought over and over again trying to imagine the answers to such a weird threat.

The day went the same. Nothing but difficulty keeping my focus on my tasks as worry about her threat plagued me. By lunch time I thought I may throw up from the fear of having to be anywhere near this nut case. However, before I could think of escape, I saw Julie at the door of my class as the lunch bell rung. She was there to 'walk' me to meet the other girls in this unholy clique. I shook so bad I could barely pick up my backpack to fall in behind the monster Julie.

Crystal, Stephanie, and Joni were already at the table waiting to my delight. I hated these girls but the thought of being alone with Julie was really getting to me. At least these other psychos would be a distraction to her. Maybe, keep her off me until I could get this straightened out. I tried to remind myself the day was half over. I only needed to hold it together a bit longer and this would be resolved. I took a deep breath as Julie told me to sit down at the table with all of them.

I sat down and looked at the table. Julie was trying to look into my eyes, and I did not like that. She sighed as I watched her from my peripheral vision reach into her purse and get out another stinky joint.

"Oh shit, feeding her psychosis," I thought nervously. I calmed myself by reminding me that if I just sat still and quiet all would be okay.

Joni who was sitting across from Julie and I, next to Crystal and Stephanie said, "Pass that shit, girlfriend. Damn that is good weed. So, any trouble with your pet lunatic?"

This caused a stir of anger within me. I tried to quell it, but it was like an ember that was growing rapidly. Joni seemed to know just how to push my buttons.

Julie blew out the smoke from her drag of the joint abruptly at Joni's question, "Damn Joni. Girl you are killing me. Pet lunatic. That is fucking hilarious," she began to laugh and cough as did the other girls.

They all found that very funny as they all stared at me and repeated that name. I was unsure what to do so I laughed too. That made them laugh even harder. I was getting angrier by the second. It was not funny. However, they are crazy, they cannot help that. So, I did not know if I should laugh or kill them all. It was so fucking confusing

Crystal still laughing added, "damn she is so fucking Psycho, she even thinks it is funny. You know Julie she maybe is retarded too, has anyone thought of that? I heard once that schizos are retards."

Now that was too far. I did not care if these assholes were cracked, I would not stand for being called retarded on top of being called Psycho. I stopped laughing as the anger ember flashed into a fireball of rage. I jumped over the table swiftly grabbing Crystal by her arms. She let out a scream and tried to get away.

Julie grabbed my waist and pulled me as I nearly drug Crystal across the table with me by her lower arms. "Let her go, Psycho. Now," she yelled, trying to get me off the girl.

I heard Julie loud and clear. The memory of her strange threat along with the knowledge that if I killed Crystal, Dr. Scott would never believe my story that these people are crazy.

I let go my hold pulling back while pushing Julie away from me, I am not retarded. I am not schizo. You are," I said to the now hyperventilating Crystal. Turning to Julie I said, "and you keep your fucking hands off me, you nut case."

Julie looked at me for a second, then without warning slapped me across the face, "I told you to stop acting like a fucking loon! Do those medications they give you do any fucking thing at all?"

I grabbed my burning cheek and glared at her. I wanted to kill her right there. My anger was an inferno inside me, the heat was making beads of sweat rise up on my white make up. This psycho was pushing me to the limit of my tolerance. The slap was more humiliating than it was painful, but I was sure it demanded retaliation of some sort. Even if I was dealing with a severely mentally ill person.

"I said do not touch me," I bellowed at Julie as she pulled back and slapped me in the face again. This time I actually almost lost my balance and fell (what is with these small-town assholes and the slapping).

That was it. My inner demon burned me down as I recovered and punched Julie in the stomach and pushed her down as she went forward heaving having lost her wind. She landed with a thud.

I walked over and kicked her in her back as she writhed in the dirt, "Call the cops, darling. You know what? Call the morgue if you come near me again." With that I grabbed my backpack and headed back into the school to my next class to wait for the bell to ring or for my arrest. I no longer cared.

My anger subsided as I waited for whatever was to be. To my relief the bell finally rang and the class all straggled in. No one seemed to be wise to the Julie attack at lunch. I smiled knowing the pothead had decided to not give me up just yet. However, I made a bet with myself she would not so quickly lay her nut ball hands on me any time soon. This leashed "pet loony" was a biter.

The rest of the day was peaceful. I did not see any of the psycho squad nor did I see any uniforms of the cops coming to haul me off to jail. Each hour made me surer that I was right, these girls were the schizophrenics.

The day came to an end to find me anxious to see Mary's station wagon and Dr. Scott. It made me chuckle as the bell rung that I would ever think of those two wanting to see them. The humor of the whole situation was not lost to me. I walked out among the clamoring student body to see Mary waiting as I had hoped. My relief was quickly dashed as I saw Julie approach the station wagon and get into the back seat.

I blinked my eyes at that. "Huh?" I felt the earth start to tilt as I walked to the car full of confusion at why this monster was going too. This was not her appointment.

Mary was scowling at me as I opened the passenger side door and looked in glaring at the monster glaring back from the back seat, "what is she doing here," I demanded to know.

Mary scoffed, "She is part of your therapy, stupid. You were told this or did you forget already with your daft brain?"

Now the tilting world actually shifted making me stagger just a bit. I got into the station wagon feeling as if I had been hit over the head by a hammer. I did not recall such a thing, but I did know these two liked to play trick on me. I would wait and see if Dr. Scott could fix this insanity once and for all. Until I could speak to her it was best to play along with these delusional people.

During the thirty-mile ride I was forced to endure Julie's retelling of my uncalled for" aggression, odd behaviors and "attacks" on her. Mary listened to that bullshit practically getting a nut at the thought that Julie was hitting me back. Of course, Julie lied and said all of her hitting me back was in self-defense (whatever).

Mary then took her turn to report of her woes at my "sinning hands." I heard of my acts that resulted in her fall from the social mountain top (of what, a shit town}, my physical abuse of her person, and of course her "many sleepless nights" of worry over my welfare.

They discussed my locker head bashing" as Mary and Julie pontificated that I must "get pleasure from pain" as it appeared it was the only thing that got me to behave "less crazy."

Julie agreed with that, "Yeah, maybe she is one of those sexually twisted perverted types you know?"

I blew a raspberry as she said that, "You wish, Julie. You freak." This made Mary frown and look over at me.

I smiled at Mary and then made a masturbatory gesture to an imaginary penis "Stroker, darling," I said.

She made an overly dramatic disgusted looking face, "You filthy demon. You whore," she blurted pretending to retch.

I started laughing, "there once was a whore who pulled tricks. Who at one time could take five pricks. One day she did cry, as she pulled out her glass eye. Tell the boys I can now take six."

Mary screamed out, "Filthy sinner. Shut your hellish mouth," as I heard Julie gasp in the back seat at my little poem.

Now that I had her attention, I could not help myself but to share another ditty that I was sure would be a crowd pleaser, "there once was a man name Dave. Who found a dead hooker in a cave. She was ugly as shit and missing one tit, but think of all the money he saved." I smiled big as Mary swerved the car nearly running off the road in horror.

To be honest, I have no idea how I even knew those poems. I was not sure why I was being so nasty either. All I knew is that I could not stop myself from tormenting these two by behaving the very way they seemed to view me. As a filthy sinner, a whore, a mindless foul creature willing to bash headlong into lockers just because it apparently felt good, I would be expected to blurt dirty limericks, wouldn't I?

"Oh my God, psycho. You are sick," Julie gasped, appearing to fain disapproval at my most underappreciated poem recitation.

I really started laughing at that, "You love it, you creep. Stop acting all righteous. You love Mary and Jane, and probably Tommy, too," I said in a sing song fashion.

Of course, neither of the two said another word after that showdown of insults. I would like to think I had won the battle, but to lower oneself to your enemies level: I would think I only debased myself with no victory. They still thought me crazy. They still thought me foul. Now they had the proof, didn't they?

Once we arrived, I went inside abruptly as I usually did. The two hell hounds came quickly yapping at my heels. This time I did not talk with the secretary at the check in window but signed in and sat down. Some amount of shame for my little blurting in the car was surely coming but to my amazement I could not feel anything. I really did believe they had that coming.

When my name was called, I got up and so did Julie. She came up behind me and I stopped at the door and asked the nurse to tell this girl she was not welcome. The nurse looked a bit surprised. To my extreme relief, the nurse told Julie if I did not want to have her with me then she would have to wait. If the doctor wanted to speak to her, she would be called. I flashed an evil smile at Julie as I followed the nurse back, I even gave her a mock wave. I watched the anger in her eyes as the door was shut between us. Now, it was time to set things right.

Dr. Scott looked up as I entered the room still smiling my evil smile. She smiled back appearing a bit pensive and unsure of this odd facial gesture of mine.

I sat down and she looked me over as she usually did. "So, you have gotten into some trouble I hear. Dr. Huff said you have charges and received a shot of Prolixin. I think we have a lot to discuss now, don't we?"

This did not bother me. I was sure she would hear what I had to say. Then together we could get this all cleared up.

"Well, it was Julie and the other girls. They are mentally ill, and they have been picking on me trying to convenience me that I am crazy like them. Mary started it and now they have joined. I understand why all this happened. I just got mixed up is all. Now I get it. I need my name cleared, and for you to get my records to say I am not sick at all," I spewed out feeling so much better that the truth was finally out there. I smiled big at Dr. Scott sure she would be proud to hear she would be able to finally close this case as "misdiagnosed."

To my surprise and horror, I watched her jaw drop. She sat back in her desk chair hard. Then grabbing both sides of her temples she brushed back her hair closing her eyes as if she were getting a splitting headache.

Okay, this is not going to work. The Prolixin is not working apparently. Do you hear yourself," Dr. Scott finally asked opening her eyes to stare hard at me, "Is Simon real? Tell me did they make him up too?"

I was confused by this question, "Simon? No, they did not make him up. He is afraid of Julie, and I thought it was the purple and ginger but now I know it was because she is insane."

"No. That is not right, now is it? Simon was around before Julie wasn't he. Think on that a minute. That doesn't work in your explanation does it," she said gently never taking her eyes off me.

"Yes? I mean, no?" I was very confused now, what is she asking me?

Dr. Scott leaned back again appearing to relax a bit, "What did the girls say to make you think they are crazy and trying to make you crazy? Do you remember?"

I thought on it for a minute, "they said I was schizophrenic. They said that I was in a hospital and that I talk to Simon." I was grateful she finally asked something I could answer without confusion. This doctor is a tricky one.

"But wait, if Simon is real then why would they call you a schizophrenic for talking to him? And you were in a hospital. You have been in a few. You want to see the records?" She reached grabbed the open folder on her desk lifting it so I could see they were my records.

I shook my head no as a feeling of despair began to fill me from the chest to my head. Something is wrong here, "Simon is real. Just because they can't see him, they are crazy you see, and they want me to think I am too."

Dr. Scott looked very sad suddenly, "you are the one with schizophrenia and wishing that were not true is not going to make that go away. You cannot hide forever in the unreal world from that very real fact, honey." She looked to see if I was hearing her.

I shook my head no. She is wrong I know that.

Dr. Scott continued, "I am so very sorry for you but it not ever going to go away. These girls had no right to make you feel bad about it, but that is going to happen. People do not understand your disease. It is my job to help you find a way to live a life as independent as possible given the severity of your schizophrenia." She paused again.

I felt the despair inside crushing me as the walls began to breathe and writhe in response to my agony. I tore my eyes from hers and looked to the floor as it began to pulsate with flashes of light. I tried to cover my ears with my hands, but I could still hear Dr. Scott.

"You are in both the real and unreal world that is very scary I know. You are trapped in a nightmare; I know that too. I truly am empathetic for the pain you must be in. Now I see I will need to teach you how to deal with the stigma of your illness. You are going to have to live with this for likely the rest of your life.

Please, you have to stop denying it or you will continue to suffer more than you already do," she said still talking very softly but loud enough I could not block out her words.

"I do not have schizophrenia! I am not psycho," I roared back at her rocking in my chair while crushing my ears with my hands. I should have known she was in on it. What a fool I had been to think she was going to help.

Dr. Scott did not speak. She sat silently watching me waiting for a sign that I had calmed down.

Slowly, as her words stopped eating away at my heart, I pulled my hands off my ears and wrung them while rocking watching the room come to life with the delusional powers the Higher Power had cursed me with.

I decided if I could not get her to help me clear my name, she could at least get rid of Julie. I took a deep breath, "Please tell Julie to leave me alone. You don't have to believe me, but she is crazy. I was out cold for hours yesterday and she took all my clothes off while I was passed out. She is a pervert."

This caught Dr. Scott attention. "You were out cold? Why did you pass out? Tell me what happened. I need to know more if I am to help you," she was still talking very soft. I found that odd, but comforting.

"I heard the whirling of the shock machine and saw the flash. Julie said that I peed my pants, but I know she used that as an excuse to take off my clothes while I was asleep," I said purposely leaving out my transmissions with the Higher Power. She did not believe in Simon so she surely would ignore that I was also a prophet. So, why bother telling her?

Dr. Scott started to write down something, "They gave you the Prolixin on Friday, right?"

I nodded my head yes. She wrote that down. Then looked at me again, "You had a Grand Mal seizure. If this happens again, I need to know. I will talk to your Guardian about taking you to the ER immediately if this ever happens again. In the meantime, I am going to give you some pills to stop any more seizure activity. You have to take them, okay?" She was still writing.

I did not care about any more fucking pills, she was not listening to my wanting Julie gone, "I need you to get Julie to leave me alone Dr. Scott. She is a pervert," I repeated, hoping this time she would listen.

Dr. Scott looked up from her notes, "Brian and Cindy Sloan, Julie's parents, are taken Guardianship of you. They are now your caregivers. Mary has filed a petition for termination of Guardianship. The Sloan's have kindly come in to take that before you end up as a ward of the state in a group home. We both know that will land you in long term institutional care. You are too ill to be without one-on-one special care. We both know you tend to believe others are trying to hurt you. That is part of your disease. Julie is trying to help you. Can you understand that? She and her family are saving you, not harming you. Think on what I have told you. Without this kindness you will be in a hospital till you are twenty-one years old. Is that what you want?" She is staring at me hard.

I stopped rocking as the room appeared to groan loudly around me. Dr. Scott began to pulsate growing larger and smaller with flashes of electricity shooting from her head down toward the ground. I stood up feeling I may explode unable to process this horror, both of her words and of the way the room had just changed into a living creature. I had been swallowed alive.

"No, no. You are lying. All of you lie," I screamed at the electronic Dr. Scott. "Leave me alone."

I began to pace wringing my hands as Dr. Scott called for the nurse to assist her. I had lost it. This was too damned much. I was never getting out. Never! The Monster had her fangs in my throat and my shitty life had become more than just a living nightmare, I was now a fucking slave to that ginger hair thing.

The nurse came into the room and with very little trouble the two ladies were able to get me to sit down as they shot me up with a load of Valium. They had no trouble because I was blown. All I could do is babble and rock. This was far too horrible to wrap my fucked-up mind around. Within a few moments of the shot, I did not give a shit about much of anything as Prince Valium took me out on a dream date. As I sat in the chair no longer pacing or wringing my hands, I looked up to the ceiling to see it was violet in color. I started to giggle. They had indeed come for me after all.

Told you to Run didn't We! Now you all know We are not a liar, but We can understand why you did not believe Us. After all, in this world within a world it is hard to know what is real and what is not right? Well, no worries, you will get another chance to decide which way to run and when to stand your ground. We are most pleased you all decided to stick with Us as the Devil now devours Our carcass.

CHAPTER 33: FEELING SO SCHIZOPHRENIC

Thank Goth you are here, Beautiful Family We have been waiting nervously wondering if you had decided to abandon Us here to our fate. You are such a glorious sight for these old Psychotic Ears...errr...eyes? Now, don't mind the chains, they are indeed heavy, but We got this. Did you bring the file We asked you for? Thank you so much. Now, if you would be so kind to assist just a bit further by looking out for Her while We try to escape? You are amazing for aiding and abiding...errr...assisting Us in this break down...errr...break out! What would We do without all of you? Okay, We have one screw....errrr...shackle loose, so while We work on cracking...errrr...busting up the other let's start on the next journey through the sewer of Our soul. You did wear your waterproof boots, right? You go ahead, We will be right behind you soon as We are completely 'unhinged.'

"It was the way they had exploited his schizophrenia to their advantage, wielding it to maim a man who was already mentally crippled."
— Vivian Barz

I continued to enjoy the company of my dear Prince Val as Julie got her chance to talk with Dr. Scott to give her side of the story. Of course, I not only was not in the room to hear it, but I likely would also not have understood any of it anyway. I was far too sedated to have given a shit if the place had been on fire. I was removed to a private waiting area across from Dr. Scott's office.

My consciousness winked in and out as I imagined I saw Julie and then Mary go into Dr. Scott's office. I vaguely understood that Julie and Mary were take their turns further turning the screws tight on the lid of my fate. This made me giggle a bit. After all none of this is real right? My dreams were certainly lucid these days, even if half the time I was not sure I was.

I became aware that the nurse who had taken me back and helped Scott to shoot me up was in the room too. She was watching me. I smiled at her still giggling mildly. The nurse looked at me with what seemed to be pity. That was so strange to me. Why is everyone looking at me like that these days? I giggled at that too.

My Prince Val had worn me out in our lovely rapid dating dance, so I was fast asleep by the time Mary, Julie, and Dr. Scott came to retrieve me from my comfortable haze of extreme tranquility. Dr. Scott was talking to me. She sounded like she was underwater. I smiled at that. I could barely open my eyes to see her blurry image.

She is snapping her fingers. I can hear it, but it is so dry. She needs to moisturize those hands I think dreamily still smiling at her.

"Yeah, she is gone. You should have no trouble out of her for the rest of the night. Now remember what we discussed, and she has to take the medication okay? Don't let her miss a single dose. Bring her back on Friday. I need to deal with this denial issue after a couple days of the new medication," I thought I heard Dr. Scott say.

Mary and Julie both took one arm as they walked me out of the clinic to the station wagon. I could not seem to keep my eyes open long, but I did my best to walk with my captors. Once inside the car I began to giggle again. This was just so fucking funny the whole thing. Crazy people are my caregivers. I am the only one who is sane, and no one believes me. Somehow, I had slipped into a rabbit hole.

When I try to tell them Julie is hurting me, they tell me I am schizophrenic. I wondered if telling them I love her would make them say I was not. Am I to forever be trapped in this madhouse? It was that thought that rang in my mind as the monotone sound of the vehicle engine sang me back to the comfortable embrace of my beautiful Prince Valium.

I vaguely recall Mary and Julie helping me into her house. They walked me to her waterbed and removed my boots. Then together they forced me to my back as I laughed at their efforts not fully understanding what I was experiencing. I was not worried. Over the last year, I had a habit of not understanding most of my sensations. Often, nothing made any sense or very little anyway.

I lay there watching Julie and Mary talking to each other. A couple of pill bottles are handed to Julie as Mary leaves the room. That seemed so very odd as Julie started to open these bottles. I wondered if she was going to take those pills. She loved her pot, but I had not pegged her as a pill popper too.

However, Mary returned with a glass of water. The two of them lifted my head and forced pills from those bottles in my mouth then forced me to drink the water and swallow them. I was incapable of fighting them off in my very sedated state. The pills tasted awful.

Finally, they left me alone in the room switching off the light which had been offending my sensitive eyes. I tried to maintain my consciousness but again, my Prince came. I drifted off peacefully into the void.

The next morning, I was awakened by the rude sound of a buzzer that would not stop. I jumped up and yell out "shut up."

Julie suddenly pulled me back down to the bed, "Stop it, Psycho. That is the alarm clock."

Now I am very confused! I look next to me and see Julie lying next to me in her waterbed looking at me drowsily. "What the fuck," I yell about to jump out of my skin.

Julie yawned and stretched as I rolled away from her now outstretched arms, "Wow, what did they give you? Must have been the good shit. Do you remember anything?"

I could not recall anything much after seeing Dr. Scott, something about a big snake, and electricity. I think the snake bit me and then I got sick or something. My memories did not seem to make sense at all. I shook my head no in response to her question. Now I am afraid to hear what she was going to tell me actually happened. Did I sleep with Julie? Like really "sleep" with her? Why would I do that? I hate her.

Julie rises and I see she is in a nightgown with pink flowers. "You wigged out at the doctor's office, and she shot you up with some drug. After that you were calm and giggling like the loony tune you are. Was pretty funny actually," she said staring at me with a mischievous smile.

"Why did Dr. Scott do that?" I also rose to see if I was naked again. To my relief I was fully dressed, minus my boots. "Why am I in this bed with you," I demanded to know getting pretty angry.

Julie laughed hard at that, "Cool it, Psycho. We were not playing tonsil hockey and shit. You were pretty out of it. All that happened here was sleep, you idiot. Mary and I put you to bed. This is your bed now. We will share it. So, get used to it." She got out of the bed stretching again.

I was about to light into her with a string of obscenities that would make a sailor blush, but she interrupted me before I could start.

"Look, don't give me shit on this, okay? You are here for good. Dr. Scott told me you now know the situation. You live here now, Psycho, and you have to do as your told or off to the loony bin till you are an adult. Likely, forever with as cracked as you are," she said glaring at me. With that she left and headed for the bathroom.

I sat there on the waterbed that was gently rocking with waves of Julie's recent departure. My mind reached into itself to seek out information regarding what she had said. With some effort I recalled being told that Julie was now my guardian, that Mary had cut me loose, and that if I did not like it tough shit. If I gave them trouble, I would be put away for a long time in some mental hospital hell.

My heart began to pound hard in my chest. I was never going home. That was now clear as glass. I felt as if I could not breath as the true horror of the situation came flooding into my understanding like a tidal wave of epic destruction. Julie was in complete control, and I was her prisoner. It occurred to me that Dr. Scott had not only not believed me about Julie harming me she had even helped Julie do it. I was feeling like I may vomit.

There were two bathrooms, but I did not bother. I bent over and puked up the measly contents of what was left of my gut on the side of the bed still warm from Julies body heat. As I retched up several times, I thought of all those years wanting a home like this. I had wanted a family that wanted me. I wanted a bedroom that did not have monsters in the darkness waiting to hurt me. I had wanted a sister to tell secrets to, a mother to hug me. Now, I see I have acquired the trappings but managed to retain the monsters in the darkness. As I always do, I had fucked up royally.

Julie came back into the bedroom to find me finally spent of my spewing on her side of the bed. She was livid and astounded at the same time. I smiled weakly at her proud of my passive aggressive way of saying what I thought of her family's "kindness" at taking me in as a slave.

"Fuck, Psycho. Why? Just fucking why," she was so angry she was stuttering, "You will clean that up right now, you hear me."

I got out of the rocking bed of water and stretched myself, "Make me." I said smiling at my evil challenge.

She may have me on a leash, but she will not find this pup compliant. I will make her life the hell she has made of mine. Julie narrowed her eyes. She is still in her nightgown but holding some purple clothing. Still fucking with Simon, I mentally note, the bitch.

"You clean that up right now or I will beat the crazy out of you. You are a stupid schizophrenic," she made sure to raise her voice on the last word.

Dr. Scott had told the bitch my suspicions. She has also told Julie I did not like to be called that word because it was not true. I was not surprised. Dr. Scott was a betraying asshole, who was in on this whole mess. I made a mental note that I would make her pay too in time.

I shook my head of that word ringing in my ears like a gong. "Bring it bitch," I said still shaking my head trying to end the ringing.

Julie came flying at me wildly she plowed me right into the wall behind me. I grabbed her throat and began to squeeze as she began to punch me in the head and sides. It hurt like hell, but I let my hatred keep me focused on ending this monster forever.

Finally, she managed to grab my elbows and pull my hands free. As she did this, I head butted her hard. She staggered back as I too stood dazed for a moment by the blow. She recovered first and with a wail she ran at me again, full on plowing her head into my stomach knocking out my breath. I feel to my knees as she began to hit me in my head and back until I was eating the hard wood floor.

She then jumped on my back and grabbing my right arm pulled it behind me to the point of agony, "Clean it up, Psycho," she demanded pulling it almost to the point of dislocating my shoulder.

The pain was ripping my head apart in a hot white explosion of terrible agony, "Okay, okay." I gave in fearing it was too late to save my shoulder.

Julie laughed as I submitted, "No, that is not good enough. Say it. Say it, or I will rip your arm off and beat you with it."

I had no idea what she wanted me to say as panic filled making the pain escalate to terror, "say what? Please, Julie, let go," I cried out begging like a little bitch.

She grabbed my left arm that I had been pounding the floor with trying to distract myself from the one that Julie was about to tear off. She pulled it back too while straddling me both crushing my breath with her weight and sending both shoulders into the orbit of planet torment. I began to choke as I felt my lungs were coming up through my throat the pain was so horrible.

Julie then leaned in close to my now bobbing head to whisper in my ear, "Say, I am Psycho because I am Schizophrenic. Say it, Psycho, or so help me."

I was beyond toleration of this now. I pulled up all my strength and tried to break her grip. We struggled for a bit until finally I was spent unable to get free. She doubled her efforts to break my shoulders.

"Say it, Psycho. You know it is true. You are a liar," she said panting from the strain.

"No. Fuck you Julie. It is not true. Break them, I do not care," I shouted back, then moaned loudly against the strain of it.

Julie let me go. She rolled off me and gave me a kick in my side with her bare foot, "You are indeed schizophrenic, you idiot. How can you not know that? Dr. Scott says you have to admit that. It is my goal to make sure you do just that no matter how many times I have to beat your ass."

She went over to her clothes she had dropped as I slowly picked myself up rubbing my very sore shoulders glaring at her, "clean it up Psycho," she said as she began to dress.

I got up and removed the soiled sheets without further argument. Julie dressed as I painfully took the wadded-up bedclothes to her laundry as directed by her. On my way down the hallway, I had only one thing in my mind, "I am going to murder this girl as soon as I get the chance."

I had not seen my best friend, Simon, in so long. As I put the sheets into the washing machine, I felt a pain in my heart as I thought of him. I wondered if he thought I abandoned him. I sent him an apology for being so mean to him all those times, calling him a toothless drunk with my mind. I hoped he could hear me. I missed him so much. I even missed my smelly old outhouse and the way the sun looked coming over the sleeping giants of darkness every morning.

I thought I had known loneliness. I of course had indeed. I had always been on my own and hurt by anyone who got near me since I could recall. Then Simon came, and I had someone to share my sorrow in my nightmarish world. Simon did not hurt me like the others always had. I had learned what love was through him. He was always there for me. He always did his best to try to make me feel safe. Simon is the only one who can touch me without causing pain. Now, without him I truly understood what being completely alone feels like because now I had someone to miss. Julie had taken him away from me. I had nothing left without my Simon.

"Psssst, hey Psycho. What are you doing?" Stephanie had slipped up on me while I was doing the laundry lost in thought of my Simon.

I shrugged. Stephanie stayed over so that must mean so did Crystal and Joni. That made me taste that sewer taste I get when I remember something from my past.

"You should stop fighting so much and stuff. Julie is too big. She will hurt you, Psycho." Stephanie was, as usual, sticking her nose into my business.

"Fuck off and mind your business, Stephanie. Why don't you go kiss Joni's ass some more and leave me be," I said not even turning around.

"Who are you talking to," Julie's voice caused me to spin around startled. "Psycho, there is no one here!"

I looked at her surprised, "I was talking to Stephanie. She was just here." Somehow, Stephanie had slipped past Julie. Likely scared Julie would beat on her next I thought.

Julie smiled at me while shaking her head no, "Psycho, Stephanie is at home. She is not here. You are hearing voices. You are sick. Only schizophrenics hear voices, and you know that. Do you see now you are lying to yourself?" She was still smiling thinking she had me.

"Liar. She was just here. Stop fucking with my head. It will not work Julie. I may be stuck here but I will not let you drive me crazy with your tricks," I said pushing past her roughly headed for her room to grab my boots and derby.

I knew this was a trick. Julie was a hateful bitch. I did not exactly like Stephanie, but I did not hate her. I thought we had been friends but now I could see she too was in on the plot to make me think myself crazy. I felt somehow sad to learn that. I knew she was not very bright but lately I had started believing maybe I had been too hard on her. Maybe she meant well but was just too ignorant to understand I was not sick. I supposed it did not matter anymore, she had chosen her side and it was not mine.

Julie followed me to her room, "drive you crazy Psycho? Did you really say that? Idiot you don't even need to walk much less drive, you are bat shit insane. Now, do you see Stephanie? You were talking to no one. Stephanie is not here in this house."

I ignore Julie's ranting as I put on my boots. Then she continues demanding I check the house for Stephanie as I put on my make-up and derby. I pretend not to hear her insults and demands. She was getting more and more frustrated. In truth, I was enjoying her wild attempts to get me to admit I had not been talking to Stephanie. I was not falling for it. Stephanie was there, I heard her. Julie wanted me to deny what I know I heard.

Finally, I was done so I grabbed my backpack and rushed past the red faced, pissed off Julie to walk to school. She grabbed my shoulder which not only was still sore but now shocked with her touch, "Do not fucking touch me, ever," I yelled at her.

Julie clenched her teeth, "So, now you hear me? I will touch you all I like, Psycho. You will stop acting stupid one way or another. You sat there and ignored me, now you say it! Stephanie is not here, and you were talking to voices."

I smiled big at her, "I would but I don't talk to voices. You say Stephanie is not here, but I know damned well I heard her. I can hear and see you too just like Stephanie earlier. So, if you say Stephanie is a voice, then obviously so are you. I told you I do not talk to voices." I left the room to a stammering Julie who now realized I had figured out her and Stephanie's game.

Opening the door, I stood smiling at my cleverness in being ahead in Julie's cat and cemetery kid game for a change. The sun seemed awfully bright for this early in the morning. I looked across the street to see the heavy fog rising from the cemetery I had slept in the night before. It was not a great cemetery, but it would do till I could get home I decided.

Above me I hear the electrical road whirling rushing about from one plane of existence to another in the tapestry either. The trees blow slightly with a light late spring breeze. The pulsating of every newborn leaf makes the landscape gleam. It appears as if there are diamonds in the outstretched arms of every tree. A small hummingbird flutters near my head looking to feed from the bright red feeder hanging from the porch overhang. I marvel as the little bird appears to grow then shrink sending a mild vibration into the force shield of the house. I see it and chuckle that such a small creature could make such a wave in the tapestry. It was just further proof that this delusional world is fragile. Any disruption could maybe send it into chaos.

I am still chuckling as Julie arrives while still appearing irritable about our earlier disagreements. I had already shaken off my anger. My emotions are as fragile as the tapestry. I would feel emotion rapidly. They are severe and intense but then they would disappear to nothingness just as quickly. For me, any emotion is felt at painfully high levels. However, no emotion ever lasts for very long. Most of the time lately, I feel complete indifference. Not too much made it to my heart anymore, nor did I even seem to care that it did not.

The only emotion that was immune to this apathy was fear. That deadly emotion was driving my world now as a vehicle of total terror. Fear constantly coursed in my veins. It was the emotion that kept causing me so many fails. Even my sudden agitation, anger and laughing fits were just masked expressions of a horrid all engulfing panic from within. This was the true secret to all my odd behaviors. Everything I do now is an attempt to alleviate the abominable anxiety that never ends.

I had to get to school and get a break from this crazy girl so I could think of a plan to get home to Simon. Today, I was in a usually good humor. It seemed I had forgotten the troubles of the morning and my situation already. That was lucky for Julie, as I would not murder her today, but definitely would consider tomorrow as a possibility I thought, as I watched her lock the door.

She sees me there smiling at her, "What do you have to smile about Psycho? I am really dying to hear what a fruit loop has to smile about." She sighed as I start for the road ignoring her insult. What she thought was not important to me.

Julie catches up quickly as we walk quietly for a bit. Less than half-way she stops appearing to need to tie her tennis shoes, "Wait up, Psycho. Hey, come here and carry my stuff for a bit."

I turn look at her briefly, but I keep walking leaving her there. I was not her dog. She could carry her own damned stuff. Her desires were not my problem.

I did not hear her as she came up rapidly behind me. Before I knew what was happening, Julie had grabbed me. Once more she grabbed my very sore right arm pulling it hard behind my back as I kicked and struggled, cursing her for this trick. The pain was doubled thanks to my tactile issues with touch. The shock was driving me into a fit.

"Let me go you bitch. I swear I am going to kill you," I screamed now angrier than in pain. I'd had enough of these constant squabbles with this idiot.

"Psycho, I have had enough of your shit. So here is how it will be, so you had better listen and listen close. You will do what I say, you will admit you are a schizophrenic too. Not just to me but to Joni, Stephanie, and Crystal or anyone else who asks. You will stop acting crazy or I am going rip off your arm, then you will be helpless with only one of them," she said in a harsh voice.

"Fuck you," I shout back, ready to blow into a thousand pieces from her very touch much less her nearly breaking my arm.

Julie laughed in my ear from behind, "You will do what I said you will do. Because let me make this clear, you don't then I will tell Dr. Scott, my dad and mom and the law you tried to kill me. Who do you think they will believe? A psycho like you or an honor student like me? They will take you away to the criminally insane unit. Do you know what they do to pretty schiz's in those places? Want to find out?" She let go my arm as she pushed me forward.

I nearly fall but recover. However, the world is tilting so violently I almost fall from that alone. Julie's words had struck me dumb. I was trying to understand them, I did understand them but did not want to believe she would stoop so low. I turn and look at her with total confusion in my eyes.

She is smiling with her arms crossed, "You heard me Psycho. Try me. Now say it God damn it."

I look away from her into the ditch next to the road. Then I look to the woods. I was not sure what I was looking for, but I needed to look for something to fix this situation. Things had just gone unexpectedly bad. Chaos and confusion kept me looking rapidly from side to side and behind. I could not seem to get it under control.

Julie was unmoved by my obvious stress, "say it or, Psycho, I am going home right now to call and report you. I have bruises you know. Wonder what they will say about that?"

"I have bruises too," I said with my voice obviously distressed. I already knew they would take her word over mine.

Julie laughed, "Okay. See you later...oh wait nope guess I won't." She waved and started back toward her house.

I watched her but then looked towards the woods. "I will have to make a wild run. Maybe at dark go back for Simon and he and I could hobo it out of this shit town," I think wild with terror.

"Oh and run all you like. You know Dr. Scott put a radar in you so they can track you down. They tag all loonies you know," I heard Julie yell not even looking back or slowing down.

"Huh," I thought as terror pulled at my bladder. My chest tightened as I thought of the hospitals, all the times on Thorazine, the surgery people in the shock shop. "Oh my God. She is right. They did do that, they tagged me."

I fell to my knees beaten soundly. Julie had me and this time there was no solution for X, not this time. I looked hard at the ground and for the first time since I had first gotten sick, I felt my eyes fill with (OMG) tears.

My heart ached and what was left of my stomach knotted, "Wait, come back, Julie," I said watching the dirt road begin to moisten with the first drops of salty fluid I had thought I could no longer express.

Julie stopped and turned around to come back. I knew she would. I kept my eyes to the ground. I imagined she had a smug smile as I heard her approach. She had known all along I would relent to her demands. No one wants to be locked in a cage with mad dog criminals for life. My life may have been shit, but that was beyond even the hellish fate I was currently trapped in. At least here, I still had a chance to find a way out. If they locked me up for trying to kill Julie, there would never be an escape.

Julie stood over me I saw her begin to tap her foot, "Okay, don't have all day here, Psycho. Say it or stop wasting my time."

I was about to go into a full-on crying jag at this point. I swallowed hard and barely choked out, I am...uhm a schizophrenic."

Julie laughed, "Not good enough I did not hear you. Say it right, I am a schizophrenic. I am Psycho. I am the liar. Say it. Go ahead you can do it."

My light shower of tears became a raging spring storm. I covered my ears with my hands so I could not hear myself say those words, "I am a schizophrenic. I am Psycho. I am the liar," I said loud enough for her to hear this time.

I began to rock back and forth feeling I would surely die. I was full on crying now with a fit of laughter threatening me from deep down. The stress of having to admit this nightmare was setting a misfiring in my shattered senses causing synapses to shoot in every direction. Suddenly, I could taste the road under my knees. I could feel the chirping of the birds on my skin. I could smell the sunlight around me and hear the electrical grid above me rushing loud as a waterfall. This upset me as extreme and painful confusion overtook me. My head began to split open as I could feel my brains oozing from my ears.

"Stop being stupid, Psycho. See how easy that was? Now get up. We will be late." Julie reached down and grabbed my wrist that was still trying to hold my ears.

I let out a guttural cry as I leap on Julie knocking her to the ground. I am on top of her hitting her with all I have, over and over again. She grabs my wrists as my blows are wild and mostly ineffective. I am too confused to be able to aim. I cannot determine where she or I actually am, as my senses whirl in all the wrong directions. Julie is able to easily subdue me while she obtains the upper hand for the second time this morning.

She holds my wrists as she rolls over putting me under her switching our positions. Once she has the advantage, she begins to slap my face hard one side to the other. I try to grab her arms, but each slap knocks my confused senses into orbit.

After several series of slaps to the face, she grabs my wrists again and holds them to my chest with her body weight demanding I, "snap out of it."

I continue to struggle for some time but Julie does not let go. Eventually, my energy is spent. My face hurts as do my shoulders. Slowly, my senses begin to settle down, still errors everywhere but not as intense. She feels my body begin to relax beneath her. Waiting a bit longer to be sure, she finally gets off me letting my wrists go.

I lay there spent and feeling utterly defeated. I had wanted to die that day so long ago over the Bob business. This moment I wanted to die more than I had on that day. However, I did not get the chance for the pity party.

Julie walks up and drops her backpack as well as mine next to me with a thud startling me from my moment of despair.

"Psycho, get the fuck up. You are a pain in the ass just as Mary said you would be. Well, Mary doesn't know how to handle crazy. I do. Wait till you meet my mom. Now pick this up. Let's go," she said appearing more bored than angry at me.

I did as she told me to do. After such a humiliating confession, I did not want to have that undone by having it go bad refusing this easier command. We walked the rest of the way to school without a word until the schoolhouse was in view. We amazingly were not late as I saw tons of students still milling about in front. even from our vantage.

Julie turned to me (I had just followed behind fuming and confused a bit the whole way), "Psycho, fix your make-up, you are a mess. Now, no crazy shit in school. I mean it. At lunch you will tell the girls you are bat shit crazy as agreed, and this whole acting nuts is over. Got it?" She took her backpack from my grip.

I nodded my head yes, I understood as I got out my purse. I fixed my make up the best I could given the limited mirror of my compact. Julie stood silently waiting until I finished.

When I was done, she looked me over, "One good thing about this crazy look you have is no one sees the bruises now do they," Julie chuckled at that.

I just looked away. My mom used to say that to me.

We arrive just as the first bell rings. I had never been so glad to get to my first period class in my life. The classes actually went very well. As each lesson began, I got the codes more clearly than I had been the day before. No one bothered me, though as usual notes were passed to my desk constantly. I ignored them. I was starting to feel better with my senses recovering but for some reason I could not focus on trying to solve the Julie problem.

Something seemed off. Whenever I tried to think of Simon or getting away, I would feel as if I were going to have another sensory overload. So, for that time it would have to wait. I could not afford to lose it in class as I had done before. I certainly did not need any more trouble.

Instead, I focused on the delusional lies doing my best to ignore the heaving walls, the pulsating students and the electrical field whirling just above my head. Ignoring their thoughts was harder.

I had not been using my mad box, but now I pulled it from my backpack while stealthily putting the noise in my ears. It helped to scramble their disgusting thinking but not completely. From time to time I had to cover my ears with my hands to help cut back the noise.

I watched the clock finally hit the dreaded lunch hour. As I expected, I saw Julie waiting for me at the door of the classroom. For a split second I thought of running again, but then remembered the radar. At least I now understood that damned electrical field above my head. I had not realized that it was the transmissions of my radar causing that.

I had not had any transmissions from 'they' or the Higher Power today. I found that odd, but then again, nothing was as it should be anymore. Maybe they had decided making me a prophet was a mistake. Maybe 'they' has no new information. Whatever the reason, both were as silent as my Simon. I felt utterly alone as I followed Julie out to the picnic area for my stint as today's entertainment.

As the day before the other girls were already there. However, to my horror there was another girl with them. I had never seen her before. This girl had, like Mr. Greene, a resting bitch face with a weak jawline. This gave the black-haired girl the appearance of early aging. She was like Julie, large with a booming voice.

Julie and I sat down across from the four of them. Julie seemed to like that our side was only for she and her "pet loony." Like a queen holding court, the discussions did not begin till Julie arrived. Pulling out their lunchtime joint Julie asked about this new girl.

Stephanie (of course) pipped up, "this is Vicky. She is cool and stuff. Joni has known her like forever."

Julie eyed Vicky, "You cool? If not, I suggest you blast off, understand?" She glared at her.

Vicky nodded, "Yeah, I smoke. That is why I am here. Joni said you chicks are like starting up a group. I want in. I just transferred in from Carter," she boomed appearing unafraid of Julie.

Carter was the school nearest to this one, only seven miles away. Still in the county but even smaller in size. Joni had also transferred two years earlier. Vicky was an old friend of hers.

Julie just nodded at that as she lit the joint and took her drag then passed it to Crystal across from her. Crystal was still suspiciously eyeing me. I kept my eyes to the table and was quiet. I hoped Julie would forget her plan to humiliate me.

At first, it seemed as though all was indeed forgotten as the five of them discussed their favorite bands, ex boyfriends and movie stars. I never moved a muscle and ignored the blather as I always did. My anxiety at Julie making me say those words in front of these nasty people kept my mind silent for a change too. It was quieter than a snowy morning, which was in its own way unnerving. My mind had not done that since I was just a little kid. I began to wonder if I had blown a gasket for real.

Of course, I knew eventually, they would get to the entertainment portion of the group meeting. Vicky started the torment session by asking about my "odd make-up."

This caused the group to break out in laughter. They tended to laugh more than me when stoned so I was at first not too alarmed. They also would forget what they were discussing rapidly if the laughter went on too long. Well, I have never been lucky. This day was no exception.

"Well, you see, Vicky that is the infamous Psycho sitting across from you," Joni said in a mocking voice.

Vicky looked at me wide eyed in awe, "Seriously, oh my God. Okay, yeah, I can see the rumors are true. Groovy man."

Julie looked startled at that statement, "What? You heard rumors all the way at Carter? What did you hear?"

Vicky began to repeat of my escapades with my brutalizing police, chewing off fingers, breaking lockers, and, of course, eating small children.

Each rumor (some were true, some exaggerated) brought riotous laughter from the four original demon bitches. Vicky was enjoying the attention so much she continued talking and I am sure added her own spin when appropriate. I continued to silently stare at the tabletop. I was not laughing. It is hard to hear what others are saying about you behind your back when you are a 'normal,' for a paranoid schizophrenic it made me sure that both towns were in on the plot to end me.

Despite my abhorrence at their laughing at my obvious difficulties handling, well whatever the hell was going on with me, I was grateful that Vicky was eating away the lunch hour. I was becoming sure I might be home free until Joni joined in the discussion once more.

"Vicky, so get this, all that shit is truth. I saw some of it myself. Now, this crazy bitch does not even think she is fucking bat shit crazy. Can you imagine. She almost beat the shit out of Crystal yesterday for calling her Psycho. And freaks out if you even bring it up; Now how funny is that shit," Joni spewed out of her foul mouth as Vicky looked at me in total surprise hearing this information.

"No fucking way. Look at her. Shit, she looks like a fucking Psycho." Vicky gestured a full body look with her hands as the group laughed hard.

Julie leaned forward suddenly. I felt my heart stop dead as it turned to ice. I could read her mind. The time had come, she was going to force me to say those horrid words.

"Yeah, well she is going to fucking admit to it. Because she is a fucking loon. Aren't you," Julie said now looking at me? I could feel everyone eyes on me waiting to see how I would respond.

I nodded my head yes, never looking up from the table hoping that would be enough to satisfy Julie. However, I never was a lucky one as I have said.

Julie smiled at that. She then said, "Yeah, she is. So, tell Vicky here what is that mental thing you have? Oh, and what do you prefer to be called?" She sat back smiling at her clever push for her blackmail demand.

Something inside me stirred. My senses all suddenly decided to work together for a change. It was almost as if they had met for an arcane ritual designed to call on the Gods of Vengeance. The righteous indignation at this most extreme cruelty conjured up a new demon within. I felt the demon rising through my chest as suddenly maniacal laughter erupted from my mouth.

I looked up right into Vicky's eyes. I could feel the madness vortex in my blue eyes as they captured her gaze. She stared deep into them entranced by things she could not ever understand. If they wanted insane, well Psycho here will deliver it wrapped in a polka dot bow.

"Wait, did you hear that too? What? Oh yes, I am a schizophrenic and so am I. Who said that? You can just call me Psychoooo!" I undulated my voice tone and howled out laughing like a basket case.

This scared the shit out of Vicky, but more than that it scared the shit out of the other four girls too. I continued to stare at her allowing a bit of giggling then appearing to stifle it by covering my mouth, I would remove my hand and giggle again. I rocked my head back and forth as if punch drunk and even turned it to hear transmissions I was not actually hearing. In a sentence I behaved like the Psycho they wanted me to be.

Julie was livid. She glared at my very crass and overly dramatic display of "classic" psychotic symptoms, "Cut the shit, Psycho. Vicky, ignore her. That is not how she acts. It is way more fucked up when she is being really crazy." She apparently did not believe I should deserve an Oscar for my performance.

Vicky yelled out stunned, "Fuck she is mad as a hatter God Damn. Aren't you people scared? She may kill you and bury you in the basement."

Crystal and Joni also looked angry as Julie did. They also knew I was "acting." Stephanie, however, laughed at my silly display. "Oh my God, that is so funny. I love it Psycho you are killing me. Fuck I am going to die laughing." At least someone knew how to appreciate my efforts.

I looked at Julie still hamming up my role as the Psycho and turning up my mad box I got up from the table. My sudden movement startled her as I stood up and posed like a ballerina. Catching the beat of the song in my ears I took off in a fast a furious dance right there for my most captivated audience. I did not have Simon but since he and I danced so often I 'pretended' he was with me the best I could.

I caught glimpses of the girls as their jaws dropped. Even Julie did not know what to do for a change. She wanted me to be schizophrenic so bad, well fuck her, I was giving it to her. Good and hard

Stephanie recovered first and yelled out, "whatever you do, don't go near her right now. She will go off and try to hit you and stuff." She had true concern in her voice. I almost smiled at that. Almost.

I then began to randomly yell "shut up" and "leave me alone" as I continued to dance with my pretend Simon. I almost did crack up on that one. From my peripheral I could see the girls no longer found me a thing to joke about. Oh no, they were quickly discovering that mental illness is not funny at all. It is scary, ugly, unpredictable, painful, and worst of all, humiliating. My nightmare was not a laughing fucking matter. As I danced wildly the rest of the lunch hour the girls sat still fearful to move and 'set me off.' I had taken back a bit of control even if just for a moment. I will not lie, it felt great.

The bell rung finally, and everyone headed off to class. I stopped dancing smiling wickedly at Julie. She looked at me irritated, "What the fuck was that Psycho?"

As I grabbed my backpack and headed in, I answered back, "What you asked for darling. See you after school. I have detention. Simon will keep you company, no worries." I entered the school smiling bigger than the Cheshire Cat.

Whew! We are sweating like a psychotic in a straight jacket here, what a busy chapter. Again, thank all of you for joining Us here in the bowels of this prison within a prison. We almost got away this time, but alas Our struggle still has a long way to go. Still want to hear more? We are off to chew off Our feet and hands to escape these bonds. See all of you soon in Book Three, entitled "Motor-Psycho".

Alexandria May Ausman was born into a dangerously neglectful home environment. She was the helpless victim of numerous incidents of psychological, physical, and sexual assaults by her parents and peers. She dressed in an unusual manner to 'fightened' off bullies and to appear less attractive to sexual predators. Despite her cries for help her pleas for aid were ignored until she was finally placed in foster care at age fifteen. In her sixteenth year, her mental health began to deteriorate. Alexandria was quickly abandoned by her foster parents when she was diagnosed with Schizophrenia. While still only a teen, she was forced to battle this devastating illness alone.

Alexandria has struggled with lack of a support system, numerous psychotic episodes, exploitation, homelessness, and an uncaring mental health system.

Alexandria raised two healthy children. After obtaining her bachelor's degree in psychology she worked as a child abuse investigator and became a diagnostic psychologist while acquiring her Master's in psychology. Alexandria never forgot the experience of 'slipping through the cracks.' Her life's goal is to help people suffering abuse and/or mental illness have access to necessary services. In 2018, Alexandria's fashion expression gained notice. By accident, she became a model of 'gothic attire'. That summer she won the World Gothic Models contest. Henceforth, dubbed the Goth Queen, Alexandria didn't miss an opportunity to offer a helping hand to those in need.

She began writing a fictionalized account of her life experiences after a catastrophic return of psychotic symptoms. Today, Alexandria is retired, and homebound due to crippling symptoms of Schizophrenia. She currently lives in Tallahassee, Florida, with her loving husband and a loyal support dog.

Made in the USA
Columbia, SC
17 October 2022